"Kyle, you are so…good, honorable, kind."

Like a jab to the chest, that was the wake-up call he needed. He wished he was good, honorable and kind, or at least wasn't carrying this secret around with him. Because he wanted to be all of those things for her—and he was beginning to believe they could be perfect together.

Cupping her face, he smoothed a thumb across her cheekbone. "I want you to know that I didn't arrange all this because I expect anything from you."

Harper gave him a contented smile that had him wanting to kiss her all over again. "I know. I believe you. And that's huge for me. I, um…"

Forcing the words past the painful guilt building inside his chest, he said, "Harper, you can tell me anything. I hope you know that."

"I think I do. I, um, I have…trust issues. The details of which I wish I could share with you. But I can't. At least…not yet."

Dear Reader,

I don't know about you, but I think trust is one of the most vital yet elusive feelings in the entire playbook of human emotions. Trust is difficult to define, yet you know when it's there. And it's essential in order to have a genuine connection with someone. But once it's lost, can you get it back again?

Harper Jansen has a lot of reasons not to trust people. But her new security consultant, Kyle Frasier, seems to be the most trustworthy man she's ever met. Soon she finds herself trusting him with not only her safety but also her heart. The problem is, he's also her deceased fiancé's best friend.

Kyle wants to keep Harper safe, but also learn the truth about his best friend's death. Except things get complicated when he finds himself falling for Harper. Can he somehow get to the truth and keep her trust?

Thank you so much for letting me know how my stories have touched you and who you want to read about next. I love hearing from you! For contact info and a complete list of my books, please visit my website: carolrossauthor.com.

All my best,

Carol

HEARTWARMING

Keeping Her Close

—

USA *TODAY* Bestselling Author

Carol Ross

⟨H⟩ HARLEQUIN® HEARTWARMING™

Recycling programs
for this product may
not exist in your area.

ISBN-13: 978-1-335-51087-7

Keeping Her Close

Copyright © 2019 by Carol Ross

www.Harlequin.com

Printed in U.S.A.

Carol Ross lives in the Pacific Northwest with her husband and two dogs. She is a graduate of Washington State University. When not writing, or thinking about writing, she enjoys reading, running, hiking, skiing, traveling and making plans for the next adventure to subject her sometimes reluctant but always fun-loving family to. Carol can be contacted at carolrossauthor.com and via Facebook at Facebook.com/carolrossauthor; Twitter, @_carolross; and Instagram, @carolross__.

Books by Carol Ross

Harlequin Heartwarming

Summer at the Shore
Christmas at the Cove

Seasons of Alaska

In the Doctor's Arms
Bachelor Remedy
A Heartwarming Thanksgiving
"Autumn at Jasper Lake"
A Family Like Hannah's
If Not for a Bee
A Case for Forgiveness
Mountains Apart

Return of the Blackwell Brothers

The Rancher's Twins

Visit the Author Profile page
at Harlequin.com for more titles.

For Dan.

Wow. What a year. Like Harper says to Kyle, if I didn't already love you I definitely would now. Thank you. You really are the best.

PROLOGUE

"Save the salmon! Don't dam our dams! Don't dam our salmon! Dam the salmon! Dam you, Bellaire!"

Clearly, the dam was a hot-button issue, Kyle Frasier thought with not a small dose of amusement. He found the chants funny partly because it was so difficult to distinguish the protesters from the supporters and partly because he knew the man they were shouting at, Dr. David Bellaire. He also knew that Dr. Bellaire tolerated the attention because it was good for business and the environment, the two things, after his daughter, Harper, that he was most passionate about. The fact that he'd successfully merged the two seemingly incompatible aspects into one highly profitable business was considered genius to some and unforgivable to others.

There'd been a group of reporters already milling around the Bellaire Building when Kyle had arrived an hour ago and headed upstairs to Dahlia International for his interview. On the way inside, he'd dodged people holding signs bearing similar slogans to the ones they were shouting. Through the tall windows fronting the lobby, he could see that the crowd had swelled exponentially since then, and now that the controversial scientist and billionaire businessman himself had entered the building a frenzied tension electrified the air.

Dr. Bellaire was the owner and CEO of Bellaire Environmental Solutions & Technology, or BEST, as it was more commonly called. Bellaire owned the entire Seattle skyscraper with the company's headquarters comprising the top seven floors right above Dahlia International. The doctor's recent provocative statements about hydroelectricity and the health of native salmon runs had managed to rile both sides of the environmental debate. He insisted dams and salmon could successfully coexist. BEST was working on a solution, some details of which they would be revealing soon. As far as Kyle could tell, neither faction could grasp the concept of a harmonious coexistence, both sides perhaps too distracted by their well-meaning devotion to their respective causes to truly consider the possibility.

Under different, less chaotic circumstances

Kyle would approach the doctor and say hello, but it was going to be enough of a challenge to navigate through the mass of people and get to the exit as it was. Last year, Kyle's best friend and former navy SEAL teammate, Owen, had introduced Kyle to Dr. Bellaire. Kyle would never have believed that four months later Owen would be dead.

The memories of Owen were still impossibly sharp and painful, like a knife slicing at his heart. At the time, Owen had been alive and well and so full of life and optimism that Kyle had been a little envious, even wondering if he'd made the right call by remaining in the military while Owen returned to civilian life. His friend had spent nearly three years working for Dahlia, one of the most respected military contractors in the world, where he enjoyed an exciting, high-paying job. He'd been walking on air after meeting Harper, the "love of his life," who also happened to be the daughter of Dr. Bellaire.

At Dr. Bellaire's invitation, Owen had brought Kyle here for a visit to BEST where the doctor had taken them on a tour of his labs and then treated them to lunch. Not long after, the three men had met again in Amsterdam while Kyle was on leave. Dr. Bellaire had been in the Netherlands on business and Owen between assignments. They'd had dinner together and then spent the evening touring the city. Kyle had found the brilliant scientist charismatic, witty and refreshingly down-to-earth. He understood why people were so fascinated with the man.

In his pocket, Kyle felt his phone vibrate. A glance at the display showed it was his friend Josh Avery. Another former SEAL and close friend, Josh now worked for Dahlia, too. Kyle had texted Josh after the interview to let him know they'd offered him a job. Stepping away from the elevators, Kyle moved toward an adjacent window out of the traffic flow. In the middle of the lobby, near a life-size metal-and-glass sculpture—ironically of a school of salmon leaping a waterfall—he watched Dr. Bellaire turn and face the crowd. A man in a suit announced that Dr. Bellaire would accept a few questions from the press.

Reporters started shouting as Kyle answered the call, "Hey, Josh."

"Congratulations, man! I'm so… Wait. What's that noise? Are you out celebrating without me?"

Kyle grinned. "Thanks, buddy. Not celebrating. I'm still in the lobby of the Bellaire Building. Dr. Bellaire just walked in."

"Ah, protesters."

"And supporters and newspeople and a fair share of civilians getting in out of the rain, too, I think."

Josh chuckled. "The man knows how to fan flames, that's for sure. This dam stuff is crazy. But back to the point—I'm so stoked we're going to be working together again!"

"Me, too," Kyle said. The crowd had quieted with some semblance of order established as Dr. Bellaire began answering questions.

"Not quite like the old days, but as close as we can get without Owen, huh?"

"Yeah," Kyle said because that was all he could manage at that moment with the grief twisting hard in his chest and clogging his throat. Being here in the Bellaire Building, interviewing with Dahlia, he should have been better prepared for these reminders of Owen.

After a pause where Kyle imagined that Josh was also paying a silent tribute to their fallen friend, Josh asked, "When do you start?"

"Not until next month. Travis said he wants me on the Tri-Star job with you." Travis was Dahlia's operations chief and Kyle's future boss. "Not sure what that is, but I'll be ready. Just need to sign my contract."

"That's awesome. What are you going to do until then?"

"More of the same. Hang out with my family on the Oregon coast. I've been bunking at my sister Mia's house in Pacific Cove. My brother-in-law, Jay, has a construction business and I've been working for him. I suppose I should find my own place now that I know I'll be based here in the west." Even though he'd be working overseas for weeks at a time, at least he'd be able to establish a home base near his family.

"I've got a spare room..." Josh went on, urging him to move to San Diego where he lived. Kyle listened, but he'd made up his mind to settle near his mom and sister. He knew he couldn't make up for lost time, but he needed to try to mend the relationships he'd damaged through the sheer force of his neglect. Not that his relationship with his sister had ever been great.

Kyle glanced up to see that Dr. Bellaire had finished his impromptu press conference. The crowd was beginning to thin, due in large part to the two uniformed security guards now herding people toward the exit. Dr. Bellaire and his entourage briefly congregated to one side before heading in his direction en masse for the elevators, presumably on their way upstairs to BEST.

A clean-cut stocky blond man in a nice suit slipped away from the larger crowd and followed them. He wore a badge around his neck that suggested he was with the press. Kyle wouldn't have cause to take another look except the guy's dress did not match his demeanor. Too fidgety, his body tense and twitchy, his gaze bounced around but always paused on Dr. Bellaire. Squirrelly. That's how he and Owen used to describe this type of nervous, jittery, shifty-eyed manner.

Warning bells pinged loudly in his brain. Of course, there were a lot of causes for this kind of behavior: drugs, alcohol withdrawal, PTSD, chronic insomnia, schizophrenia or a myriad of other mental disorders. Maybe he was new to his job and nervous about approaching Dr. Bellaire. Even too many energy drinks could make a person anxious and wired. And yet, Kyle couldn't talk himself out of the trepidation he felt.

A woman kept pace at Dr. Bellaire's side. A quick once-over told him she wasn't Bellaire's daughter, Harper, but that made Kyle wonder how Harper was doing. Many times in the months since Owen's death, he'd thought about reaching out to her. Kyle had never met her in person, but he'd seen plenty of photos via Owen. For most of Owen and Harper's relationship, the couple had been in Africa where Owen was working. Kyle had still been on active duty himself at the time, stationed at various overseas locales. Guilt and regret weighed like a stone in Kyle's gut. He made a vow to contact Harper soon and see how she was doing.

Dr. Bellaire drew closer, his focus zeroing in on Kyle. Recognition transformed his scowl into an expression of cheerful surprise.

Kyle returned the smile and added a wave. "Gotta head out, Josh. I'll call you later." Kyle ended the call and slipped his phone into his pocket.

Dr. Bellaire approached, reaching out a hand. "Kyle! How are you?" Ten feet behind him, the blond man halted, too. He removed a phone from his jacket pocket and stared down at the display. Kyle kept him in his line of sight, taking note of his accelerated respiration, sweaty brow and the way he kept swallowing repeatedly. He could almost smell the guy's fear.

"Hi, David. Better than you, looks like." Kyle tipped his head in the direction of the lobby. Odd, Kyle noticed, that the guy was still staring at his phone but had yet to touch

CAROL ROSS 15

the screen. He glanced up, noticed Kyle and quickly refocused on the phone.

David's smile was cheerful, his tone appreciative as he remarked, "Passionate, aren't they?"

Kyle chuckled. "Quite." The man had such a unique view of the world.

"I thought you were still overseas. What are you doing here in Seattle?"

"I was discharged a couple of months ago." He didn't add that Owen's death had hit him hard, prompting him to evaluate his life and his relationships, including the desire to reconnect with his family. "I'm here interviewing for a job with your downstairs neighbor."

"Ah, Dahlia, of course. You'll be a great fit there. Such a tragedy about Owen. I'm so sorry for your loss."

"Thank you." Kyle wanted to ask about Harper but was distracted by the lurker again who'd tucked his phone into his left pocket and was now slinking closer, a determined expression on his face. Kyle went into high alert. Nearly a decade in Special Forces had taught him to trust his instincts.

"Are you living here in Seattle now?"

"No, I'm staying in Pacific Cove, Oregon, for the time being. Spending time with my family."

Dr. Bellaire said, "Did you—"

The lurking guy's right hand slipped into his pocket and came out holding a short cylindrical object. In one smooth movement, his arm lifted up and back like a major-league pitcher gripping a baseball. His target was obviously Dr. Bellaire, but Kyle was already in motion. David was shoved aside as Kyle went airborne, crashing into the attacker, his left hand seizing the guy's wrist. As they went down, Kyle twisted his arm back and up, subduing him completely. Shattered glass lay on the floor, accompanied by balls of a pink jellylike substance. Kyle recognized the distinctive odor of cured salmon eggs.

For a few beats, the entire lobby went quiet before erupting with renewed chaos, screams and cheers. The crowd surged toward them, but Bellaire's security detail was already escorting the doctor away. Kyle handed the guy off to one of the security guards. "Those are salmon eggs on the floor, I think."

The police were called. Dr. Bellaire was fine. Kyle was fine. Everyone was fine. With the exception of the would-be attacker, who'd landed hard on the marble floor and was whining about an injured wrist.

It was all over in a matter of seconds. Just another day at the office for Kyle. It should have ended there. And it would have. Except for the fact that an eager reporter from Channel 11 had filmed the whole thing. That, and then Kyle received his second job offer of the day.

CHAPTER ONE

Lip-synching to Carrie Underwood while baking (okay, and eating) cookie dough will be weird with a stranger in my house. No more yoga in my pajamas. No more whale watching from the deck in my pajamas. Binge watching Tiny Dancer *while practicing my hip-hop moves is probably out, too.*

A bathrobe-clad Harper Jansen searched around her living room and let out a panicky bark of laughter, a sound she hoped *not* to make on the first date she was about to go on in months. Spotting the lotion she'd been seeking, she shoved the bottle into her pocket, secured the robe's lapels firmly around her and hurried through the house to her bedroom.

"Bodyguard," she said aloud and cringed. Even the word felt personal and intrusive. "Body. Guard," she tried again more slowly and then realized she was gripping the robe so tightly around herself it was hard to breathe. *See?* There was an inherent threat to her well-being in the very word itself. Although, her dad insisted the position was that of security consultant. "Feels like a bodyguard to me," she muttered.

She considered canceling so she could mentally prepare for this looming and indefinite invasion of her privacy. Yes, she should stay home and relish her last evening of precious aloneness. As the only child of a single dad—one who worked a lot—Harper was no stranger to being alone. She'd been alone here in Pacific Cove for three months now. Sure, it was a feeling she'd been wanting to shed lately, but it suddenly seemed both essential and precious. Then she remembered she didn't have the guy's number.

"Brilliant, Harper." Lotion forgotten, she donned her carefully chosen outfit.

When her yoga acquaintance and sort of friend, Samantha, had arranged the date, right before leaving for her six-weeks-long honeymoon, Harper declined to take his number, so she wouldn't be able to freak out and cancel at the last minute. Like she had the last time. It had seemed like a good idea at the moment—a symbol of her courage and commitment to "getting back out there," as Sam liked to say. The problem for Harper, however, was that "out there" only led to disappointment and heartbreak. She wasn't sure if she'd ever recover from her last relationship. Owen's betrayal had taken heartbreak to a whole other level. His subsequent death had exacerbated and complicated those emotions to the point that she'd wondered if she'd ever fully heal. But she had. Or at least she was way, way better. That's what today was supposed to prove: a better Harper ready to move on.

That's when the next depressing thought struck her. *This will likely be my last unchaperoned outing of any kind for weeks, if not months.*

What she needed to do was make this date a good one. Like epic. Technically, there was no making up for lost time, she knew that, but she could make the best of the time she had left.

Fueled by this notion, Harper channeled her frustration into determination. Frantically, she changed out of her dressy clothes, trading skinny jeans, tunic and boots for leggings, T-shirt and running shoes. She twisted her auburn waves up into a bun and tied a long-sleeved fleece top around her waist. She was going to have a good time tonight if it was the last thing she did. Now that she thought about it, even if her date didn't want to go along for the ride, she'd take that ride on her own. She'd enjoy her final hours of freedom, all right, and not at home fretting and pouting.

Basic security had always been a part of her life. Her father's house on Seattle's Lake Washington included a state-of-the-art security system as did the offices and labs at his company, Bellaire Environmental Solutions & Technology. But Harper had always felt like that was more about the important, proprietary nature of her dad's work and the general safety of her surroundings than about her.

Even so, when she'd moved into her house a few months ago, Denny, her dad's head of security, had brought the system up-to-date. She used it maybe half the time and not very well at that. The facial recognition technology functioned so that whenever a human stepped onto the property, the cameras began recording, and if it was a person who'd visited before, or was already in the system, their name would pop up on-screen. If not, a close-up still shot was recorded, cataloging the face for later. All visits were logged along with the time and date. The app chimed while Harper was tying her shoes, shooting a surge of nervous adrenaline through her bloodstream.

The irony did not escape her that this was a blind date. Probably, in addition to getting the guy's number, she should have looked at his photo when Sam offered it, urging her to see how "gorgeous" he was. But Mikhail was a good friend of Sam's husband, Colin, so Harper had waved the phone away, telling Sam that was enough for her. If they liked him, no doubt she would, too. Looks didn't matter, she'd asserted, Owen had proven that a beautiful facade did not necessarily harbor a beautiful soul.

But now, phone in hand, she used the app to study the man standing on her porch. Sam was right; he was good-looking if a bit somber. She'd been sold on Mikhail because, like her, he was an artist, a professional musician and successful songwriter. According to Sam, he was also a microbrew master who enjoyed traveling, concerts and long rides on his vintage motorcycle. Also like her, he was a bad relationship survivor. Sam had revealed that his ex-wife had cheated with his best friend and left him devastated. This was Mikhail's first post-heartbreak date, too. They had so much in common.

As a photographer herself, she thought it would be nice to be with someone who understood her dedication, intense focus, odd hours and the often-transient nature of her job. Someone who could relate to the inherent challenges of putting your work on display for others to critique and value.

A little spike of yearning accompanied this pep talk. She took a second to gauge it, trying to determine if there was more yearning than fear. When she couldn't decide, she reminded herself that it would be good to socialize again, to find a nice guy who was exactly what he claimed to be. Unlike Owen, who had deceived her and left her way more bitter than she wanted to be. More bitter and distrustful than a woman should ever be. In retrospect, she suspected that he'd intended to use her from the start. With her history, and her dad being her dad, she should have known, or sensed, that something was off, or at least exercised a bit more caution.

"Stop beating yourself up, Harper. Not all men are users," she muttered and headed toward the door. Inhaling a deep breath, she put on her game face and opened the door.

"Harper Jansen?"

"Yes! Hi!" she said with possibly too much enthusiasm. Dialing it down a notch, she added, "I'm Harper." Why was he frowning? Nerves, maybe? She rather liked that, the notion that he might be sharing her trepidation. "Please, come in." She waved him forward.

Tipping his head thoughtfully, he paused for a few seconds before moving inside where he stood stiffly, looking like he was trying to decide what to say.

It seemed prudent to take the reins. "So, I'm just going to come right out and tell you that I'm super excited about this."

After a beat, he asked, "You are?"

"Of course, I am!"

His mouth turned down at the corners while his gaze narrowed with what might have been skepticism.

Wow, she thought, *Sam was right, he has been out of the social scene for a while*. She went on, "And I have a fun idea how we can get to know each other." Gesturing at herself and then him, she went on, "I'm glad you went with casual. Jeans are perfect for what I have in mind."

"Uh, okay." Brow furrowed, voice hesitant, he said, "Generally speaking, my wardrobe will vary according to whatever activity you're engaging in."

Harper felt herself grinning at this odd reply. She wondered if he'd been reading up on dating etiquette. Poor guy. She could hardly hold it against him if he'd been seeking out some tips. Undoubtedly, she could use a few of those herself. A superpower would be better though, and, as long as she was wishing, she'd like the kind that allowed her to see right into the heart of a person. Yep, super judgment, that's what she needed.

"Sounds like a good policy," she said, wishing he'd relax. "I hope you don't think this is totally outrageous, but I was thinking we'd go zip-lining and bungee jumping."

"Bungee jumping," he repeated flatly.

"Yeah, like a modern-day, adrenaline-charged parlor game. Nothing like mutually shared abject terror to break the ice, right?" she joked.

Blank stare.

Harper went on, "I know a guy who has a place where we can do both. I took some photos for him a while back, and he was so happy that he offered me a bunch of services for free. Isn't that cool? Then, I thought we could head into Astoria. Have dinner, stroll around the Spring Fling Festival. Have you heard of it?"

"No, I have not." He appeared confused now and sounded almost surly.

Harper swallowed, nervousness was rapidly overtaking her enthusiasm. Possibly, these epic date aspirations were overkill. She didn't want them to be, though, and she found herself rushing to sell it. "It's an art and sea-food festival. It kicks off tonight with ships that cruise by on the Columbia River, all dec-orated with lights, like a boat parade. Ven-dors set up along the waterfront selling food, crafts, antiques…" Recalling his profession, she added, "Oh, and a band!"

This only seemed to puzzle him fur-ther, kicking her anxiety up another notch. "Maybe you could get up there with them and sing a song or two." Reaching out, she gave his forearm a quick little squeeze. "Ha-ha, just kidding."

Harper wanted to melt into the wall at this point because his eyes followed the path of her hand and he flinched at her touch. It was slight, but still, she noticed, and it was def-initely a flinch. She could feel her cheeks heating with color. *He's been here two min-utes, and he's already trying to get away from me. Maybe if I tell him my dad is a billion-aire, he'll come around. That seems to im-press the men I date, or maybe that's what attracts them in the first place. Chicken, egg, Harper, heartbreak. No matter the order. Same outcome.*

Desperation had her blurting, "Oh, and there's a beer garden featuring microbrews from all around Oregon. You'll love that, right? I can drive, so you can sample *all* you want. Maybe that'll get you up on stage. Ha-ha!"

Okay. He was glowering now, and Harper wondered if maybe it wasn't her. Maybe his problem was social awkwardness? Was it a language barrier? Mikhail sounded like it could be Russian or Eastern European? Although, she hadn't noticed an accent.

Raising her voice in that clumsy way a person does when faced with incomprehension, she enunciated slowly, "Does any of that sound fun? Or maybe you had something else in mind?" She hoped he wasn't one of those guys who had to be the one to plan every detail. Control freaks were not in her wheelhouse.

Finally, he shifted on his feet, gave his head a little shake and answered, "No, honestly, none of that sounds like fun tonight. Under the circumstances, this entire plan of yours sounds like a complete and total nightmare."

KYLE'S FIRST THOUGHT upon meeting Harper Jansen was that she didn't recognize him. Maybe not too surprising as they'd never met face-to-face. Although, he'd seen photos of

her and figured she'd seen at least a few of
him. He would have recognized her. The second thought, however involuntary and unwel-
come, was that she was every bit as beautiful
and alluring as Owen had claimed. But then
she'd started this disjointed rambling that left
him equal parts confused and concerned. No
wonder Dr. Bellaire wanted him to start as
soon as possible. The woman needed protection from herself.

Owen had waxed on about Harper's virtues:
smart, beautiful, talented, fun-loving—these
were just a few of the many, many adjectives
he'd used to describe the woman he'd met,
fallen in love with and proposed to in a matter of months. As he had then, Kyle couldn't
help but wonder if Owen had let infatuation
cloud his judgment. No one could fall in love
that quickly. An engagement that fast seemed
impulsive, if not reckless. Now he wondered
if this woman was in her right mind.

"You don't like bungee jumping?" Her tone
had lost a touch of its previous zeal.

"It's irrelevant whether I like it." In fact, he
did like it, but that didn't matter right now.
They weren't going. Did she not comprehend
what had happened to her father that very
morning? So much about this "plan" of hers
was wrong. One element, in particular, was

bothering him so he had to ask, "Why would you think I'd want to go out and drink so much beer that I'd need a designated driver?"

Dark brown eyebrows just a touch darker than her hair dipped in confusion. "Don't you like beer?"

Okay. This was too weird. Before he could form a response, the doorbell rang.

Harper frowned and glanced in that direction.

"Are you expecting someone?" he asked.

"Um, no, just you." She started to move around him like she was going to answer it.

"Then wait." Kyle caught her elbow. "I'll get it."

"What, why?"

"I think that's obvious."

"Not to me." Blue-gray eyes narrowed in on him as her expression turned thoughtful. "Why would you answer my door?"

"Because it's my job," Kyle returned flatly. "Or it will be soon if you agree to hire me."

"You…" She went wide-eyed, and her face lost some of its color. "You, your, job," she stuttered, before cupping a hand over her mouth. "Oh, no…" More muffled words followed by a groan.

Kyle shook his head and pulled his phone from his pocket. "What's the password for your security app? Your dad said you change it weekly."

"Of course, you already have the app," she said in a resigned tone, not about to admit that she never changed it. "It's *chiaroscuro* and then the number 282. Chiaroscuro is spelled *c-h—*"

"I know how to spell it," he said, a bit sharper than he'd intended. But a stranger showing up at her door right now was alarming, to him at least. He held up the display for her to view. "Do you know who this man is?"

"Maybe," she answered hesitantly, studying the screen with an expression Kyle could only describe as painful. Seriously, what was wrong with her?

"Maybe," he repeated, his patience beginning to fray, "is not an answer. Yes or no?"

"I said maybe." Her tone held an edge now, like he'd done something to irritate her. But then she sighed, and said, "He, uh… He might be my date."

"You don't know what your date looks like?"

Her answer was quick and sharp, "Haven't you ever heard of a blind date?"

Kyle's gaze met hers, and he realized then that he'd mistaken embarrassment for irritation. Cheeks splotched with pink. She was grimacing. Understanding dawned, about the odd conversation that had just transpired and her ensuing mortification; she'd mistaken him for her blind date.

Trying not to allow her discomfort to thaw his concern, he answered, "I'm aware of the concept, yes." He couldn't let himself feel sorry for her because why would she be going on a blind date considering the circumstances? It was risky if not downright reckless. Until the police were done investigating the guy who'd tried to attack her father, she needed to lay low. And she needed an education about safety procedures. Dr. Bellaire was right to hire him, or almost hire him.

The doorbell chimed again.

"You need to stay here, please," Kyle stated. He strode toward the door and reached for the handle only to find her hot on his heels. Pulling his hand away, he swiveled toward her, "What part of that did you not understand?"

"Seriously?"

He wanted to laugh at this whole unfortunate misunderstanding, except it wasn't funny. Not really, not when he thought about what could have happened here. So instead, he quirked an eyebrow, trying to find a way to make her understand what she could have conceivably gotten herself into.

Chin squared, a touch of indignation played on her features. "It's not necessary to speak to me like that. I don't care if you are my bodyguard."

"You're right. I apologize. The position is for security consultant, and technically, I'm not even your employee yet." She was right on more than one level. Not only was it unprofessional, but he also couldn't let his preconceived notions or his personal concerns about her interfere with his job. He needed to think of this like a mission where emotion had no place. When his apology was met with a distrustful glare, he lifted a consoling hand and tried to smooth his tone. "Listen, Harper, I am sorry. My people skills are a little rusty. I'm used to giving orders. But I promise you, this isn't some power play on my part. This is about keeping you safe. As I'm sure you're aware, a man tried to attack your father today, and very likely would have succeeded if I hadn't stopped him." He swept a hand toward the door. "I don't know for sure who this is, and neither do you. Now, would you, please, move away from the door?"

Her head tilted, her face scrunched thoughtfully, but the meaning seemed to get through to her. "Fine," she said, nodding and taking a couple of steps back. "I'm sorry. You're right."

He pointed. "Waiting in the kitchen would be best. What's your date's name?" When she didn't immediately answer, he added, "You do know that much, I hope?"

"Yes," she said with a resigned sigh. "Mikhail." Then she turned and walked down the hall.

Kyle opened the door to find a man standing on the porch. He made a quick assessment: thin, medium-height, dark blond freshly trimmed hair that appeared damp. The scent of soap and aftershave suggested a recent shower rather than too much product. His friendly smile and neat appearance contributed to that overall clueless, hopeful first-date air. Kyle relaxed slightly.

"You must be Mikhail."

"Yes, I'm looking for Harper, we—"

"Harper is going to have to cancel on that date tonight."

"Uh, okay, you must be her…?"

Kyle stared blandly, not about to fall for the old fill-in-the-blank trick. In Kyle's world, information was divulged on a need-to-know basis.

"Brother?" the guy finally asked.

Kyle declined to confirm or deny. Although,

he knew Harper was an only child. The only child of a single father who'd raised her on his own from the age of four when his wife, Harper's mother, had died suddenly after contracting meningitis. He knew this because he'd spent the train ride from Seattle to Portland reading about the Bellaire empire, and the drive from there to the coast reviewing every detail in his mind. But then, both because he could see where this initial meeting between him and Harper had gone wrong and because he felt a tiny bit sorry for the guy, he said, "Harper isn't feeling well. She'll call you when she can."

Kyle shut the door, locked it and headed to the kitchen where he found Harper staring at a tablet screen. She looked up as if seeing him for the first time, which he soon realized, she sort of was.

"You're Kyle Frasier," she said, and the words were like a choke hold around Kyle's heart because they sounded like an accusation.

CHAPTER TWO

"You—" Harper broke off the word to clear her throat. "You really did save my dad this morning." Reverent-like, she offered up the tablet in her hands. "I mean, you saved him, *saved* him. This guy with the salmon eggs…"

A mix of relief and unease swept through him. The first because her tone didn't have anything to do with her disappointment in realizing who he was. And the second because, presumably, she'd watched the news footage. Despite declining to be interviewed, he'd made the national news. Josh had texted him a screenshot along with a message: Dude. Nice. Did your interview come with an audition? Seriously way to go. You rock.

More texts had arrived from friends and former teammates, as well as one from his mom telling him "they" were calling him a hero on TV. His sister, Mia, had even messaged to make sure that he was okay. Kyle had absolutely no interest in watching the story himself.

"I was just—" He almost said "doing my job," but then paused because that was no longer true. He tried not to think about how unsettled that fact made him feel. Still, the action had been second nature. He could no more *not* help someone than he could breathe air. "Anyone would have done the same."

Twirling a helpless hand, she scoffed. "Yeah, no, I don't think so. A few people might have tried, a few others may have thought about trying, but that guy was really fast. He was no match for you though. You're like a ninja."

"I'm just glad I was in the right place at the right time." Uncomfortable with her praise, he attempted to put the focus back on the pertinent issue. Hitching a thumb over his shoulder, he said, "You let me inside your house thinking I was that guy, didn't you?"

"Yes, but I can explain." With a little cringe, she added, "Sort of."

"I could have been anyone in the world walking in here." Kyle put some scare into his words and tone, "That fanatic's brother or cousin or buddy or whoever else might be scheming with him." Frowning, he shook his head. "I could have been a random serial killer, for that matter."

"I realize that, but…" Dipping her chin, she studied the tablet before lifting her gaze back up to look at him. Slowly, she repeated the whole process. That's when Kyle realized that she'd put all the pieces together. He'd wondered if, when, she would or if he'd have to tell her. If he was going to be working for her, they needed to get this conversation out of the way, to clear the air between them.

Placing the tablet on the counter, she brought one trembling hand up and laid it palm down across her forehead. Voice a little shaky and unsure, she said, "But you're not. You're none of those things. You're Owen's SEAL friend Kyle." Her gaze collided firmly with his and Kyle watched as a slideshow of emotions played across her face, most he couldn't identify, but the distress and the curiosity were unmistakable. No matter what had happened between her and Owen, his presence was clearly upsetting her on some level. Between that and the news story—he now suspected that she hadn't known the extent of her father's brush with danger—she was probably reeling. Kyle felt terrible about that and hoped that his ultimate purpose for being here could rectify some of these feelings.

"Former SEAL, recently discharged."

"I can't believe I didn't recognize you. Owen had photos of you. Of the two of you in Iraq, Croatia, Pakistan, Afghanistan, the

Netherlands…" With narrowed eyes, her gaze latched firmly on to him, traveling slowly, analyzing in a way that made Kyle feel unsettled. With a shake of her head, she whispered, "You're *Kyle*," almost like she hadn't meant to say it out loud. And definitely like she couldn't quite believe her eyes.

"Yes, ma'am," Kyle said because he wasn't sure what to say, how much to say or where to start.

She studied him for a while longer before declaring, "You look different now."

He shrugged a shoulder. "Older, no uniform."

"No," she said firmly and with a confident shake of her head, the shock easing into curiosity. "That's not it. It's…" Then her expression changed; gathering herself together, she seemed to set that puzzle aside and demanded, "What are you doing here?"

HARPER WAS HYPERCONSCIOUS of the beat of her heart as she stared at Kyle Frasier. It wasn't fast so much as it was hard and painful like all the still-wounded parts were pounding and grinding against each other in discordant harmony. Barely resisting the urge to grip her shirt above the offending spot, she waited for his answer and struggled to sort the key points: Kyle had been Owen's best friend; Owen's best friend was standing in her kitchen; her dad had chosen him to be her security consultant. Questions followed: How much did Kyle know about Owen? How much did he know about her? And her and Owen's relationship, especially the end? What had Owen told him about his "side business" and Harper's part in it? Why hadn't her dad told her that her new bodyguard was showing up today?

Some of this must have been evident on her face because Kyle said, "We have some things to discuss. Harper, I'm sorry. I didn't mean to blindside you like this. As I'm sure you know, I was supposed to show up tomorrow morning so you could conduct a final interview, a more formal one, and decide whether you wanted to go ahead with this. With me, I mean."

"Yes, that's what my dad said. But he didn't tell me your name. He was going to send the details in an email. He's probably already sent it—I haven't checked. I figured I would have time to review it all in the morning."

Kyle nodded. "Obviously, I messed that up. I was driving right by here anyway, so I decided to drop in and introduce myself. I thought you might be feeling anxious after the attempted attack on your dad. And, honestly, I didn't know how you'd feel about hiring me? Specifically. Because of Owen."

Jaw tight, mouth a hard, flat line, his eyes blazed with intensity as they searched her face, his expression saying so much, and revealing so little at the same time. She chose to ignore the question because she couldn't answer it. Not yet. Not until he answered a few of her questions first. Her attention was drawn to the news story still on her tablet. Shifting her focus to the headline, she read it again: "BEST CEO Bellaire Attacked." Her father had called it "an incident." Lately, episodes like this had been happening more and more, where some extremist got in his face screaming about dams or salmon—depending on which side of the issue they stood.

That much, at least, she could explain. "Yeah, he downplayed the *incident* significantly. That's what he called it—an incident. He never said 'attack,' or even 'attempted attack.'"

"I doubt he did. More likely, the news is overdramatizing. I'd call it an incident. The guy didn't even touch your dad."

"Because of you." This person undoubtedly had intentions to hurt her dad. You could see the anger all over his face, the hatred in his body language. Gratitude and appreciation mingled with her shock. She wanted to hug the man standing before her, except he was the opposite of huggable. So *not* warm and fuzzy. More than once, Owen had said that he'd never seen a better soldier than his friend Kyle. Nor had he ever had a better friend. He worshipped the ground this guy walked on.

If there was one positive thing she could say about Owen, it was that he'd been good at his job. Thanks to his navy training and experience, he knew how to move people and supplies and keep them safe. And other things, she thought distastefully, like he'd done in Africa. If Owen thought Kyle was the best, then he probably was. But that still didn't answer her question.

"But why you? I mean, why were you there? And how did you—? I have..." *So many questions.* She glanced up at Kyle and felt her pulse accelerate again. What she had were too many feelings. Could she handle having this living and breathing reminder of Owen in her life every day for the next however-many weeks?

But Kyle had seemed to anticipate her emotional quagmire, and he sought to untangle it. "I was in your dad's building because I had an interview with Dahlia International."

At the mention of Dahlia, Harper tensed, a familiar feeling of frustration stealing over her. She may have scowled, but thankfully Kyle didn't seem to notice.

He went on, "I'd met your dad twice with Owen. Had lunch in Seattle and spent some time with him in Amsterdam. You're really lucky. He's an extraordinary guy. Anyway, I saw him in the lobby, and he'd just walked over to say hi when this guy went after him. And I… I helped out. Afterward, your dad and I talked some more. He expressed his concerns about your safety, I gave him some advice and he offered me this job. I don't start with Dahlia for another month or so. So, here I am."

Harper exhaled a breath. This all made sense. In the way that cosmic jokes, or colliding fates, or whatever this encounter might be made sense anyway. Inexplicably, she felt herself both repelled by and drawn to Kyle Frasier. More proof that her own judgment was not to be trusted. In this case, she supposed only time would tell. *If* she chose to hire him, that is… *Time*. Oh, jeez, she'd forgotten all about Mikhail!

Snagging her phone off the counter, she

pointed it at him as she sidestepped toward the doorway. "You know what? We'll talk about this later." She picked up her bag from the floor where she'd placed it earlier and slipped the strap over her shoulder. "Tomorrow morning, okay? When you come for your interview, we'll figure all of this out and—"

"Harper, I think we should talk about it now," Kyle countered smoothly. "The sooner we work out some of these details, the better." That voice. Deep and low with just enough compassion that Harper found herself wanting to comply. Or maybe the compassion part was her imagination, her hope, that this guy was only like Owen in the good ways. That he might be as willing to help her as he'd been to help her dad. But how likely was that? *Like brothers*, she'd heard Owen say countless times about himself and Kyle. Just because birds had similar feathers didn't mean they always flocked together, right? Or maybe they did. See? Clearly, she needed to sort this through.

"Okay, tonight, then. After my date." She gestured toward the front door. "I've kept the poor guy waiting and confused long enough. We'll skip the bungee jumping, go and have a quiet dinner somewhere, and then I'll come back, and you and I can have a proper interview."

"Oh. Your date is gone."

"Gone? Where is he?"

Kyle shrugged. "In his car cruising down Highway 101, I'm guessing."

"What did you tell him?"

"That you'd call him later."

"I don't have his number."

"You don't—" He broke off with a sigh of frustration. "What *do* you know about him? Did you have him checked out?"

"He's a friend of a friend," she answered evasively and yes, a little defensively. At the flicker of disapproval that crossed his face, she added, "I agreed to the date a week ago." Somehow, she needed to explain her rationale. But how uncomfortable and awkward to admit that she'd been excited (sort of) to go on the first date she'd had since she'd been involved with his deceased best friend. Where they'd been in a relationship based on deception that had ended very badly. This was insane. What was she doing? What was *he* doing here agreeing to babysit his best friend's ex, anyway? Who did that? Why would he do that?

"Well, from now on, you're not going out with Mikhail or anyone else until they've been vetted. That includes a background check and all the accompanying intel. And an…assessment."

"An assessment?" Her voice went high and a little shrill.

His expression seemed to thaw slightly. "Yes, I'll want to meet them. But don't worry, they won't know they're being assessed." Kyle offered up a hand in a placating gesture. "No one has to know you have a…security consultant working for you. As far as your friends, and dates, know I'm an old family friend staying in your guesthouse and helping with some maintenance. Your dad, if you agree, has hired me temporarily with the hope that this will quickly blow over. In the meantime, I'm going to teach you how to take care of yourself."

"Take care of myself?" she repeated, taking advantage of the unintentional gaffe. "Are there cooking lessons involved? What about laundry?" He went wide-eyed, and Harper almost laughed.

"No, I meant… I mean security-wise. I'm going to help you be more aware of your surroundings and potential threats and what to do if you are threatened. I'm going to teach you how to use every feature of your security system and—"

"Kyle, I know what you meant. I was joking. I'm sorry, I'm a bit stressed, and I tend to…" She cut herself off because she didn't need to point out her habit of making bad jokes under duress. She'd already provided him with ample evidence when she thought he was her date. "Let's, um, do you want to sit down?" Harper gestured toward the living room.

"Sure."

Harper watched him walk into the next room. As much as she didn't want to, it was impossible not to compare the two men. On the surface, they had similar features, brown hair, brown eyes, same olive complexion. But everything about Kyle, including his expression, was darker. Kyle didn't possess Owen's extreme good looks, but he'd be plenty handsome if he weren't so…severe. His thick brown hair wasn't quite a buzz cut, but it was still a little too short for her taste, too militaryish, too Owen-like. But then again, he'd just gotten out of the military. His physique certainly backed that up, that he hadn't slacked in his conditioning was obvious. And he had Owen on that score. A couple of inches shorter than Owen's six foot two inches, he was broader in the shoulders, bulkier everywhere and much more defined. The cut of muscles outlined beneath his T-shirt reminded her of an MMA fighter she'd photographed last fall. She told herself it was the artist in her noting these details and not the woman who'd barely socialized, much less dated, in six months.

His gaze traveling around the room, Kyle took a seat in one of the two chairs adjacent to the gas fireplace. She'd already noticed his eyes were an arresting shade of brown, but so dark it made them difficult to read. Like the rest of him. Although Harper suspected he did that unreadable thing on purpose. The whole time he'd been here, he had yet to crack a smile, or even offer much in the way of emotion at all. Except for confusion, but she couldn't blame him for that. Maybe it was a good thing. Like a robot sitting in the corner, she could forget he was even there. What she did not need in her life was another man with an overabundance of charm and charisma. Those were the very traits that had suckered her in time and again.

Harper settled on the sofa and asked, "Can I get you anything? Something to drink maybe?"

"No, thank you."

"How about a snack?"

"No."

"Would you like—"

"I'm fine."

"Okay, so…" She offered her sweetest smile, the one she used on her most anxious, reluctant, camera-shy clients. And then waited for him to return it. Nothing. No reaction whatsoever. Just that same somber expression. When the moment threatened to turn awkward, she finally gave up. "So, I'd like to explain my behavior. Earlier when you first arrived, I thought you were my date."

"I caught that."

"I want you to know that I'm not normally so impulsive and…enthusiastic. Well, maybe I am, to a degree. But not like this. This was…" Shifting around she tried to form an explanation that didn't make her sound like an irresponsible flake. "You see, I was—"

"Harper," he interrupted with an outstretched hand. "You don't need to explain. I know what you were doing."

Harper chuckled self-consciously. "I doubt that."

"You were going to have some fun on your last night without your new security guy watching your every move."

Huh. Well. Points awarded for insight, if not personality. "I can only imagine how terrible you think that is."

He squinted his eyes slightly like he was

trying to decide how to respond. Finally, he seemed to make a decision, and said, "What happened already happened. Or didn't happen in this case. There was a miscommunication between you and your dad. I intend to speak to him about that. I imagine that he didn't divulge all the details because he didn't want you to worry, but I don't think it does you any favors for him to sugarcoat any threat made against him."

Harper liked that, that he wasn't intimidated by her dad. That, and he seemed to be a proponent of honesty.

He went on, "You're fine for now. Meaning you're safe. The episode was good in a way. It told me a lot about how much work we're facing here. My goal is to instill specific habits in you so that you won't need a bodyguard 24/7 for the rest of your life. So, as far as I'm concerned, we can forget about what happened here today and move forward."

Harper felt her anxiety ease slightly. Did he mean that in a larger sense? Moving forward was what she wanted. But the Owen factor did need to be addressed.

He must have thought so, too, because he said, "I know that it didn't end well between you and Owen, that you wanted different things."

"That's what he said? Different things?"

"Well, he called me the day before he died. He was…upset. You'd left the country, and he felt… He said you guys had a fight and you'd ended your relationship."

Harper barely held on to her scoff. It was beyond strange to hear Owen's version of a "fight" that, for Harper, had been so much more than that.

"But he didn't say what kind of differences we had?"

"No, but I know he was hoping you'd work them out. If he hadn't died maybe you two would have…"

Harper froze. All her previous tension rushed back in and then some, blazing with a brand-new ferocity. Her skin prickled uncomfortably. Had Owen said that? Because their issues were impossible to work out. She'd never wanted to see him again, would never have spoken to him again even if he hadn't been killed in that car accident.

She'd been studying Kyle carefully, listening, watching for any clue that he knew about Owen's enterprise. Owen had told her in confidence, sworn her to secrecy. He'd said that no one from Dahlia knew about his "side business." But he needed to bring someone else on board because it was growing so fast. Customers were clamoring for the exotic plants and animal parts he was selling. Mistakenly, stupidly, he'd believed Harper's love for him would allow her to not only accept this endeavor but to help him. Specifically, with the use of her dad's jet. He took steps, he assured her, to confirm that his dealings were technically legal. But Harper suspected otherwise. At the very least, it was both unethical and immoral.

Kyle said that Owen didn't specify what their differences were. If he'd told Kyle, it seemed like there'd be no reason not to mention them now. But still, she had to know.

"Did you, um, did you know much about Owen's work?"

"Uh, yeah, sure. I've been offered a job with Dahlia. I don't start until next month, but I also have another friend working there. So I have a pretty good grasp of what the work entails."

"In Africa? Did he talk about his time there much?"

"No..." he drawled, his face twisting with discomfort and confusion. Further evidence, Harper decided, that he didn't know. She wondered what he'd think about the venture. Had Owen not told him because he didn't think Kyle would approve? She hoped so.

A more burning question followed and seared her conscience. Was it Harper's place to tell him the truth?

CHAPTER THREE

KYLE'S INTENSE BROWN gaze caught Harper's as he started speaking, derailing Harper's train of thought. "Harper, what I'm trying to say is that I know you loved Owen, too. He was a great man and my best friend. He was like a brother to me, and I wouldn't be here if it weren't for him. I don't know if he mentioned it, but the last mission we did together, he saved my life. He could have been killed. He should have been. We both should be…" His voice trailed off, and Harper was staggered by the emotion she saw, the sincerity she heard, the love and grief he so obviously felt for his friend.

Inhaling a breath, he gathered himself and continued, "Despite your breakup, I know his death had to be hard on you, too. I imagine with how things ended, it was probably even more difficult in some ways than it would have been otherwise. Owen made it clear to me that it wasn't over between you two."

Tears welled in her eyes, and she barely

managed to blink them away before they spilled over. The Owen she knew did not deserve this kind of devotion.

Sympathy was evident in the deep brown depths of his gaze. "Harper, I, um, I'm just so sorry. Those are words I should have said to you a long time ago. I thought about reaching out to you after Owen died, but I didn't, and I'm sorry for that, too."

Harper nodded because she didn't know what else to do; her tears, her pain, did not exist for the reason he believed, but she couldn't find the right words to explain. But that wasn't quite accurate. She had the words; she just didn't know if she should use them.

"I'm sorry for *you*," she finally managed. And that, she realized, was true. She'd often thought about how differently she'd feel about Owen's death if she hadn't learned the truth. If he'd died before revealing his true character, before their breakup, she would have been devastated. Of course, she realized now that she'd fallen for a man who didn't exist. It wasn't the first time she'd been fooled.

This man seated before her was no robot bodyguard. Her heart went out to him, but at the same time, she was almost jealous of him, of this pure emotion born of unsullied memories. She didn't see any reason to spoil that for him, to cause him more pain. She decided she couldn't do it, knowingly tarnish his memory of Owen. What possible purpose could that serve?

Clearing his throat, he said, "You don't have to talk about it. We don't have to talk about this anymore. That's not why I'm here. I did want to apologize, but your grief is your own, as is mine. And I want you to know that as far as I'm concerned, whatever happened between you two doesn't have anything to do with you and me, with our relationship." After a pause, he clarified, "Potential working relationship."

She could live with that. And him, she decided, going with her gut. She couldn't imagine anything else that he could have said that would have eased her anxiety as much as the speech he'd just given. And he was right; she didn't want to discuss Owen.

"Okay," she said, "You're hired."

Instead of appearing happy to get the job, he frowned. "Are you sure? Do you want to ask me some questions first?"

"No. I've heard—and seen—all I need to know."

He gave his head a little shake. "Please, don't let that news story sway you. You know how the media spins everything."

"It's not the news story," she said, even though it was a little. "My dad trusts you." The fact that he'd risked his own safety to protect her dad counted for a lot. "And I'm sure you met Dad's head security guy, Denny?" At Kyle's nod, she added, "Then you meet his standards, too, which are very high." Weighing her next words carefully, she said, "You're right that I don't want to talk about what happened between Owen and me, but I will tell you that he trusted you. More than anyone. He had nothing but wonderful things to say about you. According to him, you were the best man and the best soldier ever."

Dipping his chin, he scrubbed a hand across one cheek before meeting her gaze again. "The feeling was mutual."

"I can see that," Harper said diplomatically. She inhaled deeply and slowly and then eased out the breath. Was she crazy to agree to this? Maybe. But there was something so solid and comforting about this guy, and, if she were being honest, she wanted him to be for real. Without a doubt, she needed some help. He was right that she could have easily let some unknown, potentially dangerous person into her house tonight. Much of the time she didn't even bother with the security system anyway. When she did, she often wasn't sure if she'd done everything properly. The notion was rather sobering and lent an extra dose of urgency to his employment. She realized her dad knew all of this and had probably been experiencing something similar when he offered Kyle the job.

"So…" she drawled. "How are we going to do this? Lecture and then lab? Or do you have like a personal security textbook, *Stay Safe 101*? Just to warn you, I'm awful at pop quizzes. After the first one, I will resent you for the entire semester and not perform to my highest capability."

Kyle sat back in his seat, seeming to relax a bit as he pondered her tongue-in-cheek questions. And probably her. Had he been nervous that she wouldn't agree to hire him? That thought was rather endearing. It made him seem both human and normal, and it gave her confidence in her decision.

But only briefly because his expression went stony again. Like granite. Hard, scary granite.

Leaning forward, he placed his forearms on his thighs and tented his fingers. "It's all lab, Harper. One hundred percent hands-on. And we're going to start by getting you in shape. Calisthenics for one hour every morning at 4:30 a.m., followed by a five-mile run on the beach." Tipping his head, he added, "But not your typical run. Every other day, we'll add an obstacle course to simulate tactical evasion. And three days a week, we'll have what I like to call target practice."

What. The. Whatty-what? Harper opened her mouth, shut it and finally managed to stutter, "Um, target what? I don't know how to... I mean, I don't—"

He straightened, interrupting her with a stop-sign hand. "Relax, it's not what you think. *You* won't be doing any shooting. I'll be shooting *at* you with a paintball gun while you try to dodge it. The less paint on your person, the more lunch you earn. Positive reinforcement can be helpful in specific, isolated training situations."

Harper knew she was gaping. Was he out of his mind? Had the word *normal* actually crossed her mind in conjunction with this lunatic? He was as messed up as Owen. More, possibly. She was still trying to decide how to proceed when his face broke into a wide smile, or at least she hoped it was a smile. The whole time he'd been here she'd yet to see it, so she couldn't be sure. She kept still, waiting, in case she was misinterpreting the gesture. Maybe he was wincing or had something stuck in his teeth.

Finally, he said, "Harper, I'm joking. I do have some basic protocol that we'll cover. Your dad wants you to become an expert with your security system. But otherwise, we'll just plan on doing this situationally, taking it one day at a time. Does that work for you?"

Huh. She had not seen that coming. But she also liked it. A grin crept over her, and she laughed. He joined her, and Harper was momentarily mesmerized by the deep, rich sound. The smile that lingered transformed him. Harper met his gaze and warmth spread through her chest, making her head a little light, her thoughts a bit fuzzy. She couldn't remember the last time she'd laughed like this, felt so at ease.

That thought was sobering in itself, melting her laughter away. Because this situation was anything but easy; she officially had herself a bodyguard.

"ONE SOYSAGE, SPINACH and kale omelet." Nora Frasier proudly set a plate in front of her only son. "Protein packed with two servings of veggies tucked inside."

"Thanks, Mom. Sounds delicious," Kyle

lied as Nora turned and sailed back into the kitchen.

Soysage? Kyle mouthed the word to his seventeen-year-old quasi-nephew, Levi, who was sitting across the table from him in his sister Mia's dining room. Kyle sniffed at his plate, and then whispered, "Does she think it will make it more palatable by having it sound more meat-like? Or that we'll be so impressed by the clever play on words that we won't be able to resist?"

Levi let out a snort of laughter, which he convincingly covered with a cough. Or maybe he was choking. Poor kid had already taken a bite of his omelet. Levi lifted his glass of orange juice and took a sip.

Adamantly refusing to put anyone out, Kyle had been crashing on the couch in Mia and Jay's downstairs family room for the last few weeks since arriving in Pacific Cove. Last night, he'd left Harper's with the plan for them to meet back at her place this morning. They'd agreed on 8:30 as his official start time. Kyle smiled to himself as he thought about the look on her face when he'd proposed his "fitness plan." He hadn't been able to resist teasing her; she was so obviously nervous about this whole security thing. That easy laugh of hers was contagious, even though he recognized her joking around as a defense mechanism. He'd have to be careful about keeping her on track, emphasizing the importance of their task.

Mia was a veterinarian and co-owned a clinic in Pacific Cove. Her husband, Jay, was a former Coast Guard flight mechanic who'd recently started his own construction business. Their home was a large four-bedroom bungalow overlooking the ocean, but it didn't feel nearly as large as the actual square footage. Two of the bedrooms were filled with Jay's teenaged siblings, Levi and Laney, who Jay had legal custody of.

Until recently, Nora had occupied the fourth bedroom, but now she lived in a plush apartment above the garage that Jay had recently added on. Nora's old room was now Jay's office, which doubled as a sometimes bedroom for Jay's youngest two siblings, Dean and Delilah, who lived with their other sister, Josie, but visited often and liked to sleep over.

Two dogs and four cats rounded out the total of occupants. And Mia's dog, George, was roughly the size of two people. Currently, the mastiff-bloodhound mix was camped out under the dining room table with his massive head resting on Kyle's feet. George was the sweetest dog in the world with a bad habit of eating anything that would fit between his massive jaws. Which gave Kyle an idea.

Leaning backward, he glanced under the table. "Georgie," he whispered.

"I already tried it," Levi said, reading his intention. "George won't eat it."

"Really? Dang." That did not bode well. Kyle had seen George eat chunks of rotten seaweed like they were gravy-covered biscuits. Kyle picked up his fork and used it to flip up the top layer of the omelet. Taking a peek inside, he whispered, "What are the grayish-brown bits?"

"Pepitas," Levi answered.

At Kyle's confused headshake, Levi explained, "That'd be a pumpkin seed to you and me."

"In an omelet?" The eggs at least would be good, courtesy of Nora's cage-free, organically fed laying hens.

"Nora thinks they go in everything. She even puts them in those cookie things she makes." To Kyle's way of thinking, the "cookie things" weren't truly cookies because they didn't contain sugar. Still, he'd decided he could handle the sugar-free life better than the meatless one.

Kyle let out a dramatic sigh, and said wistfully, "You know, Levi, there was a time in my life when my mom made the best ham-and-cheese omelets on the planet."

"Ham?" Levi quirked a skeptical brow. "You're telling me Nora Frasier once ingested nitrite-laden, sodium-infused pork products?"

"Those were good times."

They shared a chuckle.

"I still can't believe you have *two* jobs!" Nora called from the kitchen.

Exchanging concerned glances, Kyle and Levi both hurriedly shoveled in several bites of omelet before Nora reappeared.

"I'm swallowing the *peptides* whole," Kyle whispered. Levi laughed outright at his deliberate mispronunciation.

Soon after he'd arrived in Pacific Cove, Kyle had discovered that Levi also was not a fan of the meat alternatives Nora liked to ply them with when he'd come in late one night and found him frying bacon. The real stuff. No *fakon* for this kid. Kyle enthusiastically offered to help. They'd feasted on bacon sandwiches after which Levi showed Kyle his processed meat stash in the spare fridge in the garage. They'd taken to clandestinely going out for burgers whenever they could manage. No way would either of them risk hurting Nora's feelings by confessing to these transgressions.

Nora hustled back into the room with her own plate. "*And* you found a place to live."

"One job at a time, Mom." Kyle grinned at Nora. "And the housing is temporary. In exchange for helping out a friend's daughter, I'm going to stay in her guest cottage for a month. After I start at Dahlia, I'll be able to find more permanent lodgings of my own."

"And it's right here in Pacific Cove?"

"Basically. It's several miles south of town."

"Who is it? Do I know these people?"

"I doubt you know them," he hedged. Of course, his mom had heard of David Bellaire, but after Harper revealed that no one in Pacific Cove seemed aware of the association between her and her father, they decided to keep it that way. This was made easier because Harper used the last name Jansen, her mother's maiden name, as her professional moniker. "They're from Seattle, and the daughter has only been living here a few months."

His mom had met Owen a couple of times when Kyle had brought him home with him on leave. But that had been years ago; she didn't know him well. To his knowledge, she hadn't been aware that Owen had been in a relationship. Kyle didn't mention the association now because it would be a lot to explain without revealing Harper's parentage. "Need to know" was ingrained in him right along with his sense of loyalty. Like a lot of habits that had kept him alive in his military career, he doubted he'd ever break that one either.

As it had too often since he'd been here in Pacific Cove, it struck him once again how little his family knew about him. Understandable to a degree, considering the circumstances of his career. The sad part was how little he knew about them. He'd been a terrible son to his mom and an even worse brother to Mia. He hadn't even come home for Mia and Jay's wedding. A fresh twist of regret and guilt tightened his chest.

"That's great news! Isn't that great news, Mia?" His mom, at least, didn't seem to hold it against him. She tried so hard to make him feel like he belonged. Too hard, Kyle thought. He didn't deserve to be forgiven so easily.

Kyle watched Mia in the kitchen beyond pouring a cup of coffee. Ten years in the military, eight of those in Special Forces, numerous life-and-death missions, and his big sister still made him nervous. As kids, they'd never had a great relationship or even a good one for that matter. Now, as an adult, Kyle understood why. Their dad, William Frasier, now deceased, but who they'd only recently learned was not Mia's biological father, had always favored Kyle. Worse than that, he'd basically ignored Mia.

On an unspoken level, Kyle had known it was unfair, but he'd worshipped his navy officer father, so he'd never questioned his dad's unequal treatment of his kids. Partially because, painful as it was to admit, he'd been the one to reap the benefits. He regretted that, and especially the wedge it had driven between him and Mia. Kyle wanted to fix it, or at least make it better; he just had no clue how to go about it. He wasn't sure it was possible.

Mia entered the dining room and sat at the table opposite him. "That is good news," she said in a tone that told Kyle the words didn't equate to how she really felt. "Congratulations. But, when you start at Dahlia, you'll be gone all the time anyway, right? So basically, it will be like you're still in the navy."

"Not exactly," he said, even though his stomach pitched at the truth behind her words. He'd figure out a way to make it work.

"Dangerous assignments where you spend weeks or months overseas," she intoned wryly. "Yeah, totally different."

"I'll be paid a lot more, and I'm out of uniform." That sounded lame even to him.

"So, you're doing it for the money?"

Kyle was grateful for the military training that kept him from reacting to his sister's challenging stare. There didn't seem to be much they could discuss without disagreeing. "I couldn't make anything even close to what I'll be making at Dahlia anywhere around here." That was another evasion. The truth was that he didn't really have an answer to Mia's question, other than he and Owen had planned this for years. From the time Owen had left the military, they'd begun discussing it. They'd wanted to work together again, and maybe someday start their own business. Owen had been gearing up for it already, planning, waiting for Kyle to join him at Dahlia. Irrational as it was, he couldn't shake the notion that if he'd started at Dahlia sooner, Owen would still be alive. The day before the accident, when he'd called, Owen had once again said how much he wished Kyle was with him. Bottom line, he felt compelled to take the job. Just like he did where Harper was concerned. The obligation, the drive to somehow make this right, was something he couldn't explain.

He hadn't realized how much Harper represented unfinished business until he'd seen Dr. Bellaire. The thought had only intensified when he'd met her face-to-face. Now it felt like his duty to make sure she'd be okay, to give her the tools to stay safe. To be happy. From their conversation the night before, Kyle could see she was hurting, no doubt dealing with her own regrets and grief. Fate, in the form of Dr. Bellaire, had given him an opportunity to ease his conscience by helping the love of Owen's life, and he was going to take it. Owen would want him to. He owed it to him.

Mia was frowning, and Kyle knew she was gearing up to counter his argument. Jay saved him, strolling into the dining room with Duke, his fluffy camel-colored cat, in his arms. Kyle could hear the cat purring from several feet away. Coastie, Jay's Brittany Spaniel, and constant companion, trotted beside him looking every bit as intelligent and vigilant as Kyle knew her to be.

Jay smiled at Kyle. "Hey, there's our hero. Just saw the story on the news again this morning."

Kyle gave his head a shake of bemused exasperation.

"Heard you got the job," Jay said, and Kyle appreciated that his brother-in-law understood that he didn't want to talk about it anymore. Not that he ever had. "Welcome to the civilian life of the gainfully employed."

"Thanks, man."

"Sucks for me though—no more free labor."

"Not exactly free." Kyle had been filling most of his days by working with Jay on construction jobs. Ironically, he now knew his brother-in-law, whom he'd only met a month ago, better than he did his sister. "I appreciate you guys letting me bunk here."

Jay waved off the thanks. "I have an old Coast Guard buddy who works for Dahlia. I've heard the pay is outstanding."

Mia let out a quiet sigh.

Kyle nodded at Jay. "It is."

"What's outstanding pay?" Lanie, Jay's sixteen-year-old sister, strolled into the room.

"Kyle's new job with Dahlia International." This came from Levi who, enviably, had finished his omelet and moved on to a bowl of fruit.

"What is that, like a florist?" Laney gave Kyle a doubtful frown. "Retiring from the military is one thing. Taking up flower arranging is altogether another. That's a total waste of your soldiering skills, Uncle Kyle."

Kyle laughed. Soon after meeting him, Laney had started calling him "Uncle Kyle," declaring that she'd always wanted a "cool uncle." Kyle had no idea how he'd passed the cool test with these teens, but he already adored them both.

Levi chuckled and answered, "Dahlia International is not a florist, Lanes. It's the fourth largest military security and intelligence contractor in the world. Kyle will be working security detail."

In the short time, Kyle had been in Pacific Cove he'd been continually amazed by Levi's maturity and intellect. Studious, thoughtful, responsible, he reminded Kyle of Mia when they were growing up. He even wanted to be a veterinarian.

Hands on hips, Laney gave Kyle the stare-down. "So that means you'll still be in combat-type situations, right?"

Kyle tried not to smile. Laney, on the other hand, was more like him: confident, adventurous, athletic, but also fearless in a way that might border on reckless if not kept in check. She'd quizzed him relentlessly about his life as a SEAL. No matter how much he downplayed combat and tried not to glamorize it, Laney remained fascinated. Just like he'd been by his dad and all things military.

"Not as much," he answered carefully.

"I still wish you'd teach me how to handle a firearm. Jay's not comfortable doing it."

Mia's frown deepened. Laney's interest in military life, and with him, seemed to irritate Mia.

Laney often talked about joining the military or law enforcement, with the FBI or CIA as her ultimate goal. Kyle thought with the years of life experience college would bring, she'd be an excellent candidate for the profession.

"That's because a professional instructor would be best. There are classes you can take."

"Yes! A class is a great idea."

Mia went wide-eyed and pinned a glare on Kyle.

Yep, it was entirely possible he'd worn out his welcome. The timing seemed right to get out of Mia's hair, not to mention that it would be nice to have his own space at Harper's, even if it was only temporary.

"Hey, Annie Oakley," Nora said, stepping out of the kitchen and grinning at Laney. "You want pepitas in your omelet?"

And ham. Unlimited access to bacon and ham would also be a bonus.

CHAPTER FOUR

NOT ONLY WAS it not in Kyle's nature to panic, the navy had honed his tactical response to one of logic and action. Granted, he'd never been in this specific situation before…unable to locate the woman he'd been hired to protect.

After breakfast with his family, he'd collected his stuff, which consisted of a backpack, a duffel bag, a suitcase and a cardboard box. The first two pieces he'd loaded into his vintage, someday-to-be-restored pickup. The remaining items he'd stowed at his mom's apartment before driving to his new place of employment where he arrived a half hour before the agreed upon meeting time.

Kyle assessed Harper's house again and approved of the fact that while spacious and well-kept, nothing about the older, two-story beachfront home screamed ostentatious. It was painted an attractive dove gray with frosty-white trim. The large lot provided privacy and plenty of space but not enough to draw undue attention. No one would guess the daughter of a billionaire lived here.

Harper had given him the key to his temporary residence the night before, so he let himself inside the guest cottage next door. With one spacious bedroom, and an open kitchen, dining, living area, the space reminded him of a swanky bungalow at a fancy resort. He was pleased to discover that it was fully stocked with household essentials.

To pass the time, he placed a shortcut to Harper's cell phone on his home screen and then played with her security app. He made a list of topics to cover with her over the next few days. When 8:37 rolled around with no word from her, an uneasy feeling began to creep over him. He tapped the icon to call her phone; it went straight to voice mail. Five minutes later, he tried again. He left a message and followed that immediately with a text. After an additional five minutes passed without a response, he pulled up the app again and checked the security footage from that morning.

Within seconds, he was watching Harper leave her house via the back door, the time display glowing 6:21 a.m. Why hadn't she called or texted to let him know she was going somewhere? More to the point, why hadn't she called or texted to let him know she'd be late for their meeting? Why wasn't she answering his calls now?

Kyle reviewed the footage carefully, looking for clues as to where she might have gone. The sun hadn't yet risen, but the deck was lit with well-placed motion lights. A daypack was secured on her shoulders, visible when she turned and paused briefly outside the door, locking it, he assumed. She paused for a moment before turning away from the door, and then hurried toward the set of stairs leading down to the beach where she disappeared from sight.

None of these actions would be causing him much concern if she'd answer her phone. Because if she'd simply gone out for a morning stroll on the beach, why wouldn't she pick up? He called again, and again it went straight to voice mail.

Internal alarm bells now ringing loudly, Kyle grabbed his sweatshirt and headed out the door. The air was thick with mist. Slipping the garment on while jogging down the steps, he quickly realized he should have worn his rain jacket. At the bottom, he discovered the thick fluffy sand littered with footprints. He could see that most of them appeared to be roughly the same size, suggesting they were Harper's, but the varying age of the tracks told him this was the accumulation of days and days of excursions onto the beach. Toward the ocean, where the softer sand turned firmer, he could make out a fresh set of prints more distinctly outlined than the rest and heading south.

He followed the tracks. The unmistakable scent of the beach's many tide-swept offerings drifted around him on the damp air, fish, seaweed and assorted moldering marine detritus. The combination was distinctive and familiar. The son of an ambitious navy officer meant his family had moved often, but they'd never lived far from the ocean. For most of his life, the beach had been his playground and his livelihood.

The wide expanse of sand appeared deserted. Jagged rocks jutted here and there, many the size of cars and larger. With the tide out, each monolith would now harbor tide pools, trapping marine animals and luring hungry seabirds looking for an easy catch. They were also a draw for curious tourists. And the perfect place for some ill-intentioned kidnapper to lurk around and snatch an unsuspecting billionaire's daughter. Concern gathering rapidly now, Kyle took off running along the wave line, following the tracks.

Minutes into his search, he cursed himself for not bringing binoculars. It was bad enough that his very first morning on the job he'd lost his subject. Being unprepared was inexcusable. In the field, it could get you killed. In this case, it could get Harper killed, and that would be worse.

The mist had turned to drizzle and soaked his sweatshirt through. His blue jeans were already heavy with moisture and sticking to his skin. A swirling haze of light fog rolled in from the ocean, cutting the visibility. Water droplets trickled along his scalp and down the back of his neck. As a SEAL he was no stranger to cold and discomfort, but that didn't mean he liked it.

Kyle estimated he'd jogged about a mile when the tracks veered off up the beach, ending at a rockier patch above the shoreline. He stopped to check his phone again. Then he turned a full circle before heading east toward the heavily wooded area between the beach and the highway. He decided to continue that way, although he knew she could have traversed the rocks before veering back down to the beach. She could have hiked into the forest. The coastline was littered with caves and rocky outcroppings. She could have ventured into one of those, as well.

Before reaching the tree line, he picked up her tracks again heading north on a distinct trail. As he started to jog, his phone rang in his hand. Harper's name flashed on the display.

"Harper," he answered, "where are you?"

"At home," she said like there was no other place she could possibly be.

"Are you okay?"

"Yes," she answered hesitantly, sounding almost confused. "I'm fine."

Kyle exhaled a relieved breath. "I called you. Why didn't you answer?"

"Yeah…" she drawled, "I just now saw your calls and text. I was on the beach with my phone off. I keep it off when I'm working."

"Why would you do that?"

"Um, I started doing it because the ringing disturbs wildlife. Even the sound of it on vibrate can startle an animal. A few years ago, I missed a shot of an osprey that still haunts me. Birds are called flighty for a reason," she quipped. "It's become a habit."

That made sense. But they would have to figure out a better system than her turning her phone off. Until then, she needed to not take off without him.

"Where are you?" she asked. "I knocked

on your door when I got back. Your pickup is here, but you're not, are you?"

"I am not."

"Oh, good." She sounded relieved and completely clueless about what she'd just put him through. "I thought I was late. Would you like a cup of coffee when you get here? I don't know if there's any in the guesthouse."

"Yes, I would like coffee. Harper, why did you sneak out of your house at six thirty in the morning without telling me where you're going? Or at least letting me know you'd be late."

A spark of surprised laughter crackled in his ear. "I didn't sneak. And I left you a note."

"A note?"

"I left a note on my door. You didn't see it?"

A note? Not a good idea. Kyle silently added note writing to his list of topics to cover. "I did not."

"Ah. That's why it was still here. I thought you'd come to the door if you got here before I came back."

A soaking wet, cold, extremely relieved and mildly exasperated Kyle stood in the rain, shaking his head. This really wasn't her fault. He let out a small sigh. "I would have done that, but I didn't want to wake you if you were still sleeping."

"That's very thoughtful. If I weren't a photographer, I'd appreciate the gesture, but I'm usually up at the crack of dawn. You know, because of the morning light."

Morning light. Sure. Unquestionably a learning curve here, for both of them. At this moment, mostly him. Memorizing her schedule would be a good place to start. "Don't go anywhere else. I'll be there in ten minutes or less."

Kyle hung up, hurriedly picked his way across the rocks to the sand and started running in the direction from which he'd come.

ROUGHLY TEN MINUTES LATER, Kyle's knock coincided with the sound of the back door opening.

"Harper?" he called. "It's me, Kyle."

Harper chuckled softly because who else would it be? "In here," she called from the kitchen.

Kyle stepped into the room looking serious and gloomy, which was a little disappointing. She'd been hoping for the lighthearted guy she'd gotten a glimpse of the evening before.

Sweeping a hand toward the back door

where he'd just entered, he said, "The door was unlocked."

His shoes squeaked on the tile as he moved closer and that's when she noticed his disheveled state. "You are soaking wet." She eyed him up and down. "Where have you been?"

"Harper," he said, ignoring her question, "you need to keep your doors locked at all times."

"But I was expecting you. Were you on the beach? What were you doing out there with no jacket? Aren't you cold? Do you need a towel?"

With a deliberate tone he answered, "Yes, I was on the beach. I have no jacket because I left in a hurry. No, I am not cold because I was running while searching for you."

Opening her mouth to reply, she quickly closed it again as she realized what had just transpired. She breathed out an "Oh." Then, squelching a chuckle, she added, "I'm sorry. That explains all the calls. I was thinking, wow, he is super impatient to start bodyguarding me."

He didn't laugh. But he did take another step closer, and she was able to get her best look yet at those dark brown eyes. Framed with inky black lashes, they weren't quite as monochromatic as she'd initially thought. You just had to be close to see the subtle swirls of color. A droplet of water trickled down his cheek. She stared at the spot, a bit mesmerized by it, and maybe by him a little, too. Was he so numb he couldn't feel it? He had to be freezing, and he'd ignored her towel question. A muscle twitched in his jaw. She wondered if he was cold or irritated. Both, she guessed from the tight lines along his face.

"I was worried. I didn't see your note, which we will circle back to in a moment."

Worried? A warm feeling radiated outward from her core. *Of course, he was worried, Harper, that's his job now.* So why did hearing him say the words give her the feels? Ridiculous. Possibly she'd been living this semi-isolated existence for too long. Probably, she needed to make some friends, too.

"I should have kept my phone on, but I was taking photos and I..." Another drop rolled down his cheek, forming on his chin. She couldn't take it. Reaching across the counter, she tore a wad of paper towels off the roll, hesitated for half a second before gently dabbing one on the spot and handing them over. "There, that had to be driving you crazy." She gave him a tentative smile. "I can understand why you were concerned. I should probably tell you that I don't really like my phone. I'm one of those people who wishes I didn't have one even as I relish the convenience." Pulling one shoulder up into a shrug, she added, "It's hypocritical, I know. Instagram is good for my business."

Paper towels in hand, he stared back, studying her, his sharp, impossibly dark eyes traveling over her face while his mouth formed a little frown above the sharp angles of his square jaw. Harper imagined that he probably hadn't needed any other weapon in the military, that expression alone could scare the enemy to death. Fortunately for her, she wasn't easily intimidated. Her upbringing had been good for that; her father's work, notoriety and travels, his habit of bringing her along with him everywhere and all over the world, had subjected her to all types of people, including commanding military types like the one standing before her.

"Thank you," he said softly, before dipping his head to mop his face. Then he looked at her again. "If you turn your phone off, then not only can you not be reached, it can't be easily tracked if you get lost or hurt. Surely, you know that? Doesn't it have a do not disturb option?"

"Yes, I do know that. I've been living here alone for a few months now, and I guess I'm a little out of practice." She felt herself wincing. She needed to lay it all out on the line so that he could help her. "No, you know what? That's not it. To be honest, I've never felt like I needed protection. Not personally, I mean. My dad is the one who's in the spotlight." She took a step forward. "Growing up, we always had a security system, and I went through the motions, you know so that I could get in the house." She added a little laugh. He didn't join in. She sighed. "But I probably didn't take it as seriously as I should have. And this highly controversial stuff with my dad didn't start until I was in college. That's when he got a full-time security detail. During the last few years, I was overseas a lot."

"I understand that." He paused to nod, taking a couple of breaths while he was at it. "Let's consider these lessons one and two." He held out his thumb to count. "Cell phone on, number one. And number two is a habit you should never *ever* relinquish. I don't care who you are. I'd tell my sister the same thing, and she's not a billionaire's daughter whose dad was almost assaulted."

"You have a sister?"

"Yes."

"Is she—"

"Stay with me here," he interrupted with

an impatient shake of his head. "It doesn't matter where you are or who you're with—you keep the door locked. And don't answer the door if you don't know who it is like you did for me yesterday, okay? I don't care if you see the cable guy, the UPS man or a little old lady holding a giant bouquet of flowers."

"Got it."

"Not even if Santa Claus is standing out there on your porch do you open that door."

Nodding, she set her tone to overly serious, "That fat guy can take his bag of gifts somewhere else. What a weirdo." She swiped a careless hand through the air. "Who wants presents and flowers anyway?"

The chuckle that escaped his lips seemed to surprise him. He shook his head, but his mouth remained curled at the corners like he was fighting a grin. The struggle appeared real, and Harper felt an inordinate amount of satisfaction at causing it.

"I'm serious," he said, his expression turning stern again.

"I know you are and so am I. Despite my... jokiness, I do want to know this stuff. I understand the value. I appreciate your efforts already, and I'm committed to changing my habits."

"Good. Then we're going to talk about

your note-writing venture, as well. Why would you leave a note on your door letting *everyone* know where you are?"

Harper didn't miss the implication. Holding up a finger, she countered, "I didn't say where I was, only that I was gone and would be back in time for our meeting."

"It wouldn't be difficult to look in the garage and discover that your vehicle is here. Anyone could deduce that you were on the beach, wait here for you and—"

"Except," Harper interrupted with another finger point, "the security system covers the entire property and would alert me that someone was on my property." If she only knew how to use that feature, she was sure it would come in real handy. But Kyle didn't know that she didn't know.

"You didn't have your phone on, so how would you get the alert?"

Busted. "If you were a bad guy, you wouldn't know that."

"Harper—"

"Fine, I see your point. No more notes."

Bobbing his head slowly, as if he wasn't sure whether he could trust her sincerity, he said, "Talk to me directly, okay? Which brings up another point, we'll figure out a code word or phrase when we're talking or texting so that in a potential emergency situation, I know it's you and you know it's me and that you are, or aren't, under duress. We'll also come up with an 'I'm okay' wave or hand signal as well as distress signals."

Yikes. "All right."

"I'm going to go change. I'll be right back."

"Sounds good," she said. "How do you like your coffee?"

"Hot."

He left, and Harper heaved out a breath, grateful for a moment to gather her wits. She retrieved a towel and wiped up the water Kyle had tracked inside. At the back door, she noticed her shoes had made a puddle, too, so she opened the door and set them outside. She headed back to the kitchen where she poured coffee into two mugs and wondered what she'd gotten herself into. She'd barely sat down in the living room when Kyle returned, scowling again, she noted with disappointment.

She'd just taken her first sip of coffee when he said, "The door was unlocked again." He gestured in the general direction of the back door. "I locked it behind me."

Harper choked on the liquid, and after a nice long cough, she wheezed, "You're joking, right?"

"Absolutely not."

"But you were coming right back!"

His response was another menacing stare.

"Wait, were you testing me somehow? Did you leave on purpose to see what I'd do?"

"No! I was soaking wet. Harper…" With a quick shake of his head, he took a seat across from her. Leaning forward, he placed his forearms on his thighs. "This is not a test. It's a lifestyle."

"All right. I get it. From now on, I will lock you out every single chance I get."

"You can't lock me out, I have a key, but I promise you I will relish using it."

She chuckled, but he held fast to his serious face. Why did she take that as a challenge?

He said, "For today, let's start with your schedule. Can you give me a copy of your weekly schedule?"

"No." What did he think, she was a dentist or an accountant where she could list her hours and appointment times? At his frown, she explained, "That would literally be impossible. I'm a photographer. My schedule varies a lot. Right now, I'm taking photos for a book about the Oregon Coast so it's all about the scenery and wildlife."

"Right." Kyle nodded, looking thoughtful. "Let's do it day by day, then. Can you give me a schedule each morning? Write down what you're going to do that day, and we'll talk about all the ways we're going to make sure you're the safest you can be while you do them."

"Uh, I can try, but it's—"

"Great," he interrupted. "Can you do that now? Give me your schedule for today, and we'll get started?"

Taking care not to let her exasperation show, she answered, "Sure." Better to show him anyway. She stood and walked into the kitchen where she scrawled a few lines on a notepad before tearing off the page. Back in the living room she handed it over and resumed her seat. "Here you go."

Kyle bent his head and studied the words. Across the top, she'd written the date and underlined it. Underneath that she'd added, "Office Work—8:37 a.m.—until I get hungry (usually around 11:30)."

Keeping his chin down, he looked up at her, eyebrows raised in question. If Harper knew him better, she might describe the expression as sardonic. Possibly, he was amused.

"Like I was trying to explain earlier, my life is currently focused on the scenery and wildlife, which revolves around the weather. And I'm sure you know how unpredictable the weather is here on the coast. When the weather is good, I'm out taking photos in the mornings and again in the late afternoon and sometimes into the evening. Or I might be out all day."

"Where is *out*, usually?"

"Oh, that varies, too. It can be right down here on the beach or hiking in the woods or the middle of town—or some other town or interesting location along the coast. Occasionally, people book me for photo shoots. I've been traveling to the various lighthouses and historic buildings and forts. I take an occasional boat trip up a river or out on the ocean. Today is simpler because of the rain. But if the weather clears, which it's supposed to do this afternoon, then…" She broke off with a helpless shrug.

"Okay," he answered, and Harper knew he was trying to absorb this information. She wondered if he was regretting taking the job at all. "We'll just worry about today for now. What is office work, exactly?"

"Today, it's editing photos, returning emails and bookkeeping." She made a show of checking the time on her fitness tracker. "In fact, I better get going. It's 9:22. Shoot, I'm late."

His eyes lit with something she couldn't

quite identify while the left side of his mouth curved up. She already liked that side because she'd learned it was a sign that he was fighting a smile, elusive as it was. Harper decided she better cut her losses before he lectured her again about taking all this safety stuff seriously. Which she was, truly. She wasn't sure why she felt the need to provoke him into lightening up like this.

He cleared his throat. "So, after lunch…?"

"I'll update the schedule for you then, or even before that if it stops raining." With that, she added a wink, pushed to her feet and took her coffee cup off the end table. Then she sauntered down the hall and into her office where she shut the door behind her with a soft click. Once safely ensconced within the room, she spun a circle and sighed a huge breath of relief. Despite her determination to not let Kyle Frasier intimidate her, he made her feel…something. Some *things* actually. What those were exactly, and what they meant, had yet to be determined.

IN THE LIVING ROOM, Kyle sat frozen in his chair, staring at the spot where Harper had just disappeared and feeling both relieved and unhappy. Less than an hour on the job and he was already reconsidering this decision.

Just when he'd thought he'd discovered a way to ease his grief and remorse over Owen, he'd managed to add another layer of guilt instead. It was also going to increase the level of difficulty in accomplishing this mission. And that's exactly the way he needed to view this job. As a mission. Where there was no place for emotion. All of which would be so much easier if Harper would stop touching him and making him laugh.

Kyle lifted both hands and raked them through his still-damp hair. Why hadn't he anticipated this? He and Owen had always had so much in common; it only made sense that they'd be attracted to the same woman. He tangled his fingers behind his neck, taking a moment to absorb the repercussions of this revelation. He'd spent his life performing some of the most dangerous military missions in the world. He could handle this, he assured himself. All he needed to do was keep his guard up, remind himself that, dead or alive, Harper was Owen's girlfriend. Just because his buddy had died, it didn't change that, at least not from his perspective. And just like him, Harper was still grieving Owen's death. Kyle's one and only job here was to help keep her safe.

CHAPTER FIVE

"It would be so cool to go back in time and see this place like Lewis and Clark did, don't you think? Except without having to schlep the four thousand miles to get here."

Kyle pressed his lips together in an effort not to smile as he and Harper strolled along the sidewalk in Astoria, a historic, artsy, upbeat little city located a few miles inland from the ocean and perched right on the edge of the Columbia River. As predicted, the weather had cleared, and Harper had decided to spend the afternoon at the town's Spring Fling Festival since she'd missed out the evening before.

Kyle estimated they'd walked roughly five miles with Harper snapping photos of everything from the boats on the river, the eclectic mix of people, their pets—including one pig, a ferret and too many dogs to count—to several of the beautiful Victorian homes and historic buildings. Also included were some of the artwork and crafts for sale at the booths, as well as the artisans who'd labored over the creations.

Kyle used the time to instruct her on some basic precautions: how to be aware in a crowd, what dangers to watch for and the most vulnerable positions at their various stops. He encouraged her to utilize her artistic eye and memorize details and faces. He taught her how to tell if someone might be following her and what to do if they were. They agreed on their hand signals and practiced those.

In between Kyle's directives, Harper shared fun facts. Did he know Astoria was the oldest city west of the Rocky Mountains? The town was named for the fur-trading mogul John Jacob Astor whose great-grandson later died on the *Titanic*. The Astoria-Megler Bridge was over four miles long, and they close it once a year for a fun run. The 1985 cult classic film *The Goonies* was filmed here. On it went. And Kyle enjoyed every second. She had a way of imparting information with a mix of enthusiasm and wonder, which she interspersed with a smattering of the ridiculous that made even the otherwise mundane seem interesting. Or funny. The challenge was keeping his commentary to himself, refraining from asking follow-up questions and just generally trying not to engage on a personal level.

Possibly breaking his own guidelines, he added, "I'm not so sure about going back in time that far. I'll also pass on the camping out for three months in the wintertime without proper provisions."

"Same. No thanks. I think I read somewhere that it was an unusually wet winter that year. Imagine that without your rubber boots and Gore-Tex. Do you like camping?"

"With the right supplies."

Kyle did like camping and backpacking. He'd spent his childhood camping with his dad whenever they could get away. He was grateful for the skills his dad had taught him as well as the time they'd spent together. That knowledge had given him an advantage when it came to his Special Forces training. But he didn't share any of that even as he wondered what she'd say next.

"Can you believe I've never been camping?"

"No, I—" he said, biting back the offer to take her. He was surprised, seeing how her dad was such an environmental advocate. "Everyone should try it at least once," he added, pleased with his self-restraint and diplomatic reply.

"I don't feel cheated or anything. Not everyone gets to grow up in a lab like I did, which was very cool. My toys were discarded microscopes and old lab equipment. That's actually how I discovered my love for photography. My dad gave me a camera that had outlived its usefulness." After a pause, she added a wistful, "That camera became my best friend."

Her tone held the customary lighthearted tenor he was already accustomed to, but there was something about the joke that fell flat. The sincerity of it, he decided. And the picture of loneliness it presented. The vision of Harper as a little girl in an empty lab with a camera as her only playmate appeared before him, tugging and twisting at his heartstrings. Ready to break his own rule, he started to ask her about that, about what her life was like as the only child of an eccentric, ambitious scientist.

The vibration of his phone in his pocket stopped him. A text from Josh. Kyle's stomach took an anxious dip as he stared at the display, rereading the message multiple times, Call me ASAP. Something we need to discuss. It's about Owen.

Owen? What could that possibly mean? He had no idea. But for Josh to go all ASAP on him meant it was important. His finger hovered over Josh's grinning avatar. But he couldn't leave Harper in the middle of the street to make the call. And he didn't want to talk about Owen in front of her.

Kyle looked up to find Harper studying him curiously. "Is everything okay? Do you need to take care of something?"

"Oh, uh, yeah. I mean, no, it's fine." He tapped out a response, Can't talk now. Will call when I can. And then, as was his habit, he deleted both messages before slipping the phone back inside his pocket. The conversation would have to wait until later when he got Harper home and settled in behind her security system and he had some privacy.

"It's a good idea to get in the habit of deleting messages on your phone that might give someone an idea of future plans and where you'll be at any given time or date. That sort of thing."

"Makes sense," Harper said agreeably. "Do you want to grab a bite to eat before we head back? There's some great food in this little city."

"Sounds good," Kyle said, realizing he was getting hungry.

They continued on, and Harper asked, "Do you like sushi?"

Ugh. Sushi was fine, but it meant he'd be grabbing a burger later. It tasted okay, but it didn't stick with him for long. "Sushi is fine," he said. "If that's what you like."

"Oh." Harper flashed him a quick apologetic grin. "I don't actually."

Kyle responded with a questioning frown. "Then why—?"

She pointed, and Kyle saw they were walking past a restaurant with a sushi sign in the window. "I was just wondering if you did. I don't get the craze. It's not very filling, is it? It's more like an appetizer to me. Don't get me wrong, appetizers are fun, but they're not a meal. Sushi *and a sandwich*, sure. But just sushi and I'm already planning my next meal."

Kyle couldn't help but smile at that. He forced himself to turn away to avoid sharing a moment. He looked out toward the wide expanse of water that was the Columbia River and the over four-mile-long bridge spanning its width. He wondered if she'd be interested in running over the bridge with him someday? Because that sounded fun and she'd probably make jokes the entire way. He wanted to ask about her favorite foods. He wanted to know all about her, including the camera that served as a substitute for a little girl's best friend.

Kyle had hoped that spending time with her would curb his growing attraction. Not happening. She was so…easy to be with. It was tempting to let his guard down and establish a friendship. But he knew that getting to know her better was not a good idea, not when he already felt the way he did. This was discouraging.

A woman pushing a stroller emerged from a shop on the sidewalk ahead of them. A little boy pranced next to her, clasping an ice cream cone that was rapidly melting into his sleeve. A slightly older girl munched on a paper-wrapped cookie she held in one hand while clutching a leash attached to a giant dog with the other.

"What about ice cream?"

"What about it?"

"Do you like it?"

"Yes," he answered without elaborating, all the while speculating about her favorite flavor and hoping she'd volunteer it.

After a pause, she said, "Me, too. The chunkier the better, like the kind with cookie dough bites, or chocolate chips, or gobs of brownie. Although right now, I'm feeling a cheeseburger. With bacon."

Kyle barely managed to stifle a sigh. Of course, she liked bacon and cheeseburgers. No matter what bad things he'd done in this life, he didn't think he deserved this kind of torture.

Up ahead, Kyle focused on the girl now being pulled along by the rambunctious dog. The little boy's top scoop leaned precariously to one side. Kyle stepped forward, ready to come to his rescue when, *plop*, it hit the ground. Stopping in his tracks, he stared down at the calamity. "Mommy! My ice cream..." He broke off with a sob.

Mom glanced over. "Oh, no," she said, crouching beside him. "It's okay, Henry." She slipped an arm around his shoulder. "Shh, don't cry, sweetie. We'll fix it." Eyes scanning the sidewalk ahead, she called, "Marnie, don't cross the street yet, okay? I need to help your brother."

"Okay, Mommy."

The dog had other ideas. With a quick backward shuffle and tip of his head, he slipped out of his collar, leaving Marnie holding an empty leash. The dog bolted into the street. Marnie screamed.

"Oh, no!" Mom cried. "Marnie, stay here. Indy!" she called to the dog. Thankfully, the light at the nearest intersection was red, and the cars in the street were at a standstill. Kyle knew very well that would change all too soon.

Asking Harper to follow, Kyle rushed forward until they'd reached the frantic mom.

"Hey, I'm Kyle and this is Harper, and we're going to help you," Kyle said quickly, noting the dog was now on the opposite sidewalk. "I'll go get your dog. Do me a favor and don't call for Indy anymore, okay? The light is going to change, and the cars will start moving, and I don't want him running back out into the street."

With wide eyes on the verge of panic, Mom nodded. Ice cream momentarily forgotten, little Henry gawked up at Kyle. Marnie, who'd run back to her mom, held on to the stroller, crying softly.

Kyle turned and ran across the street. Once on the other side, however, Indy seemed uninterested in his plan, darting here and there, pausing only long enough to sniff interesting smudges on the sidewalk. Mimicking the singsong voice he'd heard Mia use with dogs, Kyle talked to him the whole time. He'd get close only to have Indy slip out of his grasp. A few times, when he stopped long enough to gobble crumbs, Kyle almost caught up to him. His quest for kibbles would be funny if the dog's safety wasn't in jeopardy. Cars were now driving past on the street.

When Indy stopped to sample what appeared to be a partially eaten hotdog, Kyle remembered a trick he'd seen Mia do with her dog, George. He let out a short, sharp whistle. Indy, already moving again and seeming intent on nosing his way inside a bakery, turned curiously.

"Hey, Indy," Kyle called. He crouched down and tapped the ground. "What's this?" He cupped his hand like it held a yummy treat. Tail wagging, Indy trotted over to inspect the offering. Kyle gave the dog an affectionate scratch. Indy licked his ear and sat like this had been *his* plan the whole time.

"Good boy," Kyle cooed. He glanced up intent on asking Harper to bring him the collar and leash but found that she was one step ahead of him.

Handing it over, she said, "Here you go. Well done. Your next career could be as a *doggyguard*."

"Very funny," Kyle said with a chuckle, adjusting Indy's collar. "I don't think ten minutes of cat and mouse with a runaway dog exactly qualifies me as a dog whisperer. Plus, I forgot to take the collar with me. Thank you for that piece of quick thinking."

"But it was so entertaining. I liked that high-pitched voice you were using. Have you considered auditioning for the boys' choir?"

Kyle gave it up and laughed with her. The three of them crossed the street toward the grateful family.

"Oh, Indy!" the woman cried, burying her hand in the dog's silky fur. "You scared the daylights out of me." Bending over, she planted a kiss on the top of his head. She stood and beamed at Kyle. "Thank you. I don't even know what to say. That was just… incredible."

"No problem."

"How did you do that thing at the end to get him to come to you? Did you have a treat in your hand?"

Kyle chuckled. "No. Luckily, my sister is a veterinarian. She has a dog who wants to eat everything, and I've seen her do that trick with him. Your dog is food driven. I'm just glad it worked."

"Food driven? Are you like a dog trainer or something? My name is Helen, by the way." She pointed at the kids before gesturing at the stroller, "This is Marnie and Henry. And baby Shawnie, who slept through the whole ordeal, thank the stars above. And, of course, you already know Indy."

"Nice to meet you all. Not even close to a dog trainer, obviously from how long that took. I've just picked up a few things from my sister. It does make them easier to train when they're food driven, but it can also distract them." Kyle patted Indy who was staring at him like they were best friends. "He's beautiful. Bernese mountain dog?"

"Yes, maybe mixed with golden retriever, the shelter thinks. We just moved here, near Pacific Cove, and we haven't had him long. He's a rescue, and we're still learning how to navigate. Having a dog is a little more complicated than we thought. Buying him a harness is now on our to-do list." Marnie added a solemn nod. "We could probably use some dog lessons or something."

Kyle retrieved his wallet and pulled out a card. "If you're serious, I can recommend someone. My sister has a friend who trains dogs and helps families acclimate with their rescue animals."

Helen took the card. They chatted for a few more minutes until the kids got restless. After saying their goodbyes, Kyle and Harper went to get those burgers.

"So, YOUR SISTER IS a veterinarian?" Harper asked Kyle as she secured a camera to the tripod she'd set up on the footbridge that led to the marina.

Just before daylight that morning, they'd loaded into Harper's SUV and driven south for some miles along the coast to Tabletop Rock, a giant monolith just offshore, favored by puffins and cormorants. A couple of hours of taking photos there and they'd continued here to Dungeness, a small town nestled near the mouth of the Crab River.

"Yes," Kyle answered, his gaze bouncing around, landing everywhere but on Harper.

"That's awesome. I think it's amazing that a person would dedicate her life to helping animals."

"I agree."

Harper waited, hoping he'd elaborate. They'd spent nearly every waking minute together the last two days, and he still wasn't warming up to her. She might have thought that was just his personality if she hadn't gotten a glimpse of his softer side that first evening when she'd hired him and then again in Astoria. He'd chatted up Helen and her kids more in five minutes than he had her in the entire time she'd known him. Why did that bother her?

She looked at him. He looked away. It seemed like the harder she tried, the less receptive he was to her attempts. She wondered if she was getting on his nerves. She knew she talked a lot. Being alone will do that to a person. But part of it was also because he basically didn't talk at all unless it was about safety. Maybe he just didn't like her. Or maybe the very thing she'd been afraid of was bothering him after all; she reminded him of Owen. What a depressing thought. Maybe she should just quit trying so hard. Why was she trying so hard? He had a job to do, and he was doing it very well. Since it had rained the day before, he'd spent hours teaching her how to use her security system, quizzing her and having her set it in all the various combinations. They'd also practiced using the cameras—angles, zoom, video— neat features she couldn't believe she'd over-looked.

Leaning over, she peered through the lens of her camera, adjusted the zoom and set it for the light conditions on the dock below where a group of sea lions was basking in the late morning sun. The dock was a favored resting spot for the animals and had become popular with tourists, leaving them unbothered by Harper's and Kyle's presence. In an effort to not try so hard, Harper resisted the urge to share the differences between a sea lion colony, raft, rookery and harem.

She lasted nearly twenty minutes before breaking, "Did you go to college?" she asked, deciding to make a last-ditch effort. After all, they were going to be together like this for almost a month. They could at least be friendly.

"No."

"So you joined the Navy right out of high school?"

"Yes."

"Are you close to your family?"

"Not really," he answered, squinting off in the distance.

"But your sister lives in Pacific Cove?"

"I don't want to talk about my family."

"Oh. I'm sorry," she returned and instantly felt bad about whatever hardship he'd endured where his family was concerned.

"You don't need to be," he said. "See that building right there?"

Harper followed the direction of his pointed finger to the weathered gray structure beside them. "The old cannery?"

She'd photographed the abandoned factory a couple of times now. Built over a hundred years ago and constructed on pilings stretching out into the river, the processing facility had originally been much larger. As the fishing industry evolved and began to rely more and more on large ocean processors, the factory had closed. Years later, a fire had destroyed a good portion of it, and less than half of the original structure remained, now used as a warehouse for a local fishing company. Many of the old pilings could be seen extending unevenly from the water, providing convenient perches for various species of seabirds. A few weeks ago, Harper had taken a brilliant shot of a pelican with a fish dangling from its beak on one of the posts close to shore.

"Yeah." Kyle asked, "You know about crime scene B, right?"

"What?" Harper zoomed in on a large male sea lion as it drew itself upright like it was posing. Harper chuckled as he made an ostentatious show of barking and flapping his flippers. She snapped several photos before answering, "Was there a crime committed there?"

"Probably at some point over the years. It reminds me of something I've been wanting to discuss with you. What I'm talking about is if you are ever in a situation where a perpetrator tries to kidnap you."

"There's a happy thought."

"I know," he said grimly. "But it's a consideration with family members of the very wealthy. Fortunately, it's not as popular as it once was. Not as likely as a home invasion anyway."

"That's a relief," she responded drily. "I'd take a home invasion over a kidnapping any day. There's no place like home, I say."

As usual, he ignored her sarcasm. But his mouth-twitch suggested she'd scored a victory. "The point of abduction would be considered crime scene A. You don't want to be taken to crime scene B because—"

Grimacing, Harper stood upright and interrupted him, "I get it. Because that's where the really bad stuff happens."

"That's right. So we're going to go over some of the ways you can prevent yourself from being taken to crime scene B."

"You mean like self-defense moves?" Harper liked that idea, of being able to fend off an attacker like Kyle had done with her dad. "That would be great. I am absolutely pro-ninja, especially when that ninja is me."

"Yes, we'll discuss that in a minute. But there are other things you can do, too. Often a perpetrator will threaten a victim not to scream or make any noise. That's because they don't want to get caught. If you do the opposite of what they demand—scream and struggle and make noise—sometimes they'll abandon the attempt."

"That makes sense."

"The problem is that fear can make people freeze in the moment."

Harper nodded. "Operation amygdala."

"What?"

"Where the primitive portion of the brain takes over. The old fight, flight or freeze conundrum."

"Exactly," he said, seemingly pleased that she knew what he was referring to, and possibly that she was taking this seriously. "It's a complex phenomenon. Despite what some people believe, you're not genetically disposed to one reaction or another. If you plan for a situation, you can act accordingly. Initially, it might go against your instincts, but you *can* fight. You just have to be ready. Prepared. Take away the element of shock. We'll go over some scenarios."

"Sounds good," she said, and then dipped back down to watch the sea lions. This particular camera had both an LCD and a traditional viewfinder, which made using it in bright light a breeze.

"I ordered you some pepper spray. Weapons are tricky because they can be disarmed and used against you. So we'll practice with it. Self-defense moves are better, way more effective. I've hired someone to teach you basic techniques."

Harper looked up at him again, just in time to see him shift on his feet. "Why can't you teach me?" she asked.

"I think an expert would be better. I found a guy who teaches private lessons."

"I thought you were an expert." The sun had moved and was beginning to cast a shadow across the sea lions. She decided to switch cameras so she could get some wider angles of the marina and the harbor beyond. Unhooking the camera from the tripod, she noticed Kyle gazing out at the water. She took his picture.

Slowly, he turned toward her, his expression menacing in a way that no longer unnerved her. She kept snapping away.

Digging in that scowl, he asked, "Did you just take my picture?"

"I did." She took another. "Several."

"Why?"

"I want to show you how scary you are."

His features immediately softened. What was that? Surprise? Concern? Harper was taken aback by the sight. Reflexively, she hit the shutter again before lowering the camera.

Eyes pinned on hers, he asked, "You think I'm scary?"

"Yes," she answered honestly.

Brow scrunching, he seemed to choose his words carefully. "Harper, I don't want you to be afraid of me." He added a little groan of frustration. "This is my fault. I know we need to build some trust but I..."

Harper reached out to touch him, to reassure him, but before she made contact, he took a step back to lean against the railing of the bridge. With a sigh, she pulled her hand back. "I'm not afraid of you. I was teasing. Mostly. But honestly, in general, you can be very intimidating." And not a ton of fun, she added silently. She turned the camera and held it out toward him. "See?"

Gingerly, he reached out and plucked the camera from her, his big hands surprisingly nimble as he once again avoided touching her. He reminded her of the beast in the fairy tale taking extra care with the heroine. That's when it occurred to her how extensively he avoided physical contact with her. All the time. Was that why he didn't want to teach her the self-defense stuff himself? Was it her specifically or some sort of professional line he didn't want to cross?

Harper nearly laughed out loud as she noticed Kyle glaring down at the image of himself scowling. "It's not the camera's fault," she teased.

He looked slightly embarrassed, and Harper felt kind of bad. But only a bit because she didn't understand why he was so aloof. She said, "I'm right, huh?"

Lifting a shoulder, he conceded, "Maybe. But, you know, attitude is important when it comes to being a potential target. Criminal research has shown that the more confident and unapproachable you look, the less chance you have of being assaulted. We'll talk about that *a lot* more. You're very poised and self-assured, so that's helpful."

Was that a compliment? Harper stared at him, steadily holding his gaze for a few long seconds waiting for…what? She wasn't sure. Something, some sign that he didn't find her completely annoying and repulsive.

Finally, she heaved out a sigh, and said, "Well, you're extra safe, then, because there's not a bad guy on the planet that would mess with you when you look like that. Which," she added confidently, "is often." Reaching out, she took the camera from a once again somber and silent Kyle and tucked it into her bag. Pulling out a different camera, she fastened it in place, focused on her work and told herself to give it up where he was concerned. For now, anyway.

CHAPTER SIX

As KYLE PACKED some of Harper's equipment in her SUV, he thought about what she'd said. It bothered him that she thought he was scary or intimidating or whatever. He knew she was right. At best, he was being some much harsher version of himself. At worst, he was being a jerk. That was not what he wanted. The problem here was that he didn't know how else to be at this point. He didn't know how to keep his distance and still be himself with her. Not without letting his emotions get involved.

When they'd set out that morning, Kyle had offered to drive so Harper could watch for photo ops. Again, she was already settled in the passenger seat when Kyle eased into the driver's side.

"Where to?"

"Home," she answered, the one-word response reminding him of himself, and making him feel worse.

Kyle started the car and pulled onto the

coast highway. "Let me know if you want me to pull over anywhere," he volunteered. Traveling with Harper, he'd learned, meant lots of stops and impromptu detours.

"I will."

Instead, she remained uncharacteristically quiet and still, staring straight out the windshield. Until they neared a section of coastline where a large headland stretched out into the ocean, he could see the top of a lighthouse rising above the trees. Peering in that direction, Harper shifted in her seat as they passed. He noticed a road that he assumed accessed the area.

"Do you want to go out there?"

"I'd love to," Harper answered flatly.

"I'll turn around."

She scoffed. "I wish."

"Let's not wish, let's do," Kyle said almost cheerfully, trying to coax her back into good spirits. He should be glad that she'd finally switched to subdued mode. But he wasn't. Not at all.

Harper gave him a suspicious frown. He couldn't blame her. His hot and cold behavior would irritate him, too, if he were on the receiving end of it.

"I can turn around?" Kyle offered.

"It won't do any good," Harper said, her

tone resigned. "This guy owns the entire headland there. More than two hundred acres of oceanfront, wilderness, historical amazingness, but he doesn't allow anyone on his property."

"Seriously?"

"Yes. The gray whales come very close to the shore off that point. Rumor has it, it is the best place to view them on the entire coast. There's also an old decommissioned lighthouse and a World War II bunker."

"Why doesn't he allow anyone there?"

"Nobody seems to know for sure. I've heard different explanations."

"Who is he?"

"His name is Rhys McGrath. The property belonged to his grandfather, who died several years ago. Rhys inherited, but it's been closed to the public for decades."

"Have you asked him if you can tour the place?"

"I've tried. I couldn't find a phone number. I've stopped at the gate at the end of the drive, but no one answers. And I've emailed him. Three times."

"Did you get a response?"

"Immediately. The same canned one every single time, like the response is on auto-send. It reads something like, 'Thank you for your inquiry, but Mr. McGrath is not available for consultation at this time. The lighthouse and grounds are closed to the public and will remain so indefinitely.'"

"That's too bad. I mean, it's his right, for sure. Everyone deserves their privacy." Kyle glanced over at Harper, waiting for her retort, but she was busy staring out the window behind him.

Kyle reminded himself it was better this way even as he fought off the urge to apologize, to explain, to…to what? To try and snap her out of this funk by laughing and joking around with her and getting himself even more tangled up in her than he already felt? There was no solution, no way forward, beyond keeping her at arm's length. Except, he didn't think he could keep it up.

When they arrived back at her place, they went inside where Harper informed him she'd be in her office. Kyle took the opportunity to head to his cottage, locking her door and setting the security system behind him.

Despite calling several times over the last couple of days, he still hadn't talked to Josh about the text he'd sent. Pulling out his cell, he tapped on Josh's number, the fourth one down on his contact list. It was just under Owen's, whose contact he couldn't bring himself to delete. Circumstances being what they were, Harper had taken over the top spot above his mom.

His friend picked up. Finally. "Kyle, hey! Sorry I've missed your calls. I was on a plane to Nairobi and then getting settled in here."

"No problem, but I gotta say, your message rattled me. Can you talk? What's up?"

"Yeah, I'm in my room now. Listen, here's the thing. Travis called me into the office before I left, the day I called you." Travis was Josh's boss, soon to be Kyle's, too, when he officially signed on with Dahlia. "It's Dahlia's standard operating procedure to investigate every death of an employee whether they were on the clock at the time or not. Because, as we both know, you're always on the clock with Dahlia." Josh added a laugh.

Kyle knew this to be true. The company operated even more strictly than the military where employee behavior was concerned. It was of paramount importance for them to keep a stellar reputation in the international community. "They call it an inquiry and Owen's has been delayed."

"What does that mean?"

"There are some issues." Before Kyle could ask what that had to do with him, Josh said, "One of them has to do with Harper Jansen."

"Harper?"

"Yep. So, Travis asked me if I knew Harper. I said no, but I mentioned that you happened to be doing security work for her right now."

"Yeah, and?" Kyle prodded, unable to make sense of what he was hearing.

"Travis got excited and… Long story short, he wants you to gather intel about Harper on the QT. Find out what she knows about what Owen was doing in Africa."

Kyle felt his blood go cold. Dahlia wanted him to spy on Harper? Harper's question that first day came rushing back to him, if he'd known about Owen's "time" in Africa. Kyle thought she'd been talking about her and Owen's relationship. "Why does he think she knows anything at all?"

"Owen had a notebook, like a journal or a calendar, but not super personal. Most of it is in some sort of shorthand or code, but he also wrote a few things about Harper. I guess something in there makes the investigators think she might have information that could be helpful. I guess they had a fight and broke up right before he died."

"They did. He called me afterward. Harper confirmed that with me, too."

"I don't know how to say this, but I got

the feeling from Travis that they think Owen might have been involved in something..."

"Something what, Josh?" Anxiety pressed against Kyle's lungs, making it hard to breathe. He forced himself to stay calm.

Josh let out a sound, a frustrated groan, and Kyle could hear the fear, the unease in his tone, even nine thousand miles away. "Not good, Kyle. *Shady* was the term Travis used. They're not sure what he was up to exactly. But I guess some of these notes reference Harper and suggest she might know something. Listen, buddy, I know this is a lot to dump on you right now."

A lot? Under different circumstances, Kyle would have laughed at the understatement. But there was absolutely nothing funny about his future employer asking him to spy on his current one. The answer would be an unequivocal no if they weren't talking about Owen. The idea of his best friend involved in anything shady was ludicrous. If there was something he could do to clear Owen's name, he had to try.

Kyle didn't immediately respond. Josh stayed quiet. Kyle appreciated that Josh was giving him a moment to work all this out.

Then, in typical Josh fashion, he attempted to lighten the mood. "I mean, you must be working your charm on her by now anyway, huh?"

"I'm just her bodyguard," Kyle snapped and could hear the defensive edge in his tone.

Josh muttered a soft curse. "I'm sorry, Kyle. That was totally insensitive. Not surprising coming from me. I'm not exactly known for my subtlety, am I? Of course, you're not making moves on your best friend's fiancée."

"No, it's fine. I know what you meant. This is just a lot to take in. I don't believe Owen was—"

"Don't even say it," Josh interrupted. "Of course, he wasn't. Obviously, there's an explanation. Dahlia is looking for it. That's what you're going to prove, or at least help prove. And Travis said he'd put you on the clock for this, bill it as part of the inquiry."

Kyle squeezed his eyes shut and brought one hand up to grip the back of his neck. Could this situation with Harper get any worse? Keeping his distance had been difficult enough, now someone was going to pay him to get close? So he could get information from her about his best friend?

Josh reminded him that it could, in fact, be worse. "Whatever was going on, Travis wanted me to reiterate that possibly Harper was involved, too. Or maybe she was the one who exposed Owen to a dangerous situation somehow. She knows people in Africa. And her dad is a billionaire hotshot with tons of connections. So, you have to be discreet. You can't tell her anything about this."

"I'M GOING TO CLASS," Harper announced after changing into workout clothes. She'd spent the afternoon editing photos, but her mind wasn't on the task. Especially when she'd loaded the photos she'd taken and seen Kyle scowling at her from her oversize monitor. As if his regular-size scowl wasn't bad enough. Yep, the object of her distraction was right here in her own living room relaxing in the easy chair by the fireplace. Feet up, coffee mug in hand, he was all kicked back and reading a book like he wasn't trying to annoy her by now appearing concerned. Biting back her curiosity, she refused to ask the title even though she'd noticed and appreciated that he liked to read.

Kyle lowered the book and looked her up and down. "Class? What kind of class? Where?" If Harper didn't know better, she'd think there was a hint of appreciation in his perusal. But she did know better. He was probably planning on how to get access to the studio's schematics so he could properly secure all the exits and then quiz her on the proper escape protocol.

"Yoga."

"You do *yoga*?" He emphasized the word like she'd just told him she was into swallowing hot coals or juggling knives.

It was on the tip of her tongue to defend her exercise of choice, but suddenly it occurred to her that a break from him would be a really good idea.

"Yep," she said, trying to keep her expression neutral while reveling in her brilliance. She should have predicted that Mr. Uptight would sneer at yoga. This was perfect! He could wait outside while she enjoyed an hour of physical activity and let go of some of this gnawing anger. She needed to make peace with the reality unfolding before her: he didn't like her.

"What kind of yoga?"

"Um, the stretch-like-a-pretzel, meditate, workout kind. You know…" She paused to gesture at her tank top, which read "When in doubt, plank it out." "This particular class is called yoga fit, and it's a combination of yoga and body-weight strength training. I go to this awesome little studio in Pacific Cove called Vela, right across the street from the health food store."

"Yoga fit," he repeated with a little grimace. Good sign. Maybe she'd stay for a double class. He glanced at his watch. "And you're going to this class at Vela Studio right now?"

"I'm leaving in ten minutes."

Sighing, he scrubbed a hand across his jaw. "All right. Let me get changed."

"Wait." Harper felt a little surge of panic. "You don't need to go to class *with* me. I mean, you can just wait outside in the car or…wherever. There's a coffee shop across the street, right next to the health food store."

Kyle studied her carefully, and Harper had the feeling he was making some sort of decision that was much larger than where he would be waiting while she was in child's pose.

"No, it's fine. I'll go with you."

"*You're* going to do yoga?"

"Yeah, sure, why not?"

Yes, Harper, why not? "Umm, okay, but just so you know—it's mostly women. And it's *not* easy. I know you work out and everything, but this is a whole different type of physical activity than you're probably used to. I could barely walk for days after my first class."

Kyle's assessing stare made her feel fidgety

and silly. The silence stretched between them until he finally asked in a tone that sounded almost teasing, "Harper, are you trying to discourage me from attending yoga fit class with you?"

Harper felt her cheeks go warm as she realized how obvious she'd been. Which only irritated her more. "Of course not," she lied. It had been too much to hope for that a room full of women would deter him. She doubted the man was intimidated by anything. "It'll be good to supplement your…normal exercise routine." A routine that Harper knew took place long before she ever stirred in the morning. He usually checked in on her while he was still in his workout clothes or came running up the stairs from the beach while it was still dark out. "I just thought… Never mind, just go change. I don't want to be late."

AFTER CHECKING IN at Vela Studio's reception desk, Kyle followed Harper inside the door of the studio classroom where they deposited their belongings in a set of cubbies situated neatly off to one side. Kyle removed his shoes and watched Harper choose a spot front and center of the large square room. No chance of getting lost in the back row.

Muttering under her breath, she set her

water bottle down and gave her mat an almost violent fling, kicking it into place with one bare foot. Clearly, she'd been trying to dissuade him from participating. What was up with that? Was she afraid he'd embarrass her? Little did she know he was the one with the problem if he had the timing right, or wrong as the case might be.

He didn't see anyone milling around who looked like they could be an instructor. The walls were painted a calming yellow-beige and bare of decor. Planks of honey-colored oak covered the floor. The lighting was soft, and candles were burning in two corners. Subtle scents of lavender and other unidentifiable spices floated on the air. Lavender was not a good sign.

The room was filling fast, and he needed to figure out how he was going to handle this conceivable encounter. A tall, fit man wearing snug black pants hustled into the room. His tank top bore the studio's logo, and he scanned the crowd like he was doing a mental tally. Definite instructor behavior. Kyle began to relax a bit. Maybe he was in the clear after all.

A petite blonde woman in bright purple-and-orange leggings stood next to Harper.

She waved at the guy in black, and said, "Hey, Coby."

"Hi, Tina," he said, gesturing at her legs. "How are you? Cute leggings." Then he retrieved a water bottle, called out greetings to a few more students and strolled out again. Kyle felt his hopes plummet as he then paused in the doorway to converse with someone, someone whose cheerful voice carried across the space and whose tone was unmistakable to Kyle.

He was still trying to figure out a way to handle this encounter when Nora glided into the room as only his mom could, on a cloud of happiness and positive energy. He loved his mom, and under normal circumstances, he'd enjoy surprising her in this way. Why hadn't he thought about doing this on his own? By himself. This situation with Harper was already difficult enough, he didn't want to complicate it further by introducing her to his family.

Like he was wearing a homing device, Nora's gaze latched on to him immediately. Stopping abruptly, she called out, "Kyle, honey!"

Eyes wide, Harper spun toward him.

"Hey, Mom."

With a slow blink, Harper whispered, "Mom?"

Then Nora was upon them and wrapping him in a tight hug. "I'm so excited that you're here." She stepped away, and keeping one hand on his shoulder, pivoted and announced to the entire room, "Everyone, most of you already know my daughter, Mia. This is my son, Kyle."

Kyle felt his neck go warm as waves and greetings of "Hey, Kyle" surrounded him. He smiled and waved and felt like a doofus. As if that wasn't bad enough, Harper's curious glare was singeing his skin.

And Nora wasn't finished, not even close. "He's been living overseas for years, and I'm beyond thrilled to have my baby boy home."

"Okay, Mom," he said good-naturedly, slipping an arm around her shoulders and squeezing. "I think they get the picture."

Laughter ensued, and people went back to preparing for class and visiting amongst themselves.

Nora said, "Your sister is going to be here tonight, too. Those two mats in the back corner are for her and Laney. For some reason, she always makes me save a place for her in the back row."

"That's because she's terrible."

Nora winced. "Poor thing is incredibly inflexible, isn't she? But she's improved! And I'm proud of her for trying. The meditation is good for her. She worries too much." Then Nora seemed to notice Harper standing beside him, closer than a stranger might, and watching their interplay with more intensity than was socially acceptable. She said, "Harper, hi! Nice to see you back again."

"Hi, Nora. Thank you. It's good to be here."

"This is my son, Kyle. Kyle, this is Harper."

"We've met, Mom. And even if we hadn't, the entire room is now aware that I'm your son."

"Well, can you blame me? I'm proud of you."

Kyle couldn't help but chuckle. "Thanks, Mom. Harper is um, she's the friend I told you about. The one I'm helping out."

Nora went hands on hips and smiled widely, her gaze bouncing from Kyle to Harper and back again. "Really? That's so great. Did Laney text you about dinner this weekend?"

"Uh, no."

"Well, she's going to—dinner on Saturday at four. Lanes is grilling salmon, wild caught. It's early so we can play on the beach after."

She looked at Harper. "You're invited, too, Harper. You can meet everyone."

"Oh, Mom, I don't think—"

"I'd love to, Nora." Harper beamed at her and then at Kyle. "Thank you. I can't wait to meet…" Harper added a helpless shrug "…everyone."

"Great! I'm going to borrow him for just a sec." Nora placed her hand on Kyle's elbow and ushered him away.

CHAPTER SEVEN

HARPER BARELY HAD time to register that the lovely Nora was Kyle's mom when a smiling woman, black hair piled into a messy bun on top of her head, stopped before her. She was wearing black leggings and a baggy tank top with a picture of a sleeping cat that read, I'd Rather Be Cat-napping. Harper liked her instantly.

"Hi, you're Harper, right?" She gestured to where Nora and Kyle were now chatting with two older women nearby. "Mom just told us you're a friend of Kyle's?"

A willowy, blonde, stunningly beautiful young woman joined them.

"Yes, hi. Harper."

"I'm Mia, Kyle's sister, and this is Laney. Laney is my sister-in-law but also like my stepdaughter, which makes her sort of Kyle's niece."

Harper decided not to ask about the specifics involved, thinking she'd have time to sort these associations at the family dinner.

Even though she'd already begun questioning her impulsive response to Nora's invitation. Kyle clearly didn't want her there, and she'd only accepted with the hope that it would get to him. Not well done of her. Why couldn't she just kill this curiosity of hers where he was concerned?

"Nice to meet you both."

"You, too!" Laney grinned, and Harper could see that she was much younger than she'd originally assumed. "Nora said she invited you to dinner this weekend."

"She did. I hope that's okay? I understand you're doing the cooking."

"It's more than okay. It's awesome! And I am. I love to cook! I'm making Uncle Kyle's favorite."

"Well, great. I'm already looking forward to it. Should I bring anything?"

Laney's answer was another happy grin, "Just Uncle Kyle. I miss having him around."

"If Laney wasn't cooking an entire salmon, we might say yes," Mia joked. "Since you guys are friends, you probably already know how much my brother eats?"

Harper smiled at Mia's subtle attempt to discern the status of her and Kyle's relationship. The question hinted at protectiveness on her part. And Laney was calling him "uncle" when, from what Harper understood, he hadn't earned the title through genetics. As far as Harper was concerned, that made it even more affectionate and special. Nora, Mia, Laney—these engaging, friendly women did not seem like the estranged family members Harper had been picturing. Speaking of, a still beaming Nora was strolling to the front of the room. With a promise to see her at dinner, Mia and Laney departed for their mats in the back row. Harper turned to look at Kyle who was shooting the breeze with a middle-aged woman behind them. He faced the front to focus on Nora as she began to teach the class.

Where Harper was in for another huge surprise. So much for her relaxing yoga session where she was going to let go of all her negative feelings. Instead, they blossomed and festered like a diseased lotus flower.

Reverse warrior, triangle, downward-facing dog, lord of the dance, it didn't matter, Kyle Frasier could do them all. Every pose. Much better than Harper could, which wasn't saying all that much. But he was also better than every other person in the class as far as she could see, even his mom/instructor. Harper labored through the poses, sweating and straining and trying not to grunt like a

tennis player. All of this made more difficult by attempting not to watch Kyle breeze
through the class like some sort of yoga prod-
igy.

It was official: she'd been conned. And not
only in the yoga way. She'd asked him if he
was close to his family and he'd said, *Not really.* He'd told her he didn't want to talk about
them, and he'd said it in a way that led her to
believe the relationship was strained. She'd
actually felt bad for him!

All of this prevented her from feeling sorry
for him when, at the end of class, Nora asked
him to demonstrate a "challenging series of
poses." She could tell he was embarrassed
by the attention. This was something she did
know about him; his humility had appealed
to her from the day they'd met. She could see
he was ready to decline. The hint of disappointment on Nora's face had Harper wanting
to volunteer to perform the poses herself, and
she had no idea what they entailed. Nora was
like the coolest, sweetest person Harper had
ever met and she silently willed him not to
disappoint his mom. It was difficult to believe
the woman had birthed this closed-off, hard-
edged, military disciplinarian. That wasn't
exactly fair; she knew he was a nice guy. *To
other people.*

Kyle, being the good son that he was, obviously could read Nora, too, and acquiesced to her request. Smoothly, he dropped into plank position as if he were going to perform a push-up. Then he lowered to his elbows and shifted his weight forward, lifting his legs and tucking one knee onto the opposite elbow.

"Soaring pigeon," Nora proudly narrated through the poses, giving the traditional name and the familiar English translation. Kyle stretched both legs back until they were parallel with the ground. He extended one arm, so his entire body was balanced horizontally on the other. Harper watched and tried not to gape at his muscles bulging out all over the place. The pose looked impossible, like something an acrobat might perform.

Lowering the outstretched arm, he placed his palm on the floor near the other and extended his body up into a handstand. Bending his knees and arching his back he touched the back of his head with his toes.

"Wounded peacock, handstand scorpion," Nora finished in succession. "Just beautiful, Kyle!"

"Thanks, Mom," an upside-down Kyle said, making everyone laugh.

"Can you do the grand finale?"

"Sure." He walked across the floor on his hands to the very front of the classroom and stopped. Springing to his feet, he executed a back handspring. He was pure brilliance and a stunning example of manly beauty. And Harper was incredibly angered by all of it.

The entire class broke out in applause. Dry-mouthed, probably from the gaping, Harper fumbled with her water bottle.

"Kyle was a gymnast when he was young," Nora explained. "He's the one who got me interested in yoga when he was only a teenager."

Fuming, Harper took a long drink and tried to analyze her feelings. She was upset on two fronts. The first because she'd realized a disturbing truth throughout the course of class. Kyle had deliberately kept this information from her. About his yoga abilities, not to mention the acrobatics, about his mom, his family and everything else. Despite her efforts, she'd learned precious little about him, and that's the way he wanted it.

The second part was more complicated and had to do with why this bothered her. She wanted to know this stuff about him. She wanted to *know* him. It hurt that he didn't want to share anything about himself, that he didn't want her to get to know him. Which all had to do with why it also bothered her that a shapely woman with a perky ponytail sidled up next to him and introduced herself.

"Hi, I'm Mandy. So, you're Nora's son, huh?"

"Guilty."

"What else are you guilty of, Kyle?" Mandy asked. "JK!" she said after a beat and then giggled wildly. Reaching out, she play-slapped his biceps. "I adore your mom. You are so lucky..."

Harper bent over so that she could roll her eyes and her mat at the same time. She took her time, blatantly eavesdropping, while Mandy gushed over his one-handed-whatever-pose (of course, Mandy knew its proper name!) and not so subtly quizzed him about his relationship status. Harper wanted to interrupt, but she needed to face the fact that no matter how different—how *nice*—he was toward others, he was not that way to her. She was just a job to him. She needed to accept this and treat him like he was an employee. Except she didn't care if someone was an employee, she treated everyone the same, or at least she tried to. She liked to think she did. Kyle, on the other hand, did not.

Mat tucked under her arm, water bottle in the other, and no further reason to loiter around while Kyle gave Mandy tips on how to gain the proper core strength to master the wounded peacock, Harper took off toward the cubby where she'd stored her stuff before she wounded *him* with a kick to the kneecap.

CLASS HAD NOT gone well. Harper seemed even more upset with Kyle than she'd been earlier in the day. Asking what was wrong felt like crossing a line, a line that Kyle both desperately wanted to cross and didn't want to go near at the same time. But that's what he had to do now. And it wasn't the crossing so much as why he was going to do it. He'd been easing over the line already, at least in his mind. But now that he had to make friends with her, he'd give anything if he could do it for reasons that were entirely his own. Wrestling his conscience into submission, he told himself that this was the best and the most expedient way to discover what she knew about Owen.

"Harper, is something wrong?"

Continuing to stare out the window, she droned, "I'm fine."

"You didn't injure yourself in class, did you?"

"No."

They drove in silence as Kyle tried to decide how to proceed. Deciding directness was the best approach, he asked, "Harper, did I do something to upset you?"

Tension resonated in the space between them. "Not on purpose," she finally murmured.

"What is it, then?"

"It's nothing."

"It's obviously something," he countered.

"You'll think I'm weird."

"I doubt that." *I think you're smart and beautiful and interesting without being conceited or pretentious. And now I finally get to ask all the questions I've been wanting to ask you. And regardless of why I'm asking, I still want the answers.*

"You know what, fine, why shouldn't I tell you?" She shifted in her seat so that she was looking right at him. "It bothered me seeing you in there."

"Which part?"

"Doing yoga. You're incredible."

"Well, I can teach you some stuff if you want. I work at it several mornings a week. The better shape you're in, the easier it is to elude a would-be assailant."

"Can you give the safety stuff a rest for five seconds?" she returned sharply. "This is personal."

"Sure," he replied calmly.

"What bothers me is that I didn't know that you even did yoga. We had this whole conversation about it, and you never said anything. You didn't even mention that your mom taught at the studio, or that she was a yoga instructor at all. Or that she lives in Pacific Cove. When I told you I was going to yoga class, you looked like you were going to be ill."

"Yeah, that's because I didn't want you to—" He cut off the end of the sentence when he realized how it might sound.

"You didn't want me to what?"

He tried a more diplomatic explanation. "I didn't want to start mixing up my professional life with my personal life."

"You didn't want me to meet your family, you mean?"

"Yes." *But not for the reasons you're thinking.*

Harper let out a strangled sound that went right to his heart. "Why? If you weren't nice to *everybody* except me, I wouldn't care. I'd just think you were a jerk and go on about my life. But Helen and Mandy know more about you than I do! I know I talk a lot and tend to be sarcastic during our safety sessions, but surely you can recognize that for the fear and uncertainty that it is. Am I that horrible to be around?"

"Helen?" Kyle turned on his blinker so he could pull over at the next lookout. He couldn't talk to her about this and drive safely anymore. He couldn't handle that he'd upset her like this. He wasn't sure how he was going to explain away his behavior, but he had to try.

"Yes, Helen! Indy's dog-mom. The *stranger* you helped on the street and then happily conversed with for a good ten minutes. Unprompted, you chatted about dogs and told her that your sister is a vet. I heard you tell the woman behind us at yoga that you like egg rolls, and I eagerly filed it away.

"My point here is that everything I know about you I've learned from your conversations with someone else. When I asked about your sister, you said, and I quote, 'Yes.' And then gave me a speech about crime scene B. I asked if you were close to your family and you said, and I quote, 'Not really.' If that's true, then what was that back there?" She thrust a finger toward the back window. "My son this, my brother that, I'm making Uncle Kyle's favorite dinner—those were not the sentiments of a family that is not close. I realize that our relationship is different, you being my security consultant, and technically this is none of my business, but I don't understand why you're so…cold to me. What did I do to make you not like me?"

Slowing the vehicle, Kyle turned off and steered into a parking spot on a lookout above the ocean. The moon was a nearly full, pale yellow ball on the horizon, its fuzzy reflection shimmering on the surface of the water below. He turned to face her, and thought, *Here goes.*

"I do like you," he said.

Harper gaped at him and then barked out a doubtful laugh.

"The fact is that I like you very much." Capturing her surprised gaze with his, he tried to convey his sincerity. Her breath caught as she stared into his eyes and he could see she wanted to believe him. His focus shifted to her mouth. Her lips looked incredibly soft. And the way they were parted was like an invitation. One he badly wanted to accept. Kyle was a hundred percent positive he'd never wanted to kiss a woman as much as he did in that moment. What he wanted to do was to show her exactly how much he liked her.

"I like you, too," she said softly. "That's why this bothers me so much."

Struggling for control, he swallowed his desire. Inhaling slowly, he exhaled a breath, and said, "Harper, I'm sorry. You're right. About everything you just said. I've been trying to keep some distance on purpose."

"Why?"

Why indeed. "I've, uh… Owen—" Harper winced, and he stopped talking. Perfect, he thought. Owen was his excuse. Because at the core of this, he was. Kyle was just going to twist the details a little.

"See?" he said. "That's the problem. Just the sound of Owen's name makes you flinch. I thought I could do this, work for you, get to know you, help you, I thought it was what Owen would want. I still believe that last part, which is why I'm still here. But almost immediately, I could see that it was going to be a lot more difficult than I anticipated. I don't know how to be…friends with you without Owen being right here in the middle between us. He's so much a part of me—and you, too—from what I can see, that it seemed easier for me just to avoid anything personal to keep from talking about him. To keep from reminding you about him, and maybe myself, too." That was true; he reassured himself. It just wasn't *all* of the truth.

Harper's blue-gray eyes flashed with something that looked like anger but then went soft. Sad. Kyle felt like a heel for putting even a hint of this on her. The attraction was the issue, his issue, and he needed to find a better way to deal with it because things were about to get real between them. And the last thing he wanted to do was hurt her.

HARPER STARED AT Kyle and felt her heart go warm and crowd her chest. She knew it! He really was a good guy. More to the point, it wasn't her. The regret and sincerity in his expression drew her sympathy and made her want to lighten his mood. "Well, I'm glad it's not because you think I'm annoying and difficult."

"No, Harper, I promise that's not it."

A smile tugged at her mouth.

"Although," he drawled, tipping his head to one side, "you are a *little* difficult."

"What?"

"This job would be so much easier if you were like an attorney or a florist or a telemarketer." Now she could see the humor dancing in his eyes.

"A telemarketer?" she repeated flatly, trying not to laugh.

He shrugged one helpless shoulder. "In case you didn't know this about yourself, you are an exceptionally good talker. But my point is, any job where you stayed in one place for more than five minutes would be a dream for me."

Harper barely managed to smother her laugh. "I edit photos for hours straight sometimes."

"True, but I'm on the edge of my seat the whole time," he said. "Because any second, I know you're going to come running out of your office like it's on fire and tell me we have to go because the sun is going to set. Like it's a surprise. News flash, Harper, the sun sets every single day."

She tried to form a response, but then gave in to it and laughed instead. Funny Kyle was her new favorite person.

They exchanged grins and something else that made Harper's pulse leap before Kyle went serious again. "I'm genuinely sorry. And what I said is true, I do like you. I'd like for you to give me another chance."

Harper nodded. "You're forgiven. Second chance granted. What you said makes sense. But you don't have to *not* talk about Owen because you think it might upset me. I mean, I don't want to talk about what happened between him and me for reasons I've already worked through. But I don't care if you mention him, especially if not mentioning him makes you clam up and go all stone-faced military man on me. Sharing your memories might make it better. It worked for me." *Even though they aren't happy memories like yours*, she added silently.

"Stone-faced military man?" he repeated with a playful scowl. "That's a bit extreme, I think."

"Hey, I have photographic evidence, remember? Do you need to see it again?"

With an exaggerated cringe, he said, "Ouch. That's right. No thanks. That photo isn't going to end up on some internet meme, is it?"

Pulling one shoulder up, Harper fashioned a "we'll see" expression, and said, "Just be honest with me, and you'll have nothing to worry about."

CHAPTER EIGHT

EVEN THOUGH HE and Harper had formed a truce of sorts, the impending dinner with his family was unnerving for Kyle. Kyle and his dad had been so close; he'd felt lost after his death. Nora and Mia shared a similar closeness and Kyle didn't know where he fit into that, or if he even deserved to. He'd been his father's son. By design, he realized now.

Since Mia wasn't his father's biological child, his dad hadn't wanted a relationship with her, and so Kyle had inadvertently followed his lead. It made him cringe when he thought about how uninterested he'd been in his sister's life. It was true that they'd had different hobbies and pastimes—Mia had been a loner focused on school while Kyle had enjoyed outdoor activities and excelled at sports. But the truth was that Kyle had never been interested in finding common ground. He couldn't recall ever attending one of her science fairs or academic competitions. He never asked what she was up to or invited her to play sports with him. At the very least, he wished he would have just taken the time to hang out with her once in a while. The way Levi and Laney did.

As a kid, Kyle had worshipped his dad. Reverence, he'd only realized too late, that his dad hadn't earned. At least, he hadn't deserved quite so much of Kyle's undying devotion. Certainly not at the expense of his mom and sister. Since he'd come to Pacific Cove, his mom acted like he'd been a perfect son who'd never done a thing wrong. His attempts to establish a relationship with Mia were mostly discouraging, a kind of "one step forward, two steps back" kind of thing. And he knew Nora felt the strain of playing peacekeeper between her children. While he struggled to shake the guilt of not being a better son and brother, Nora's enthusiasm somehow made Kyle feel worse. Bottom line, he felt like he deserved some of Mia's scorn and didn't deserve his mom's devotion. Bringing Harper into the middle of it felt...overwhelming.

"Are you sure you're okay with this?" Harper asked from the passenger seat as they neared Mia's house.

"With what?" Kyle asked.

"With me meeting your family."

Were his thoughts so easy to read or was she just being polite? "Why wouldn't I be okay with it?" he hedged.

"Well, you didn't exactly invite me. Your mom did. At the time, I said yes because I could tell you didn't want me to go and I thought it might annoy you if I did. Plus, I was curious. I still am."

Kyle grinned at her honesty. "That was before. If I seem edgy, it's not because of you." He sighed. "My relationship with my family is complicated."

"How so?"

Kyle pulled into Mia and Jay's driveway and parked behind Levi's car.

"It's too much to tell in the two minutes it'll take us to walk inside the house. Suffice it to say that my sister doesn't like me very much, and I don't blame her." Opening the door, he got out, giving a startled Harper no time to ask her customary questions.

She'd insisted on detouring into town for flowers, so Kyle retrieved them from the backseat and walked toward the porch.

Rushing ahead of him, Harper leaped onto the first tread and turned so they were closer in height. "Wait a sec."

Kyle stepped right up to her. The fact did not escape him that all he had to do was lean forward a few inches and he could finally taste her lips.

Just before his gaze drifted down, she caught it with hers, and whispered, "Why are we here if your sister doesn't like you? After meeting her, I gotta be honest and say I find that hard to believe."

Leaning in so his mouth was beside her ear, he closed his eyes and took a second to enjoy the enticing flowery scent of her, before whispering, "Because I'm hoping to eventually change her mind."

"Oh." With a little shudder, she breathed out the word and Kyle knew it had nothing to do with his response and everything to do with their close proximity. "Kyle...?"

But he wasn't going to kiss her on his sister's porch. He shouldn't be thinking about kissing her at all. Bobbing his head to the left where the porch led to a walkway, he said, "That way."

Exhaling an "Okay," she turned around. They followed the path that led to the back deck. With the sun shining and Laney grilling salmon, Kyle knew that's where his family would be congregating.

"Hey!" Levi called from the deck chair. Setting aside the book in his hand, he stood. "You guys made it."

An apron-clad Laney was in front of the grill where a whole salmon filleted in two sizzled over the hot coals. At Levi's words, she pivoted and faced them. "Harper, hi! Nice to see you again. You look so pretty. I love your top." Leave it to Laney to make Harper feel welcome. Pointing the oversize spatula at Levi who'd moved closer, she made introductions. "Harper, this is my brother, Levi. Levi, this is Uncle Kyle's friend Harper."

Harper greeted them both and shook Levi's hand.

"Uncle Kyle," Laney said with a disappointed sigh. "You, on the other hand, are a pig." She added a headshake as if disgusted by the sight of him. "You really need to start working out. That was a sorry display at yoga the other night. You almost turned that soaring pigeon into a crash-landed turkey buzzard. Humiliating."

"Well, you're ugly and not very bright. But it's nice that you try hard."

Laney laughed and punched him in the shoulder with her free hand. These newest members of his extended family Kyle adored. There was no regrettable history to cloud the future, and he intended to keep it that way. He was also grateful for the buffer they created between him and Mia.

Kyle turned and patted the spot. "Quick, Laney, I think there's a mosquito on my shoulder. I felt it trying to bite me. Do you see it?"

"Funny," Laney said flatly. "I'll have you know I can now bench-press my body weight."

"All eighty pounds of it," Levi quipped.

Laney punched him, too.

"Ouch!"

"Yeah, that's right," she said. "And there's more where that came from."

Kyle had to laugh at his skinny, six-foot-tall niece who looked way more like a supermodel than a tough girl. Woe to the men of her future who would undoubtedly underestimate her.

"Seriously, Laney," Kyle said. "It was a good punch. I'll probably have a bruise." He held out a fist.

"Yes!" she exclaimed and bumped it with her own.

Kyle explained to Harper, "Laney is a sure-thing for a volleyball scholarship. The only question is which university? She's been working out to ensure the best offer."

"That, and so that I stay injury free. Thank you again for all the help, Uncle Kyle. That workout plan you made for me is doing the job. I've already gained an inch on my vertical leap."

"Which universities are you leaning toward?" Harper asked.

Kyle left Harper visiting with the teens and stepped through the slider into the house to see if he could help in the kitchen. And promptly stopped in his tracks when he heard his mom say his name. The voices were coming from the kitchen and the response, presumably from Mia, was incomprehensible.

He distinctly heard Nora's rejoinder, "All I'm saying is that you could try a little harder, be more supportive."

Mia's voice went louder, "I know, Mom. I could. It's just that it's hard for me. He hasn't been around for years—by his own choice. Which he freely admits. But now he's here acting like an enthusiastic part of the family and I'm supposed to just ignore the fact that he's never wanted to be around me, which he also admits. And now he's going to take off again. I don't think it's—"

"But, Mia, honey," Nora interrupted, "you just said it, he's here now and—"

Kyle didn't want to hear the rest. He didn't know how to deal with Mia's disapproval anymore. He'd hoped that by spending time in Pacific Cove, they could find a way to bridge the gap between them. Maybe he needed to accept that the kind of relationship he hoped for wasn't possible. Regardless, his mom did not need to defend him.

Stepping into the kitchen, he said, "Hey, guys."

"Kyle, hi!" Nora said brightly even as her expression flickered with concern, no doubt wondering how much he'd overheard.

"Hi, Mom. Mia, you won't need to worry about me hanging around much longer. My new job with Dahlia starts in a month, and like you said, things will go back to being like they were when I was in the military. You'll hardly ever have to see me."

Mia looked shocked. "Kyle, that's not at all what I meant."

"Salmon's ready!" Laney's voice called through the house.

"Maybe not," Kyle said, not bothering to keep the resignation from his tone. "But that's what I heard, and it'll undoubtedly be easier for you that way." He turned on his heel and strode out of the kitchen.

FOR MOST OF Harper's life, she'd been a family of two. Her mom had died when she was four, and while she couldn't possibly love her dad any more than she did, she'd always been fascinated with big families. As a little girl, she'd longed for a sister or brother. Several of each would have been ideal in her mind.

Levi explained that there were six kids in their brood. "So, we were born in sets of two. Jay and our older sister, Josie, have the same dad. Then me and Laney—same dad. And we have a little brother and sister, Dean and Delilah…" Levi nodded and shook one finger. "I can see you're picking up on this quickly. Presumably, to make it easier for her to remember, our mom named us so that the first letter of our names matches the first letter of our corresponding dads' names. For example, Laney and I share the same father. That's Lyle."

"Wow." A million questions swirled through Harper's mind. As she tried to decide which ones were polite to ask, Levi saved her from having to choose by answering a few of them.

"Our mom is on her fifth marriage. She has a mental illness, a personality disorder, and last year she relinquished custody of us to Jay and Josie. They've raised us anyway, but family court made it official. Jay kept Laney and me, so he's our legal guardian. Sometimes I call him dad just to freak him out. Josie has Dean and Delilah. She's married to Craig. They'll be here soon, and you'll get to meet them, too. Oh, and we all call Kyle 'Uncle Kyle' because we like him and are thrilled to have a real uncle. Well, some of us have biological uncles who we never see so we don't count them."

"All right, then." Harper nodded. "I'm good with faces. This will be fun."

No sooner had she uttered the declaration than a little boy and girl came running around the side of the house, followed by a woman who looked like Jay's brown-haired, green-eyed twin. Introductions were made, and Harper felt incredibly welcome. She knew that she and Kyle were a source of speculation, but Kyle handled it well, calling her a friend and explaining that he knew her dad without mentioning his name. No one pegged her for David Bellaire's daughter, but she felt sure that if anyone would, it would be Levi.

Laney learned she was a photographer and asked for her advice on the pictures they'd posted on the Lucky Cats website. Harper learned that Mia had started the cat rescue organization with the goal to reduce the feral cat population. In addition to sterilizing strays, they also gave them medical treatment and rehabilitated them for adoption. Harper was honest about the photos, explaining how different light and composition might help. One black-and-white cat looked so thin and sickly Harper despaired of her ever being adopted.

Everyone seemed to adore Kyle, and Harper speculated that the "complicated" part he'd mentioned must go back further than the built-in family Mia had gained via her marriage to Jay.

It wasn't long before the interaction between Kyle and Mia added proof to her theory. Compared to the dynamic among Jay's siblings, Harper would never have guessed Kyle and Mia were brother and sister. They barely spoke to each other and when they did it was with excessive politeness. This was all very strange. When Harper met Mia at yoga class, she'd seemed excited that Kyle was coming to dinner. But now Mia seemed tense and edgy and totally unlike the woman she'd met. Kyle was stiff and uncomfortable—a state she was all too familiar with—but his comment when they'd arrived told Harper that he cared very much for his sister. And the vibe between them didn't *feel* like dislike as much as... She didn't know, but Harper felt an inexplicable determination to get to the bottom of it.

Her chance came sooner than expected.

After dinner, the kids recruited Kyle for a game of soccer on the beach. Jay headed down with them to light a fire as s'mores were on the menu for dessert. Harper volunteered to help clean up, and soon she found herself alone in the kitchen with Mia.

Harper rinsed the silverware and began loading the dishwasher. "Kyle said you guys didn't grow up here?"

"No, we didn't." Mia spooned leftover salad into a smaller container. "I'm sure he mentioned that Bill, his dad, who I thought was my biological father but was in reality my stepdad—although I didn't learn that until last year—was career navy."

What! "Mmm-hmm," she answered because he had told her the navy part.

"We moved often, but usually we lived near the ocean. The beach was one part of my childhood that I did like, so when I graduated from veterinary school, I came here. My mentor had started a practice in Pacific Cove, and he offered me a partnership. I jumped at the chance. Bill had passed away, and Mom always loved living by the ocean, too. She generously helped me with the down payment for this house and moved in with me."

Harper plugged the sink to start washing the dishes that wouldn't fit inside the dishwasher. "I don't blame you for choosing this place. I've only been here a few months, but I love Pacific Cove. My dad and I used to vacation here when I was little."

Mia was working on stowing the uneaten portion of potatoes au gratin. Harper was surprised there was any of the delicious dish left.

Mia said, "Kyle seems to like it, too."

"He does," Harper agreed.

"So, you two know each other through your dad? Is he in the military?"

"Yes, and no, he's not. My dad's a businessman in Seattle." Harper didn't mention the scientist part for fear it would give her away.

"Any chance you could get my brother to abandon his Dahlia fixation and stay here in Pacific Cove?"

Okay. Those were not the words of a sister who disliked her brother. "Unfortunately, I don't have that kind of influence. We're not... We're just friends." At least, Harper thought they were headed toward a friendship. Even though there'd been a few moments where it felt like it could be more. Like earlier on the porch...

"Is that his idea or yours?"

"Um, both, I guess." Harper needed to change the course of this conversation before Mia asked something that forced her to lie outright. She was attracted to Kyle in ways that she'd never felt before, ways that she'd never felt about any other friend before. Or any more-than-friend, for that matter. But attraction didn't make a relationship or mean that you should even entertain the idea of one. *So, yeah, stop entertaining, Harper.* "You don't like the idea of Kyle working for Dahlia?"

Mia scoffed. "No. That work is dangerous. I don't know why… I understand him putting his life at risk for our country, but to do it for money? I don't get it. Do you know that his best friend was killed last year while he was working for Dahlia?"

"I did. I do know about that. But from what I understand, Owen wasn't on the job when he was killed. It was a car accident."

Mia made a skeptical sound. "Maybe not. But there have been plenty of other employees who have been. And he was in that danger zone because of Dahlia. I know Kyle will be making a lot of money, but that's never been important to him. Obviously. You know him."

She was right, of course; he was trading one high-risk occupation for another. Why was he taking the job? Harper thought about his old beat-up pickup, his casual wardrobe and his decided lack of expensive gadgets. Even more telling, he'd never asked Harper about her wealth. He didn't seem to be motivated by money like Owen. The more important takeaway here was that Mia sounded like a protective big sister who cared very much for her baby brother. So, what exactly was the problem between them? Harper needed to think about this.

"How did you and Jay meet?"

"A plane crash."

"A whatty-what?" Soapy serving bowl in hand, Harper swiveled toward Mia, sudsy water flying. "Oops." A bubble drifted up toward the window above the sink. "Sorry, but did you say plane crash?"

Mia grinned. Towel in hand, she reached over and swiped at the mess on the countertop. "Yes, my mom and I were traveling in a small plane that crashed into the ocean. Jay was the flight mechanic with the Coast Guard crew who rescued us. One look into those green eyes and I was hypnotized. Of course, Mom was injured, and I was in shock, so it could have been that."

"Wow. That is super romantic-dangerous, terrifying meet-cute aside."

"Yeah." The word floated out on a laugh. "If you knew me better, you'd realize just how romantic. I would have lost a lot of money betting that I'd never fall in love with a guy in the military."

"Even though that's what your stepdad and your brother chose?"

"That's precisely why I don't like it. As a kid, I hated moving around all the time, changing schools, always being the new girl. We never had a *home* or even a hometown. It was hard. How the navy came first in our life. I hated—" Mia cut herself off.

Harper silently willed her not to stop. She could sense she was close to getting some answers here.

"I'm sorry. Get me talking about my childhood and I'll go on for ages. Even though I've learned that a lot of my feelings are tied to the way Bill treated me and not the military itself. And I still don't understand why Kyle is trading the military for a job that's so similar."

"I take it your stepdad was not a nice man?" Harper couldn't stand the thought of a man who would mistreat Nora or Mia or Kyle. The idea of any dad who was unkind to his children made her heart hurt. Was *this* why Kyle didn't want to talk about his family? This image of their life was so different from the one she'd formed based on the snippets she'd gleaned from Kyle. He'd seemed to recall his dad fondly when they'd discussed him in Astoria.

"Oh, he was a very nice man," Mia said, and waited a beat before adding, "To my mom and Kyle."

Oh, no. Harper didn't know what to say. "I'm so sorry."

"Don't be!" Mia reached out and gave her forearm a quick squeeze. "That sounded a little dramatic, I think." She added a chuckle. "I swear, I'm not normally one to discuss this with people I don't know. You're so easy to talk to. But now that I brought it up, and because you and Kyle are friends, you should know that he has a different perspective. As he should. His perspective is different because his experience was different. Bill wasn't mean to me or anything. He was just…nothing. He didn't want me, and he didn't love me. He tolerated me because he loved my mom. And my mom loved me. She was the best mom ever and did her best to make up for it but…like I said, I only learned that he wasn't my real dad last year, and I'm still dealing with it all. But I grew up thinking my dad didn't like me. But Kyle was his son, and he adored him."

Unfortunately, that was the end of the

conversation. Before Harper could respond, barking erupted from the next room. George and Coastie trotted into the kitchen followed by Nora who announced the fire was ready for marshmallow roasting. The three women gathered all the goodies for s'mores and headed down to the beach. Harper had no idea what to do with the knowledge she'd gained. Maybe with what she'd learned, and now that Kyle was being more forthcoming, she'd get more answers from him and solve the puzzle. Maybe there was even some way she could help mend this brother-sister rift.

KYLE'S BLOOD SEEMED to freeze inside his veins as the phone in his pocket blasted out a song he hadn't heard in six months. "Another One Bites the Dust" was Owen's ringtone. So why was he hearing it now? Was this some kind of sick joke? He was on his way back from fetching Nora's jacket from the house. His eyes found Harper on the beach before taking note of everyone's location. Nora, Mia, Laney, Josie, Craig and the little ones were roasting marshmallows. Levi and Jay were playing Frisbee with the dogs. All of them were too far away to be the source of the sound. Kyle knew very well the song was playing in his pocket, emanating from his phone, but his rational brain wouldn't allow him to believe it.

Pulse galloping, he removed the phone and stared at Owen's smiling face. With a shaky finger, he swiped the screen and put the phone up to his ear. "Hello?"

"Kyle?"

A woman's voice. Lungs pressing inward with a crushing weight, he demanded, "Who is this?"

"Kyle, sweetie. It's Sheila. Are you okay?"

Owen's mom. A mix of relief and understanding dawned. "I'm so sorry for my tone, Sheila. You startled me by calling from Owen's phone."

"Oh, no! Of course, I did. What was I thinking? I've kept his phone because of the contacts and the photos, and sometimes I play his message so I can hear his voice. I went to get your number from it and I just tapped it without thinking. I'm still not myself and now…" The words trailed off with a quiet sob.

"Sheila, what is it?"

It took a moment. "Someone from Dahlia called me."

"About what?" Kyle calmly urged even as anxiety welled within him.

"You know that Owen had a life insurance policy with the company."

"Yes, for you and Mattie." Mattie was Owen's eight-year-old daughter who lived with Sheila.

"That's right. They told me after he died that it would take a while to process the paperwork."

"You haven't gotten the money?"

"No, and now they've notified me that it will be a while longer yet..."

"What did they tell you? Why won't they release the funds?"

"You know about the investigation, right?"

"Yes. From what I understand, it's standard procedure."

"Not like this. Usually, it only takes about six weeks. It's been six months, and they keep giving me the runaround. Now they're saying there's a hang-up with the insurance company. I'm afraid that something is really wrong."

Kyle felt his already massive concern increase exponentially. With military contractors under the microscope these days, he knew that Dahlia had their reasons for wanting to find the truth. Employee behavior was scrutinized, and Dahlia took their reputation very seriously. If it were discovered that one of their employees was involved in criminal behavior, their reputation would suffer. The media tended to pounce on these kinds of stories. Ultimately this would be reflected in their bottom line. Kyle had wanted to help his employer avoid that as well as prevent Owen's name being smeared in the process.

But this was different. And much, much worse. Did this mean the insurance company suspected Owen of illegal activity? Kyle knew it was one of the reasons claims were denied.

This was beyond belief. Kyle knew Owen, and there was no possible way he'd been doing anything illegal. Owen was good and honorable and… Kyle needed to help clear this up, so Sheila would get that money. Money she could use to help secure Mattie's future. That meant upping his game where Harper was concerned.

"Sheila, I'm so sorry. I'll do what I can to help." Kyle knew that was all he could say. Now he needed to *do* something, more than what he'd been doing. "We'll get this figured out."

"I'm sorry to worry you about this. That's not why I called. I just heard your voice, and I lost it."

"That's okay. You can call me anytime—you know that."

"I called because I finally went through all of Owen's things. There's a box for you, Kyle. It's taped shut, but it has your name on it. I'm going to send it to you, but I need an address."

CHAPTER NINE

"Hey, Kyle? Kyle, wake up."

The hand on Kyle's knee registered simultaneously with the soft lilt of Harper's voice. A surge of adrenaline had him bolting upright to find her sitting serenely on the edge of his bed. Why was Harper sitting on his bed? Kyle flicked on the lamp to make sure he wasn't dreaming.

"Good morning," she chirped.

Nope, not dreaming. "Harper, what are you doing here?" Still, the question came out a little sharper than he intended. Clearing his throat, he adjusted his tone and gathered his wits, "Is everything okay?"

"I'm fine. Everything is fine." Smile fading, she added, "Sorry, did I scare you?"

"Yes. You did. A little. What's going on?"

"I got a phone call this morning, and I need to be at a marina in Astoria ASAP." Lips twitching, her gaze traveled over the blanket on his bed. "Is that a kitty-cat blanket?"

"Yes, Mia and Laney gave it to me. They

made it." Kyle checked the time. "Why? It's 4 a.m. Why didn't you text me?"

"It seemed easier to explain in person. I brought coffee." A steaming mug sat on the nightstand. Nice. Kyle couldn't remember anyone ever bringing him a cup of morning coffee.

How could someone be so sweet and frustratingly vague at the same time? Normally, she was all about the information. The very trait he planned to exploit where Owen was concerned. Kyle needed to push aside the uncomfortable manipulative nature of that thought and focus on the big picture. And the smaller one unfolding before him now. "No, I mean why do you need to be at the marina in the middle of the night?"

"Whales."

"What about them?" he asked patiently.

"We're going to go see some. Hopefully. A while back, I talked to the captain of a boat named *Robin's Reveler* about taking me out on the ocean."

"Who is this guy?"

"A boat captain." She said it like he'd just asked the stupidest question ever.

"What type of boat, what kind of captain?" He fired off the questions.

She answered just as quickly, "The type

that floats, the kind that drives the floating boat."

Despite his consternation, he let out a chuckle. He couldn't help it. "Harper, you can't just—"

"Okay, look," she interrupted with a good-natured huff and a little eye roll. "I know it's in your nature, and part of your job, to want to know everything and plan everything. But we need to get going, so I have to make this quick. Everyone told me this guy was the one to ask if you want to know where the whales are. I don't know about the specs of the boat, his favorite baseball team or where he went to high school. We made a deal. He would take me out when the weather was decent, and there were whales close by. He warned me that it might be spur-of-the-moment. Turns out, it's today!"

"So we're going out in the ocean." Kyle reached for the coffee mug and tried to wrap his brain around this latest outing. A day on the ocean sounded awesome.

The last two days had been busy ones. First, they'd driven up the coast to photograph oysters. At a shellfish farm, they'd donned waders and shuffled out waist-deep into the oyster beds with the friendly owner. Harper had seemed entranced by the long history of oyster farming, impressing the man with her knowledge about how the Romans had practiced it as early as the first century. He'd shown them the proper method for shucking an oyster. An enthusiastic Harper attempted the task while the man looked on like a doting father. Then he'd graciously invited them to sample all his varieties of smoked oysters: barbecue, black pepper, garlic, jalapeno. They'd parted with a promise on Harper's part to attend the oyster festival in a nearby town in the fall.

On the way home, they'd detoured to a waterfall, which had led to a hike in the foothills to capture some spectacular ocean views. They hadn't returned until after dark.

Yesterday they'd driven inland and hiked through an old-growth forest. They'd followed that up with a visit to a museum dedicated to the mythical (or not) Sasquatch with an enormous carved statue of the creature out front. Somehow, Harper had talked him into posing in front of it, convincing him she needed him there "for perspective." The smirk on her face at the final product had suggested otherwise and had Kyle suspicious of her intentions. They'd spent the afternoon at home where Kyle tackled a few of the items on his safety lesson list. They'd ended the day by strolling through downtown Pacific Cove and stopping at Tabbie's for bowls of their prize-winning seafood chowder.

"Yep, that's the schedule for today. You want me to write it down for you?" she joked. "Or, wait a second, *I'm* going out on a boat today, but you don't have to go if you don't want to. You could have the day off. I mean, what could happen to me on a boat for goodness' sake?"

Kyle took a sip of coffee, set it down and said, "I'll be ready in ten minutes."

EVEN IN THE dim light on the dock, Harper could feel Kyle's eyes on her, inquisitive, assessing. Although, she didn't mind his glower as much now that they were on friendlier terms. She'd also learned that frequently this look meant he was gearing up for a safety lesson. No matter what they were doing, he never missed a teaching moment. Except this morning she feared he'd see through her to the terror she was busy trying to keep in check. This whale outing had seemed like a great idea when she'd planned it. Now that it was upon her, not so much.

He said, "Just so you know, a lot can happen to a person on a boat."

Harper felt her stomach take a dip as if she

were already being tossed about on the ocean. "I'm sure," she said, immediately imagining a number of scenarios. If the boat were to capsize, she couldn't decide which would be the worst way to go, hypothermia or being eaten by a shark. Hypothermia would be slower and likely, ultimately, involve less pain. A shark, on the other hand, would be much quicker, but horrifically painful. Getting eaten by a shark after hypothermia set in would probably be the best bet; faster, less pain due to the numbness from the water's frigid temperature. This was one of those puzzles that she'd enjoy mulling over with her dad. She made a mental note to ask him next time they talked.

"Are you okay?" he asked.

"Yep, great!" she answered, fiddling unnecessarily with the camera hanging around her neck in the hope of distracting him. "I hope I packed my extra battery," she muttered, knowing that she had.

They were a few minutes early, which normally Harper would appreciate. Kyle might be lecture-y, but he was always ready at a moment's notice when inspiration struck her and the weather decided to cooperate. And like this morning when she'd sprung this outing on him. Initially, she'd been concerned that he wouldn't take her work seriously. That wasn't the case at all. He was a fun travel companion and an excellent unofficial assistant.

"I saw you put at least three batteries in that bag. Now might be a good time to talk about a few safety precautions. How much boating experience do you have?"

He also took *his* work very seriously. Flashing him her best "I got this" expression, she said, "When I was a teenager, my friend Cynthia's family had a boat. Her dad used to take us sailing on Puget Sound. Super fun."

"Sailing," he repeated drily. "On Puget Sound. So, you've never been out in the ocean?"

"Of course I have! A few times, actually, since I've been living here." One thing Harper had learned in her career as a photographer was that faking it went a long way where confidence was concerned, both in boosting her own and in generating others' confidence in her. She'd scored a lot of photo opportunities this way. Kind of like Kyle's confident victim speech, although she doubted that "attitude" would help where a shark attack was concerned. She let out a short, nerve-induced cackle.

Kyle gave her a sharp look. She could feel his eyes on her, keen with doubt and questions. Like some sort of silent interrogation, she was feeling the heat. Even her palms were sweating. His lips pursed thoughtfully. She imagined him analyzing her answer, looking for ways to squeeze the details from her.

"Okay!" She confessed, "I've been out in the ocean, but you should know that I've never crossed the Columbia River Bar."

Kyle's mouth turned down into a little frown.

Noise on the dock behind them halted his commentary. They both turned.

"Hey, ho! Good morning, folks." An older gentleman approached with a friendly wave. He was medium height and barrel-chested, and with his warm grin, jolly voice and shuffling gait, Harper thought he was the perfect picture of a sailor. His white beard was trimmed close, but it couldn't hide the dimples flashing in his round cheeks. He wore blue jeans, boots and a lightweight parka. A faded and frayed, royal blue baseball cap fit snug on his head with the word *Grandpa* stitched across the front.

"I'm Robin Reichman. You must be Harper, the whale seeker?"

"Yes, sir." Harper shook the calloused hand he offered. "It's wonderful to meet you. Thank you so much for calling this morning and making this happen. This is my friend Kyle."

Kyle reached out his hand. "Kyle Frasier. Appreciate your generosity in taking us out today, Captain."

Kyle and Captain Robin made small talk as he led the way down the dock to a slip and stopped in front of a sleek white boat. Fancy script spelled out *Robin's Reveler* on the stern and Harper was relieved to see that the vessel looked clean and appeared perfectly seaworthy. Of course, it was difficult to make out all the details in the dark under mercury vapor lights, but she couldn't imagine Kyle would have a problem with it.

"You kids go ahead and board." The captain swung a hand toward the craft. "I see you brought your own life vests. No need for my lecture, then. Folks love to tell me how well they can swim." Captain Robin added a hearty chuckle and headshake.

Kyle commented, "Tough to swim if you hit your head or break a limb on the way into the water."

"That's exactly right!" Captain Robin exclaimed, and Harper braced herself for a conversation about Kyle's career. Owen always bragged about his life as a SEAL.

Instead, Kyle grabbed her duffel bag full

of gear and the small cooler containing their water and lunch and climbed onboard. He faced her and Harper could tell he was staying close to see if she needed help. A combination of excitement and fear prodded the already agitated butterflies in her stomach as she boarded, but she managed to keep her cool. Stepping onto the boat felt almost menacing. Nicknamed the "Graveyard of the Pacific," the Columbia River Bar was one of the deadliest stretches of water in the entire world, and even on a calm day like today, problems could arise in the strong currents and notorious shoals where the river literally collided with the ocean.

As if reading her mind, Kyle reached out and slipped one arm across her shoulders. Giving them a squeeze, he whispered, "Did you take the meclizine I gave you?"

She nodded. She hadn't even thought about taking a seasickness pill until he'd handed it to her in the car.

"This is going to be a blast, and you're going to get some phenomenal shots today." His gentle smile charmed the butterflies into submission and calmed her fidgety pulse. Under different circumstances, she'd analyze how much his confidence and experience eased her apprehension. Right now she was just grateful.

The captain followed. "I take it you have some nautical experience, Kyle?"

"Yes, sir, a bit. I'm ready and willing to take orders."

"Excellent. Thank you. Truthfully, that's a relief. My buddy Al was supposed to be my first mate today but he canceled this morning. Down with a stomach bug. You think you can handle the job?"

"Sorry to hear about your friend. I'll do my best to fill in and help out any way I can."

The captain looked pleased, and Harper again waited for Kyle to add his credentials. Instead, he nodded politely and asked, "Should I cast off?"

Captain Robin agreed, throwing out a few specific instructions while Kyle saw to the task. The captain fired up the motor. In a matter of minutes, they were cruising out of the marina, the scent of diesel and fish and creosote surprisingly pleasant in the chilly morning air. Slivers of sunlight were peeking over the horizon behind them, the brilliant orange shade reminding Harper of a perfectly ripe cantaloupe. Overhead, a gull screeched, its grayish-white wings glowing in the morning light.

Harper didn't waste any more time. She took a seat in the stern and began snapping photos, knowing the light would change fast now. Kyle stood by Captain Robin, the two men chatting like old friends.

A few minutes later Kyle sat down beside her. "How are you doing?"

Harper mustered a smile. "Great! Will you tell me when we reach the bar? Is there a seat belt or something I should buckle? What is the likelihood of being bounced overboard like a piece of popcorn?"

Kyle snuffled out a gentle laugh as if he couldn't contain it. "I knew you were nervous."

"I know you knew. That's why I'm admitting it. Seems pointless to hide it now. How could you tell?"

"I can't tell you that." Kyle slid her a grin. "Then you'll try and change your tell. But don't worry. You're every bit as good of an actress as you think you are. I'm just incredibly observant and intuitive."

"Whatever." Harper rolled her eyes but couldn't stop her smile. "Some people would say those are the same thing, you know?"

"Hmm. You're probably right." Kyle peered out at the water for a few seconds like he was thinking that over. Then he caught her gaze again and held it. "Honestly, I'm neither of those things. I'm just becoming skilled at reading you."

The smile froze on her face while her body went warm and cold at the same time. What did he mean by that? And why did she want it to mean something? She was struck by the thought that she would love for someone to truly know her, to read her thoughts, to gauge her moods, to truly care about her feelings.

Before she could form an answer, he grinned. "Occupational hazard, I suppose."

Harper ignored the pang of disappointment and forced out a chuckle. "Ha. That's what you think, Frasier." Nervous energy had her adding, "The inner workings of Harper Jansen Bellaire's mind are intricate and complex. I am an enigma, and you will never solve the puzzle that is me."

Leaning in, mouth forming a playful smirk, he said, "We'll see about that."

"Yeah, we will," she shot back with exaggerated confidence.

"You're really cute, you know that?"

She changed her mind; Funny Kyle was out, Sweet Kyle was her new favorite. "I appreciate your efforts to distract me," Harper whispered even though there was no way she'd be overheard. "But why didn't you tell the captain who you are? That you were a SEAL?"

"Why would I do that?" Kyle whispered way too loudly, which made her grin and decide that Funny and Sweet Kyle could share the title.

"Honestly, I don't know. I guess so he would know that you know what you're doing?" She liked sitting this close to him, so she could see the colors change in his eyes. Right now, they twinkled with humor and mischief.

"He'll know what I can do when he sees me doing it. I'd rather earn his respect than tell him that I think I deserve it." Harper realized he was happy to be here, to be heading out on the ocean. That helped a bit with her nerves, too.

Harper thought about his answer, and how unassuming he'd been regarding her dad's rescue, his reluctance to talk about his service, even the way he'd failed to divulge his yoga skills. Maybe he hadn't conned her exactly. It was just that he was so…blasé about his knowledge and expertise. A fresh wave of admiration rolled through her as she realized how appealing that was. And rare. At least, she'd never known a man like him. The thought flashed through her mind before she could squelch it; why couldn't she have met him instead of Owen?

She found herself blurting, "Owen would take any opportunity to, um…talk about being a SEAL."

"Brag, you mean?" One side of his mouth tugged up.

"That's exactly what I mean. It was something I didn't like about him. Not that being a SEAL isn't amazing, because it is. It's just, he was so…"

"Conceited?"

"Yes."

Kyle smiled a little. "I know. He used to tell me I was too modest. And I would tell him that it was okay because he bragged enough for both of us. But he was so…lovable it was easy to overlook. Plus, there was his honor and integrity, too, which made up his core. Not to mention he was the bravest guy I knew."

Honor and integrity? Ha. When she'd first met Owen, he'd put on a good front, showering her with compliments and saying all the right words. He could talk a good line; she'd give him that. And he never missed a chance to talk himself up.

"You are unreal," she said. "How can you

be this superhero expert at everything and still be so…humble?"

His head tipped back in surprise. "Harper, thank you for the compliment. But I am far from an expert at everything."

"Name something you're not good at."

"Well, okay… Um, let's see, I have terrible handwriting."

"Ah," she joked. "So, that explains the anti-note stance."

He grinned and shook his head.

She pressed him, "You can't think of anything, can you?"

"Of course, I can. I'm lousy at drawing or any type of art. Which is a shame because my mom is such an amazing artist."

"Hmm. I'm not sure that counts. I think art is more of a gift."

"I'm not great at math."

"I love math. What else?"

"Well, my personal life is…"

"Is what?" she prodded.

"It's pretty much a mess," he answered. "I would put relationships in the 'needs work' category."

She wanted to quiz him about that. Was he talking about his sister? Did he have a woman in his life? Was that why he'd turned perky Mandy down? How could she pose these questions without seeming like she was too interested?

Then, Kyle reached out and touched her for the first time. A combination of heat, affection and longing blasted through her with surprising force. She stared down at his hand now covering hers. And that's when she realized that she couldn't ask those questions without seeming too interested. Because she *was* too interested. How had she let this happen? She'd promised herself she wouldn't fall again, not until she knew someone very well. She didn't know Kyle well enough. Did she? Even if she did, and he was to return her feelings, she didn't see a way forward for them without telling him about Owen.

That's when something else occurred to her. What if she told him about Owen and he didn't think anything was wrong with it? No, that wouldn't happen. His sister was a veterinarian. Of course, he would think dealing in exotic animal parts was wrong, right? Swallowing around the lump in her throat she was afraid to look up.

"Hey." Kyle squeezed her hand. "You're going to be fine. It's a nice calm morning. Captain Robin has been calling around, and it should be a fairly smooth crossing. I'll be right here with you. And I'm not bragging when I say I'm pretty good at this ocean stuff." Releasing her hand, he stood. "I'm going to go check in and see how much longer, okay?"

Harper nodded and turned away, her anxiety over the dangerous bar crossing dwarfed by the new fear overtaking her; if he could tell when she was nervous, what else would he see?

KYLE STOOD BESIDE the captain, gazing around at the beauty of the ocean before him and trying not to watch Harper too much. Captain Robin had been spot-on; the crossing had been relatively smooth. Harper was a trooper the whole way. It hadn't been a hardship to sit with her and hold her hand. He liked how it seemed to help soothe her nerves.

They'd been motoring south and west, faster now, having passed the south jetty of the Columbia River. In deeper water, the swells were long and shallow, making the trip a joy. No whales had been spotted, but Harper seemed to have settled comfortably into the ride.

Suddenly, Captain Robin cried, "Spout! Starboard."

Camera at the ready, Harper already had her camera in position. Captain Robin maneuvered the boat as close as he could. "The females have their calves this time of year, so we'll hover round here."

"Kyle?" Harper asked, without taking her eyes off the camera. "Can you come here?"

He moved toward her. "Yep."

"Can you take this camera while I get a different one? Just watch the LCD and if you see movement hold the button down."

"Got it." He took the camera.

Harper retrieved another camera from her bag. Harper peeked around him. "You're doing great. I'm going to change lenses real quick."

A burst of movement dead ahead grabbed his attention. His finger hit the button, but his focus was not on the LCD. Kyle watched, mesmerized, as a whale emerged from the water and then tipped sideways, its giant body crashing against the ocean's surface. It was so close, Kyle could see the barnacles adhered to the rubbery surface of its skin. Another one followed suit.

"Oh, boy," Captain Robin said. "These guys are getting a little close. We need to get back a bit."

"Kyle, did you get that?" Harper asked excitedly, snapping photos beside him.

"Maybe…" He doubted it. He was all over

the place. How did she do this?—keep one eye on the subject and the other on the LCD? Another whale followed. Definitely missed that one. Finger poised, he was determined to get a good shot for her. Suddenly, it was extremely important that he not disappoint her.

"I'm going to have to move us forward," Captain Robin's voice barely penetrated Kyle's concentration.

Holding the camera with both hands, he leaned over the railing… Too far, he realized too late, as the boat accelerated and his feet slipped on the deck beneath him. Falling toward the ocean, he braced himself for the cold, but his only real concern was for Harper's camera.

Not being a stranger to frigid water didn't make his accidental swim any warmer. Kyle easily broke the surface, thrusting the camera upward. The boat had slowed and was already turning around.

"Kyle!" Harper called. "Are you okay?"

Treading water, he flashed a thumbs-up with his other hand to indicate he was fine and waited for the boat to circle back. Doing a sidestroke so he could keep the camera out of the water, he easily swam to the stern where he handed the camera off to an extremely concerned Harper.

"I got your camera wet."

"Who cares? Oh, my gosh, you must be freezing. You're going to get hypothermia."

Captain Robin was more amused than sympathetic. "That's something you don't see every day."

"What's that?" Kyle asked, expecting the joke he deserved.

"A navy SEAL imitating a real seal."

Kyle laughed. "That's actually a really good one."

Harper's expression was pure concern. "I'm sorry, Kyle. I told him because he was worried when you went overboard."

"It's fine, Harper. It's not a secret." Kyle climbed the ladder and stepped on board.

"Seriously, I'm honored to have you aboard, son."

Kyle waved away the adulation. "I'm the one who's honored, Captain."

Another whale breached, farther off this time.

"At least you didn't scare the whales," the captain offered helpfully.

Harper shoved one of her bags at him. "I always pack a change of clothes. Hurry, get those wet things off. You're going to get hypothermia while you're standing around making jokes like you didn't just fall into the ocean." She mumbled something else that sounded like "shark bait."

Kyle chuckled even as her concern helped ward off the chill seeping into him. Taking the bag, he headed into the cabin where he peeled off his soggy clothes. He didn't think about what she'd packed until he was staring at the garments inside: black leggings, a long-sleeved thermal and a fleece pullover. "This should be good," he muttered and then silently thanked her for the pair of thick wool socks at the bottom of the bag. There was no way he could squeeze his feet into a pair of her shoes.

Swallowing his pride in the face of the very real threat of hypothermia, he pulled on the ill-fitting garments and ventured back onto the deck where Harper and Captain Robin stood side by side. Grinning. So obvious that they were waiting for him to emerge. They exchanged quick glances before simultaneously erupting with laughter. The leggings only stretched to his knees, and the thermal top looked as if it had shrunk to something that was kid size. Placing his palms on his thighs, Captain Robin doubled over. Camera in hand, Harper was snapping photos like a deranged paparazzi. Kyle wondered how she managed it through her delighted cackling.

"Are you two having fun?" Kyle asked, gesturing at himself.

"So much fun," Harper said and cracked up all over again. "These are the ones that will go on the internet if you don't watch it."

"I'm going to tweet it—hashtag SEAL in women's clothing." The captain snorted out a fresh burst of laughter. Harper had tears streaming from her eyes.

"Well," Kyle said, planting his hands on his hips. "I think we can officially count photography as something I'm not great at. Although, those photos I took were undoubtedly awesome. Too bad I probably ruined them all when I fell overboard, huh?"

"Don't you worry," Harper assured him. "They're all on the cloud. All my photos are on the cloud."

CHAPTER TEN

"MAYBE I SHOULD stick around, talk to your dad." Kyle watched Harper glide around the kitchen making breakfast and thought about the meeting he'd scheduled.

Most mornings he had breakfast before Harper because he worked out before she got up. Today, he'd taken a rest day and accepted her offer of sausage and eggs.

She'd charged him with mixing the orange juice and making toast. Two slices of whole wheat bread were browning in the toaster. After the effort it had taken to arrange, canceling the meeting would seem flakey and could possibly cost him the opportunity he was hoping for. He also had lunch plans with his mom. Breaking a lunch date would disappoint her, and his days of letting Nora down were through. Or at least, he planned never to do so on purpose.

"Kyle, you haven't had a day off since you started. I'll be fine with my dad." Since David was coming for a visit, Kyle knew his security team would be with him, so leaving Harper would likely be fine.

"I could find out the latest in the investigation of the Salmon Egg Stalker." That's the nickname Harper had given her dad's would-be attacker once police had confirmed the contents of the jar. Thus far, the investigation suggested that he'd been acting alone.

"I'll ask, don't worry. Dad will be here by noon, and he's never late. In the meantime, I have a ton of editing to do. I promise I will set the alarm, and I pledge to *not* open the door for anyone I do not know." She waited a beat, and added, "Except for Santa Claus. Because he might be bringing that new wide-angle lens I want."

"Funny," he said drily. Unfortunately, his accompanying grin foiled his attempt at remaining earnest. That didn't mean he would let up where the locking-of-the-door issue was concerned.

"I know," she said looking smugly pleased. Removing the sausage links from the pan, she added, "I enjoy it when you smile in spite of your tough-guy self. What are you going to do on your day off?"

"Meeting a guy for coffee, running a few errands and grabbing a late lunch with my mom. I'll let you know when I'm on the way back." He hadn't mentioned who he was meeting, and he hoped she didn't ask. "What are you guys doing?"

Harper cracked eggs into the pan. "I'm not sure. Even in this rain, we'll take a walk on the beach for sure. Dad loves it here. I don't know if you know this, but this house originally belonged to my grandparents, my mom's parents. Mom was an only child like me, so after they died, she inherited. My parents lived here for a few years after they were first married. Later, it became a vacation place for Dad and me. It's funny because my dad insisted that my mom keep the house in her name and will it to me."

"That's very cool."

"It is, especially because my dad didn't have anything then. My parents were pretty poor for the first few years of their marriage. It wasn't until after I was born and he sold his first patent that they had any money. And even then, he poured most of that back into his research. The big money didn't happen until I was a teenager." Harper scooped the eggs out of the pan.

"That explains a lot."

"How do you mean?" Harper slid their plates across the counter and then walked around to take a seat at one of the stools.

"Your dad," Kyle said, buttering the last piece of toast. "He doesn't act like some egomaniac rich guy. And you certainly don't act like a snobby self-involved rich girl." Kyle moved around the table to join her.

"Thank you." One eyebrow nudged up as she nibbled on the edge of her toast. "That's really nice to hear."

"Calling it like I see it."

Harper set her toast down and fiddled with her napkin. "You've known a lot of rich girls, have you?"

Kyle shrugged a sheepish shoulder and took a bite of sausage. "A few. And you are not anything at all like the one I knew the best. Or her friends."

Harper went very still before turning her thoughtful blue-gray eyes on him. "Kyle Frasier, did a rich girl break your heart and make us all look bad?"

"No." He chuckled and then winced a little. "I think I might have broken hers though. I didn't mean to, but we just weren't a good fit."

"I see."

"My friends thought I was an idiot for breaking up with her." Owen included, but he didn't add that part. Despite what Mia apparently believed, money was not Kyle's primary motivation for taking the job with Dahlia. It had a little to do with money and everything to do with who he was. What would he do if he wasn't protecting someone or something?

"I bet," she said and focused on her plate. Kyle sensed that he'd stirred up a painful memory. Then she looked at him again. "You know, you're the first person I've known longer than about fifteen minutes who's never asked me about money."

"No way."

"Yep, aside from my friend Cynthia, whose family is also wealthy, or other wealthy people, it's something everyone asks me about. I've been wondering when you would ask. You're not even planning to, are you?"

Kyle shrugged. "It hasn't occurred to me. What would I ask?"

"How about… What's your dad's net worth? How many cars do you own? What's it like to be able to buy anything you want? Will you buy me a car? Do you drink champagne for breakfast? But my personal favorites are the backhanded insults and comments. 'If I were as rich as you, I'd help people and give it all away.' And, 'I wish I could just work for fun.' And then there's my dad's top pick, 'It must be so nice not to have to worry about money.' That one is just ridiculous, by the way, because whether you have money or not, you have to worry about money. And often, like in my dad's case, it means you have other stuff to worry about, like privacy and personal safety. And—kidnapping, too, apparently. Although, lucky for me it's not currently the fad. Not to mention Dad's philanthropy, which he does a ton of. But you have to be extra vigilant about what organization you give the money to—If they're legitimate, what they're using it for, how much actually goes to the cause you're supporting, etcetera. One little hint of fraud or deceit and it all comes back on you."

Kyle nodded. He could easily see how all of this would be true. "Those are all real questions you've heard?"

"Yep. Most of them more than once."

"Wow."

"I know. People are weird about money. I admit it sounds like a cliché, but money, or even the possibility of it, can bring out the worst in people. People are cruel and demanding and they…"

"And they assume things that aren't true and want things from you that aren't fair?" Kyle finished for her.

Harper's eyes went wide with appreciation. "Exactly," she said. "We have the same emotional needs as everybody else. We're ordinary human beings too after all." Capturing his gaze again, Kyle had the sense that she was willing him to understand. Almost immediately, the moment evolved into something else. Her blue eyes darkened, and attraction collided between them. Chemistry, admiration, respect and just outright...enjoying her. His worst fear was being realized, and there didn't seem to be anything he could do about it.

Maybe it was good that he was leaving for the day. Getting out of here for a while would give him some perspective, ease these feelings, allow him to rebuild his defenses. Because right now all he wanted to do was take her in his arms and tell her he'd never be one of those people who'd hurt her.

Breaking eye contact, she picked up her coffee mug and took a sip. Spell broken; he felt like a heel as reality swept in. Because he wanted things from her that weren't fair, too, even though they didn't have anything to do with her dad's money.

"This is a big part of the reason I don't work for BEST anymore. His life is very complicated."

"You used to work for your dad?"

"Yep. I think he hopes I'll come back one day."

"Will you?"

"No. I want…a simpler life. A home and a family and a job where I get to be outside. I'm more like my mom in that I'm only good at sitting still for short periods of time. At least, that's what he tells me. More than anything, he wants me to be happy. I love that about him."

Kyle wanted her to be happy, too. But he wasn't going to say that. Hoping to distract them both from this intimacy, he said, "Just so you know, you are far, far from ordinary."

"What does that mean?" she asked suspiciously, yet there was a hint of amusement in her tone.

"It means that you have the kind of genuine weirdness that money could never buy."

"Kyle," she said, with exaggerated sweetness, "that is the nicest thing anyone has ever said to me." Then she threw her balled up napkin at him.

TWENTY MINUTES LATER, Kyle was on his way. Windshield wipers slapping a frenzied beat, he steered the pickup left at the end of Harper's driveway. He traveled south on the highway until he reached the headland Harper had described the day they'd gone to Dungeness. He turned onto the private drive that accessed it. Heavily wooded on both sides, the narrow lane was lined with oversize rhododendrons and dense under-brush. Fifty yards ahead, a tall black metal gate appeared, blocking his path. Kyle hit the brakes, Harper-induced amusement fad-ing, replaced by a surge of uncertainty.

If this meeting went well, it would most likely be a turning point for him and Harper. Did he want that? Yes, came the immedi-ate answer. But could he handle the reper-cussions? He didn't know. Guilt battled with anticipation until he couldn't tell one from the other. For the first time in his life, Kyle warred with his sense of duty. His head told him this was the right thing to do; his heart wished he was doing it for the right reasons.

"THAT'S GREAT, LANEY. Now hold the treat like you did before so that the kitty sees it…" Harper stood in the headquarters of Lucky Cats, which she'd discovered was a recent addition to Pacific Cove Veterinary Clinic.

Harper had one camera attached to a tripod and held a remote in her hand so she could watch the cats, keep an eye on the LCD and take photos at the same time. Their "set" con-sisted of a long table, and a light gray-colored sheet tacked to the wall and draped over the front. Down below, two black kittens batted at the sheet's edge.

"Got it!" Harper called after capturing her feline subject with her little head tipped curiously to one side. "Adorable! Next."

Harper had every intention of doing exactly what she'd told Kyle she was going to do this morning. But then two things happened: her dad called to cancel, and Laney texted. Laney and Mia had a rare free morning with only two cat rescues on the schedule, which Nora, Levi and his girlfriend, Ty, were executing. Could Harper come in and help them photograph the cats ready for adoption? Harper hadn't even considered turning them down.

Only after she'd committed did she realize the pickle she'd gotten herself into. No way would she call Kyle and spoil his day off. She tried to analyze why this meant so much to her. Getting to know his family suggested more than a professional interest in the guy. Unquestionably, it was wading into friendship territory. Trying to repair, or at least understand, his relationship with Mia felt like more than friendship. Or, maybe, it was gratitude.

She was incredibly grateful for everything Kyle was teaching her. Sure, he was being paid. But she'd come to depend on him, driving her around, helping pack her equipment, discussing ideas for what locations to explore next. They'd even taken to sharing the cooking, alternating lunches and dinners. But it was the talking and laughing and companionship she enjoyed the most. Those aspects weren't part of his job. So that was it; he felt like a friend, and you did nice things for your friends.

"Let's do Annie next, Lanes," Mia said, handing her an adult cat with black-and-white tuxedo markings.

Laney took the docile cat and set her on the table where she immediately folded her lanky form into an unattractive crouch that made her appear both frightened and skeletal. Yikes. Harper recognized the cat from the photo Laney had shown her at dinner. She studied the animal critically. More sleek than skinny with long legs and a very shiny coat, the cat appeared graceful and athletic in person. Not sickly like Harper had initially thought. The problem, Harper realized, was simply that the cat didn't photograph well. That odd resting pose and her wide-set eyes reflecting the camera flash made a deer in the headlights look relaxed.

A frowning Laney said, "It's so sad. Annie

has been here for almost a year. A lot of people think that black cats are the least likely to be adopted, but in our experience here, it's black-and-white cats that get passed over the most. Plus, Annie is shy and not a kitten, and those two aspects make her *waayyy* less likely to be chosen."

"It is sad," Mia agreed. "Especially because she's so sweet and playful. She's not antisocial. It just takes her a bit to warm up to new people. And she's super smart."

"Yeah, watch this." Laney lifted the cat again and set her on the ground. She produced a small round ball from the pocket of the apron she wore. "Levi taught her this trick." Laney cooed, "Annie?" The cat sprang to attention. Laney tossed the ball. Annie bounded across the room and pounced, batting the ball here and there a few times. Then she gave it a hard chomp, brought the ball back to Laney and dropped it at her feet.

"No. Way!" Harper watched with amazement as Laney did it again. "The cat fetches?"

Laney grinned. "Yeah, it's seriously amazing what you can teach a cat. To be fair, Levi is like gifted with them though."

"I have an idea," Harper said. "Laney, how do you feel about being in the photo?"

"What do you mean?"

"Well, I was thinking we could do a still shot of you with the cat cuddled in your arms. She seems so much more comfortable if she's being held, which makes her more...attractive. Then, we can add a short video clip of her doing that trick. We'll come up with a cool tagline and see how many clicks we get."

Mia and Laney exchanged excited glances. "Why didn't we think of that?" Mia asked. "Videos."

KYLE HAD ARRANGED to meet his mom at Mia's vet clinic. Since it was Sunday, they were closed for regular appointments, but he knew Lucky Cats would be bustling with activity. He was early, so maybe Mia could put him to work for an hour or so until Nora arrived.

His meeting had gone even better than he hoped and now all he had to do was form a strategy. Strange, how he was both anticipating and dreading what he had planned. He knew Harper would be thrilled, but that was also the problem. On one hand, he couldn't wait to see her face when she realized what he'd done. On the other, the thought of her finding out why he'd done it significantly tempered that enthusiasm.

Distracted by thoughts of Harper, he stepped through the door of Lucky Cats and did a double take because there she was. Harper. Chatting with Mia in front of an open laptop. And from the look of it, the conversation appeared serious. Her dad was not with her, which meant no security. The surge of fear that followed surprised him in its intensity. What if…? No. He wasn't going to go all worst-case scenario right now. She was fine. But what was she thinking?

Laney walked through the door that led from the clinic and spotted him. "Uncle Kyle, hi!"

Mia and Harper looked up then, too, both appearing a bit startled to see him. Harper managed a small smile. Mia waved. He wondered what they'd been discussing.

His favorite cat, Annie, was winding around his feet. Kyle leaned over and picked her up. She had the best purr.

Laney said, "Harper is brilliant and the best photographer ever. Mia, I have a message here for you."

Since his family didn't know the real reason Kyle and Harper were hanging out together, Kyle tacked on a smile and walked closer. "Is that right?"

"She *really* is," Mia agreed. "You should see what she's accomplished. A few hours ago, I put new photos of Annie along with a video of her fetching on the Lucky Cats website, shared it on all our social media sites, and we've already received eight phone calls. That's more than we've received for her in all the time she's been here. Two people are coming in to look at her today. Can you believe that?"

"That is great news. I'd adopt her if I could."

"Which you absolutely could do, if you decided to stay in Pacific Cove," Mia said in a way that didn't call for a response. She stood and walked to where Laney held out a tablet for her.

With his back now to Mia and Laney, Kyle didn't bother to hide his scowl. Careful not to reveal his surprise and frustration in his tone, he said, "I didn't know you were volunteering here today."

Harper smiled, but he could see the concern dancing in her eyes. "I didn't know I was either, but Laney called, and they had the morning free to photograph cats that need homes, so here I am."

"Here you are," Kyle repeated.

"What are you doing here?" Mia asked, joining them again.

"Meeting Mom for lunch."

"That's right. She mentioned that. Do you

guys want to have lunch with us? We're having sandwiches at Salmon Crackers. Harper has been here for hours. She's earned her first volunteer lunch."

HARPER COULD SEE Kyle's hesitation. She knew he was surprised and possibly upset about her being here at Lucky Cats without telling him.

"Sure," Kyle said, "sandwiches sound good."

"I love their hot ham and swiss," Harper added and began packing her gear. "Let me put my equipment in the car."

"I'll help." Kyle walked over and collapsed her portable studio lights. Harper picked up the tripod and camera bag and followed him outside.

Once in the parking lot, she rushed to explain, "I can tell you're upset."

"I wouldn't say I'm upset. Surprised, yes." Kyle opened the back of her SUV. "And now that I know you're safe, I'm as much confused as anything. Harper, why would you come here without telling me? Why would you go anywhere without telling me? Where is your dad?"

"Dad had to cancel. Approximately three minutes later, Laney called. I'd already promised I'd help with the cat photos, so I said yes. I realize that was a little impulsive, but I didn't want to interrupt your day off."

"Impulsive," he repeated with a shake of his head, "is not really the issue. I don't want to change that about you. It's actually very appealing how spontaneous you are."

Harper took a second to enjoy the compliment while Kyle seemed to gather his thoughts.

"But I'd like for you to be spontaneous without being reckless."

"I see your point, but you've been putting in some long hours."

"My day off could not possibly be more important than your safety. This is my job for which I am being generously compensated. *You* are my job. I can't do my job if you don't communicate with me."

Her heart sank a little at that reminder. His job. She didn't think of him as her employee. Why did she expect him to feel more for her just because she felt more for him?

"I'm sorry. I took all the precautions you taught me." Pulling out her phone, she showed him the display. "Look, I even have my phone, it's charged and on with both your avatar and 911 front and center, in case I need help."

Kyle glanced at the phone before locking eyes with her again.

She pointed at her hip. "I also have my pepper spray." He'd gotten her a holster that attached to her waist.

"Good. But please tell me next time, okay? I don't care if it's my day off or what I'm doing."

"Okay," she said simply.

Reaching out a hand, he curled it gently over her shoulder. Heat radiated from the spot, down her arm, through her body and right into the center of her heart. His next words left her reeling and gave her hope that she maybe shouldn't feel. "Harper, just... I don't know what I'd do if something happened to you."

CHAPTER ELEVEN

THE DISTINCTIVE CHIME from her phone alerted Harper to Kyle's text. Groggily, she reached toward where it sat on the nightstand and saw that the time read 4:30 a.m. A bolt of concern zipped through her. Had something happened to her dad? Was there an emergency?

Tapping the screen to open the text produced a cute GIF of the sun rising, Mandisa's "Good Morning" playing along with the animated cartoon. Relief flowed through her and left her smiling. She scrolled down to read the message: I didn't want to scare you by showing up in your bedroom at this hour. (Who would do that?!) She laughed out loud and continued reading. But I need you to get up because we have someplace to be in about an hour. I'm coming over to get you in thirty minutes. You'll need all your outdoor camera gear. Lunch is taken care of, and I'll bring muffins and coffee for breakfast.

Harper reread the message while trying not to read too much into its meaning. Throwing back the covers, she climbed out of bed and texted him a Good morning! and a thumbs-up emoji. No point in quizzing him about where they were going; she didn't care. Kyle was doing a nice thing for her and she was going to let herself enjoy every second.

Something had shifted in their relationship. Instead of the awkwardness she feared would linger after he'd found her at Lucky Cats, he'd let it go. She liked that about him, how when he said something was resolved it was. They'd gone to lunch with his family and had a great time.

Harper had found an opportunity to chat a bit with Nora who even produced a couple of baby pictures of Kyle. She was delighted to discover he was the cutest little guy ever. The ensuing discussion about family photos had given Harper an idea. Now she just needed to run it by Mia and Josie.

Twenty-eight minutes later, Harper heard Kyle let himself in through the back door.

"Ready?" he asked as he stepped into the kitchen.

"I think so. Are you going to tell me where we're going?"

"Nope. Do you have all your equipment?"

"Yes."

"Tripods?"

"Left those in the car last night."

"Perfect." He gifted her with a mischievous smile, making her stomach tighten with only good anticipation. "Let's go."

Harper followed him outside. Kyle watched her arm the security system. Inside the SUV she found a travel mug of coffee and a box from Bakery-by-the-Sea on the console.

"Did you run to town and get these this morning?" she asked. In addition to cheeseburgers, they'd discovered a mutual love for Bakery-by-the-Sea's oversize muffins. Harper liked raspberry cheesecake streusel while Kyle preferred blueberry almond-top.

"Yep, I did."

Grinning, she buckled her seat belt and then reached for the box. "I don't even know where I'm going, and I already like this day."

Before long, she was slightly confused when Kyle steered the SUV off the highway and onto the private drive that led to Rhys McGrath's property. "What are you doing?"

Kyle shot her a quick conspiratorial grin. "I have an idea."

"What kind of idea?"

"Well, as you know," he said with mock austerity, "I'm a navy SEAL and highly trained in stealth and covert operations."

"Uh-huh," she answered doubtfully. "So?"

"You're about to see me work my magic."

Kyle halted the vehicle. The headlights illuminated the tall black iron gate where Harper had stopped herself a grand total of six times in the months she'd lived here.

"But," he said in his serious, safety-lecture tone, "if something happens and I give you the distress signal, I want you to climb into the driver's seat and get out of here as quick as you can. Don't wait for me. I'll find my way back."

"Wait a minute! What are you going to do? Kyle, that sign reads, No Trespassing and that trespassers will be prosecuted. Loosely translated that means, 'no go, amigo.' Plus, I don't know if you had a chance to review it, but *prosecution* is not on my schedule for today."

He chuckled. "Harper, I'm kidding. Mostly. But if this does go south, just do what I said, okay?" Kyle opened the door, and got out. Harper watched him stroll confidently toward the gate where he fiddled with the keypad located next to the buzzer.

He turned around, shrugged and walked back to the SUV. He climbed inside. "I don't hear any sirens, so that's good."

Harper's brows went up. "What are you… out of your mind? Have you been drinking?" Then she chuckled because of course she appreciated the elaborate joke. With exaggerated sincerity, she said, "I am so shocked that it didn't work. I mean, you were a SEAL. No doubt your military Special Forces training makes your button-pushing technique superior and—" She cut herself off because the gate was moving. Opening!

His grin was nothing short of adorable. "You were saying?"

"Kyle, what is going on?"

"You're going to go photograph an old lighthouse, a World War II bunker and other historical amazingness, I believe is how you termed it."

"Are you kidding me?"

"Oh, and you get to meet Rhys McGrath. You're going to like him. But not too much I hope." He added a wink that made her insides melt like water on a sunbaked sandcastle.

Kyle drove on, and minutes later they arrived at the home of Rhys McGrath. Who opened the door and let them inside! Kyle performed introductions because, apparently, the two men already knew each other. Harper shook his hand and understood why Kyle had made the comment about her not liking him too much. (She'd ponder exactly why that would bother Kyle later.) Far from being the crotchety curmudgeon she'd been expecting, Rhys was tall, gorgeous, and while not quite as fit as Kyle (but then again who was?) lean and muscled. His light brown hair was streaked with blond. Wavy and chin length, he wore it tucked behind his ears. Harper estimated his age at midthirties.

"Lovely to meet you, Harper. I've seen some of your work. I confess I Googled you after my meeting with Kyle. You're very talented."

Meeting? What were they? Business partners? "Thank you, Mr. McGrath. I'm honored to meet you, as well. I admire the work you've done for veterans' causes."

His eyebrows hiked up onto his forehead like he was surprised Harper knew about the endeavor. "Please, call me Rhys."

All the information she'd gathered on the man a few months back when she'd hoped to arrange a meeting herself came back to her. Harper was dying to find out how Kyle had managed to get through to him.

"Your home is gorgeous," Harper said, studying the large exposed wooden beams interlocked at the peak of the ceiling and extending down the walls of the large timber frame home. "Old-growth Douglas fir?"

Rhys smiled. "Very good. Not many people recognize it."

"When I was first starting out in Seattle

as a photographer, I did a lot of weddings. There's an old timber frame building near Mount Rainier that's a popular venue. It has a similar style of construction, and I admit I was so taken with the place, I studied up on it. One of the best parts of being a photographer is traveling to new places and learning about the stuff I shoot. I find that the more I know about something, the better able I am to capture all the nuances. That probably sounds crazy."

"Not at all. I enjoy information, too. Was it the Picot Mansion?"

"It was!"

"These beams came from the same place."

"Well, don't keep me in suspense," Harper returned. "What place is that?"

"I'll tell you all about it at lunchtime."

"Lunchtime?"

"I understand from Kyle that there's a reason why you needed to get me out of bed at this unfortunate hour."

"Oh, my goodness, it is early, isn't it?" Her grin collided firmly with Kyle's. "I apologize. I forget that not everybody is quite as enamored as I am with the morning light."

THEY VENTURED OUTSIDE where Harper gawked around spellbound as that light began to cast a glow all around the gorgeous landscape. Evergreen bushes like salal, rhododendron and Oregon grape circled a tidy green lawn. Windswept spruce trees fanned out from there. Harper could see the towering, elegant form of the lighthouse and the shingled roof of the caretaker's cottage.

From her previous research and inspection of satellite photos, Harper knew the property consisted of a headland over two hundred acres in size. Extending out into the Pacific Ocean and delineated by steep cliffs rising a hundred and some feet from the ocean below, it had once been a vital lighthouse locale. And, later, the perfect placement for a World War II bunker. People still photographed the lighthouse from the ocean, but the last known photos taken from the property that Harper could find were from over fifty years ago. Excitement churned inside of her at the notion of scoring such a coup. And she owed it all to Kyle.

Happiness and affection mingled inside of her. She was certain it was the nicest thing that anyone, outside of her dad, had ever done for her.

Rhys gave them a quick description of the property, pointing out various paths and trails to the lighthouse and cottage, the old war bunker and the stairs down to the ocean below.

"They're all unlocked. Take your time exploring." Rhys paused before adding, "Kyle knows all this because I showed him around when he was here."

"Wow. Rhys," Harper said, "I'm incredibly grateful and excited. I don't know how to thank you."

Rhys shot a meaningful glance at Kyle that had her wondering what he'd had to do to pull this off. "No thanks necessary. We'll see you guys around noon." And with that, he headed back toward the house.

"You ready?"

"I think so. Believe it or not, I'm a little overwhelmed. I'm not sure where to start."

"I thought you might be, so I took the liberty of making a schedule according to how I think the light is going to move…" He explained his strategy while they gathered the camera equipment from the car.

Harper agreed with his plan. She draped one camera around her neck and slipped her pack onto her back. Kyle took the duffel bag and slung it over one shoulder. The tripod he tucked under the opposite arm.

The lighthouse stood regally on the bluff and seemed to bask in the dawn, reflecting the sun's orange-tinted morning rays. It was still painted the original white, and Harper estimated the cylindrical structure was close to a hundred feet tall. The lookout at the top was surrounded with panes of thick glass. A layer of dew lent richness to the setting. From the first snap of the shutter, she was lost in her craft and relishing every second.

Within a few hours, Harper had photographed the lighthouse, and the view there from every angle, the caretaker's cottage, the grounds, the ocean, the cliffs and on it went. Just before noon, with the sun approaching its peak, they decided to check out the bunker.

Kyle set off on a trail like he knew right where he was going, which she soon realized he did. And now that her frenzied pace of taking photos had slowed, she decided to learn some details. "Are you going to tell me how you managed this?" she asked as they walked.

"I did some research, figured out Rhys's dad and my dad served together in the navy."

"Really? But how did you get him to take your call in the first place or return it?"

"That was trickier. I reached out to a guy who'd served with them both to see if he'd kept in touch with Rhys's dad. He has, and he called Rhys's dad for me, who called Rhys. Luckily, Rhys decided to call me back."

The trail emptied into a small, roughly oval-shaped, grass-covered clearing. Taller, older trees surrounded the perimeter. A low-lying border of wild shrubs and bushes outlined the area like they were trying to crowd their way in. Rhys obviously kept the grass mowed and the brush trimmed. Located near the edge of the cliff was the bunker. Moss-covered and attractively draped with vines, it blended into the scenery almost like a natural part of the landscape.

Harper turned a circle, absorbing the beauty of the setting. "This is incredible."

"Do you want to go inside?"

"Yes!" was her immediate reaction, which she followed with, "Wait, is it safe?"

Kyle laughed. "Do you know how funny I find it that you're finally asking me if a place is safe when that place was designed specifically to keep people safe?"

"All right," Harper said along with a playful glare. "I see your point."

Once inside, Harper realized the front of the structure had been built like a half circle to obtain the best views of both the surrounding area and the ocean down below. The windows were situated high up on the walls. Stepping onto a rock ledge running along the bottom, she peered out one of the rectangular slots where she imagined guns would be placed in a combat situation. The view of the ocean was stunning. Raising her camera, she took a keyhole photo so she'd remember it. Then she snuck a photo of Kyle in profile as he gazed out at the view.

She wanted to remember every moment of this day. This day that Kyle had gone to so much trouble to arrange. And then planned down to the last detail. All the emotions that had been simmering inside her intensified. She turned to find Kyle watching her, his brown eyes penetrating and soulful, and at the same time, increasing her confidence that he felt this insane attraction, too.

"Why did you do all this?"

He took a step closer. Her heart knocked hard against her rib cage and then took off racing.

"I did it for you." His voice sounded low and a little raspy, making her skin tingle. "Because what can you give the woman who has everything? Or could have, if she wanted."

Oh. Wow. Harper didn't stop to think about what the consequences might bring. One step brought her right into his space, so close the heady scent of him seemed to wrap around her, a mix of citrus and lush fir needles. Raising her arms, she wrapped them around the back of his neck and kissed him. A mix of relief and desire rushed through her when he didn't even hesitate to return the embrace. Kissing her, he slid one strong arm around her waist and settled it on her hip. All of this combined to leave her with no doubt about the way he felt. Palm flat, he pressed his other hand to the middle of her back, coaxing her closer. His lips were soft and warm, and his actions held a sense of urgency that Harper felt, too. Like finally taking a drink after waiting way, way too long.

Slowly, she lowered one hand to explore the muscled curves of his back, appreciating the way his shirt stretched tight across his shoulders. She knew how hard he worked to look like he did, and she wanted to tell him how much she admired that, how much she admired him. Along with his strength of character, kindness, work ethic and that humility that she found so captivating. There were so many things. But that would entail talking, and that wasn't what she wanted to do right now.

With a soft moan, Kyle loosened his hold and Harper wanted to protest, but then realized he was only shifting his hold, deepening the kiss. A blast of heat combined with her emotions and left her a little light-headed. And she realized then that she never wanted to let him go.

LESS THAN TWO seconds of Harper kissing him, Kyle realized his mistake and yet did the opposite of what he should have done. He kissed her back. He knew he was attracted to her. He'd fantasized about kissing her almost since the first moment they'd met. But this was so much more than that. Getting to know her made it all so much better. He'd only known her a couple of weeks, and he was experiencing the most intense emotions of his life. How was that possible?

He'd never forget the way she'd looked at him when she'd realized he'd managed to arrange this tour. He'd done that. Made her that happy. Making Harper happy was hands down the best feeling he could ever imagine. The depth of that realization was a little startling. He'd achieved a lot in his military career, felt the heady glow of accomplishment due to his hard work, perseverance and innate abilities numerous times. And while it had been satisfying to be one of an elite group like the navy SEALS with a skill set matched by very few, this was better. Being with Harper was like all of that and so much more. It was everything. He wanted to hold her and keep her safe and make her happy like this forever.

She was incredibly soft and warm and inviting, and she tasted like happiness and freedom… And that's when Kyle finally found the strength to rein it in. Because he wasn't free. Not free to do this with her anyway. Heart twisting painfully in protest, he broke off the kiss.

"Harper," he whispered, although he wasn't sure what to say next.

Tender and hazy and full of affection, her blue-gray eyes found his. "Hmm?" she murmured, digging her fingers into his shoulders like she didn't want to let him go. And why was that so irresistible? Kyle felt his control slipping away, but in a good way, a driving-a-fast-car, cliff-diving kind of way. He couldn't help himself; he kissed her again.

She broke it off this time but kept him close. She rested her forehead on his chest, and he could hear her breath coming in little gasps, a perfect match to his own. Bringing one hand around to his chest, she spread her fingers over his still-racing heart, and murmured, "You are so…good."

Like a jab to the chest, that was the wake-up call he needed. He wished he was good, or at least, he wished he was good enough for her. Because that's what he wanted, and he was beginning to believe they could be perfect together.

Cupping one hand to her face and threading his fingers into her hair, he smoothed a thumb across her cheekbone. "I want you to know that I didn't arrange all this because I expect anything from you."

That hurt, too, because it wasn't true, was it? Although he'd known this outing would make her grateful and likely heighten her fondness for him, this kind of physical closeness wasn't what he'd been after *precisely*, and yet he couldn't help but acknowledge that taking their relationship to this level would make it so much easier to get the truth he needed. And even though he wanted this, so much he could barely think straight, obviously, or he wouldn't have kissed her back in the first place, he couldn't do this. He couldn't let it go any farther; he couldn't use her in that way. He needed to accomplish his goal and somehow learn the truth while keeping their hearts out of it. How was he going to do that and somehow undo whatever damage this kiss had done? The last thing he wanted to do was hurt her.

Harper gave him a contented smile that had him wanting to kiss her all over again. "I know. I believe you. And that's huge for me. I, um…"

Forcing the words past the painful knot of guilt clogging his chest, he said, "Harper, you can tell me anything. I hope you know that."

"I think I do. But I, um, I have…trust issues. The details of which I wish I could share with you. But I can't. At least…not yet."

Trust. Kyle's chest went tight because he knew she was talking about Owen. There was something here. There had to be or else she wouldn't be afraid to tell him. "I'm here when you're ready."

She nodded and forced a smile. "For now, we need to get going so we're not late for lunch. I would never want to take Rhys's hospitality for granted."

CHAPTER TWELVE

THE OPEN FLOOR PLAN of Rhys's home made it possible for Harper to stand in the kitchen and watch Kyle and Rhys chatting and laughing in the spacious living area like old friends. Harper had been thankful for the obvious camaraderie between the two men during lunch, a delicious treat of fresh steamed clams, crusty sourdough bread and a green salad, as it didn't call for much discussion on her part.

Harper wanted to tell Kyle about Owen. Or rather, she wanted to tell him part of it. Specifically, the part about her not being in love with Owen like Kyle believed. Her feelings for Kyle already surpassed what she'd felt for Owen. She realized now that she'd never been in love before. She'd *wanted* to be in love, wished for it so much that she'd talked herself into the emotion. More than once. Which seemed so silly now. It was like before Kyle, her soul had been smoldering, trying to ignite. Now there was a full-on bonfire raging inside of her. The world seemed brighter yet safer and more exciting at the same time. She wanted to go places, do things and share everything with him.

She'd finally found the right guy, and she couldn't have him. Not like she wanted. Could she open this can of worms labeled "Owen" and only let part of them spill out? She knew instinctively that if she wanted to have a romantic future with Kyle, that might not be possible. But telling him could ruin everything, too. And the friendship they'd built already meant so much to her. What she'd said to him was true. Trust was *everything*, and aside from her dad, she didn't have anyone in her life she could trust. Despite what she'd been through in the past, she wanted to trust him. But that was the problem, wanting and having were two different things. She needed to be sure before this went any further. Because if it did, she'd have to tell him. She didn't want a relationship that wasn't based on honesty.

Then another thought occurred to her, chilling her enthusiasm considerably. What if she told him and he didn't believe her? She didn't have any proof. She trusted him, but did he trust her?

Gathering her thoughts, reining in her discouragement and trying to deal with reality, Harper took time helping herself to a cup of coffee. When she turned around, she discovered Rhys behind her. Kyle strolled around the living room beyond, examining the artwork and photos arranged on the walls.

Harper smiled. "Your home is incredible. The craftsmanship is breathtaking."

"Thank you," he said. Harper couldn't help but notice the pride in his tone, the twinkle in his eye. He seemed like such a nice guy. "When I built it, I knew I'd be spending a lot of time here so I wanted to make it as perfect as I could. Bring the ocean inside, so to speak."

"Well done. I can't imagine anyone not being happy here."

Rhys's smile faded, the eye sparkle dimmed and Harper knew there was some underlying pain there. What was this guy's story? A hundred questions ticked through her mind, all of them too personal. Why did he secret himself away here all the time? Why didn't he socialize in the community? There was no way she was going to risk damaging this potential acquaintance by being intrusive.

Deciding to steer the subject back around to the original topic that he clearly enjoyed discussing, she asked, "Are you going to tell me about these beams now?"

It worked. Moving around her, Rhys refilled his mug and then leaned a hip against the counter. "The Picot Mansion used to be two mansions. A mansion and a smaller guest mansion, that's the one that's still there." Pointing, he explained, "These beams were recycled from the original larger mansion."

"So, you're telling me there was another mansion even bigger than the one that's there now? What happened to it?" she asked, already intrigued. "How did you get the beams?"

"Hold on there," he said, chuckling. "Good questions. Marcus Picot emigrated from France and made a fortune in logging and lumber. After scouting the area around Mount Rainier, he fell in love with that extraordinary piece of property, which he purchased for his country estate. He then logged a portion of the land and used the trees to construct two giant houses. A larger home for him and his family and a smaller house for guests."

Harper felt herself frowning because there was only one Picot Mansion. She was sure of that.

Rhys's smile blossomed slowly like he knew what she was thinking. "Not long after they moved in, Marcus caught his wife cheating with his secretary. Angry and heartbroken, he shipped her back to France. He didn't want the house anymore, nor did he want to look at it. So he proceeded to disassemble the larger structure piece by piece. But as an aficionado of wood, he couldn't bear to destroy the beams. He kept them in storage where they sat for more than a hundred years."

"Wow. So he remained there on the estate?"

"Yes, Marcus moved into the smaller guesthouse with the two children he had from his first marriage. That's the house that's now known as the Picot Mansion."

"Fascinating. What happened to the secretary?"

"Good question." Rhys grinned. "Rumor has it, Marcus sent him on a seven-year sojourn to the Yukon to scout for lumber, but I've never been able to confirm that."

Harper laughed. "The *small* house is so incredible. I can't even imagine what the larger house was like. How is it that I never ran across this story when I researched the place?"

Cocking his head to one side, he gave her an enigmatic smirk. "Ah, well, you know what they say, the best stuff never makes it into the history books."

"So, how do you know about it?"

"Family history. Marcus Picot was my great-great-grandfather. My family still owns the estate."

"You should write a book, a history of the house, or even your family. I know a photographer who'd help you out."

Rhys nodded, seemingly pleased that she'd enjoyed the story.

Kyle said, "Hey, Harper, come here a sec."

Harper crossed the room to where Kyle now stood in front of a large framed photo. Four men in uniform posed before an enormous submarine.

Kyle pointed from left to right. "That's my dad, William Frasier, Rhys's dad, Thomas McGrath, Rear Admiral Wilhausen, and you probably recognize our former president."

"Holy cow. That's so cool."

Next to that photo was a smaller one of Rhys in combat gear flanked by three men in matching attire. Facing Rhys, she said, "I didn't realize you'd served, as well?"

"Yep, also a SEAL." Tossing a meaningful glance at Kyle, he added, "A pipe hitter, like Kyle."

As Harper thanked him for his service, she realized she knew that term from Owen. A *pipe hitter*, a person who went to extremes to get a job done. Her heart cooled inside her chest. A reminder that she needed to be very careful where this tight brotherhood was concerned.

Due to their common military experience, Kyle and Rhys already seemed like old pals. With nearly a decade of that same unity, Kyle and Owen had shared a bond that she could never fully comprehend. And that's when she made a decision; while her feelings for Kyle felt real and intense, they also might be snowballing out of control. She couldn't do this again. She couldn't let her emotions control her. She'd done way too much of that in the past. She needed to slow down and think this through. Every time she'd let her guard down and trusted a man, it had turned out badly. She didn't think her heart could withstand it again. Especially not from Kyle.

AFTER RHYS TOLD them how cool it was at the bottom of the stairs "suspended only feet above the raw power of the ocean," of course, Harper wanted to check it out. Rhys reported that he'd recently replaced both the stairs and the landing. The metal structure looked and felt sound, so Kyle agreed. But like a walk to the gallows, he spent the descent in torment, working up his "we can't do this" speech. He was not great at sharing his feelings under the best of circumstances; now he had to lie about his feelings when he didn't want to. Because a romance could not happen between him and Harper no matter how much he wished it could.

He needed to figure out a way to fix this, mitigate whatever damage had been done. And fast.

Once they reached the bottom, he was still gathering both his words and his courage when Harper faced him and blurted, "Kyle, I'm sorry. I shouldn't have kissed you."

"Harper, I—"

With one hand gripping the metal railing, she raised the other palm up and out to cut him off. "Let me finish, before I can't, okay?" At his nod she went on, "I think I let my gratitude toward you and my...warm feelings cloud my judgment. The thing is, I have a history of rushing into relationships. No, it's not even that. It's more that I get into the wrong relationships. I, um, let people use me. I mean, I don't *let* them, but they do it..."

Pausing for a few breaths, she seemed to think things over before continuing, "Example, I let my high school boyfriend borrow my car, and then I caught him cheating on me with another girl. Inside the car. Then there was my boyfriend in college, Evan. I thought I was in love with him! We were discussing marriage when I caught him stealing from me. Literally, taking money from my wallet. There was another guy, an artist. I mean, artists are supposed to be sweet and sensitive, right? Not this guy. He…" She waved a hand as if brushing away a bad memory. "Never mind, you don't need all the details." Then she sort of deflated, shoulders slumping, eyes welling with tears. "And then… Owen."

Blinking rapidly, she turned toward the ocean. It took every bit of Kyle's willpower not to go to her and wrap his arms around her.

A few deep fortifying breaths later, she faced him again. "The point I'm making, inelegantly I realize, is that my judgment is off. It's like, if I like someone and they like me, that should be enough. Enough to trust them and know that they won't hurt me or use me. But now I realize, it's not. Not at all. Because people will…" With a bitter laugh, she added, "That vetting thing you've been talking about is a very good idea. And I hope this doesn't sound too cheesy, but I really value your friendship. I'm not ready to risk that."

Kyle was absolutely certain that he'd never felt worse in his life. He wanted to jump into the frigid ocean water and swim away from this kind, sweet, beautiful woman before he hurt her, too. Another part of him wanted to stay, to hug her and protect her, and show her that there was a man who wanted her for all the right reasons. Which he did. But she wouldn't see it that way because he was using her, too.

Then he thought about Owen. And Sheila. Little Mattie. He wanted to help fix that, too. Sheila needed that life insurance money. Mattie no longer had a father. At the very least, she deserved to grow up believing her dad was a hero. He owed it to Owen to get the truth.

Heart aching, he buried his own desire, and said, "I understand. Friends is good." He paused to add a resigned smile. "I'm not sorry you kissed me though. But under the circumstances of my employment with you, getting romantically involved is probably not a good idea."

Relief and maybe a bit of disappointment flashed across her face.

For added insurance, he forced himself to add, "Plus, I'm not sure I could get past the fact that you were Owen's..."

Harper looked away again, but not fast enough. Curiosity had him biting his tongue.

He didn't want to push her and make her suspicious, but he recognized anger when he saw it. And he couldn't help wondering where it was coming from.

"Now GRAB MY HAND. Firmly. That's right. And twist. Good job, Harper!"

Kyle watched martial arts expert and instructor Terry Hennessy give Harper her second self-defense lesson. Roughly half the lower floor of Harper's house consisted of a large open-style family room. One end contained a bar and a gorgeous vintage pool table. The other side was a sitting area where Kyle had moved the furniture against the walls to give them plenty of space. Currently, he was seated in an easy chair in the corner. What should be giving him a sense of comfort and satisfaction was instead tying his stomach in knots.

Terry told Harper, "Now jab like I showed you. You're not going to hurt me, I promise."

Harper threw a punch and let out a little shriek as Terry intercepted her fisted hand in his open palm. She seemed to be enjoying the lessons, which only made matters worse.

They shared a laugh. "Nice," Terry gushed. "If I hadn't known that was coming, I'd be on the ground right now."

Why was Terry still holding on to her hand? Kyle didn't like the way he was grinning down at her either. The man needed to do his job and quit gawking at his student.

"I know you're just saying that to make me feel good about myself," Harper countered.

"No, I'm—"

Harper interrupted with a breezy wave. "It's fine. I'm totally okay with it. Flatter away."

Terry laughed, and the sound was an annoying grind in Kyle's ears. "You're right that I'm not above doing that. But I promise, I'm not flattering you. You're picking up on this very quickly."

Kyle felt the mass of knots tighten even though Terry was right; Harper was doing very well. He, on the other hand, felt like he was being tortured. When he'd arranged these lessons, it had seemed like a brilliant solution. Teaching her himself would require touching her and touching her was not a good idea. A rationale underscored at Rhys's a few days prior. The unanticipated consequences, however, were far worse. Because now he had to watch some other man touch her, which Terry seemed only too eager to do.

These last few days had been difficult. Instead of getting better, the "friends" situation was only growing more challenging. Every time he looked at her, he thought about that kiss. He wanted to kiss her again. He wanted to kiss her whenever he wanted to. Like now, for example. Right after he took Terry down and tossed him out the door.

"Let me show you." Kyle felt himself scowl as Terry positioned Harper's arms crisscross over her chest, and then kept his hands over hers for far too long.

Kyle had met Terry through Josh. The two of them had gone to high school together. Also former military, Terry had served eight years in the army.

Kyle pulled out his phone and fired off a text to Josh: Hey, is your friend Terry single?

Tapping a toe, he impatiently waited for Josh to respond.

"Now," Terry said, "I'm going to approach you from behind. I'll grab you, and I want you to…"

Josh responded immediately. Yes, and he's a total smooth dog. I've never seen anyone as good with the ladies as he is. Except maybe Owen.

Kyle shot to his feet, knocking the coffee table with his knee in the process. The sound was inordinately loud in the spacious room.

Terry and Harper both stopped what they were doing to glance his way.

"Okay, that's enough for today. Thanks, Terry."

"Are you sure?" Terry glanced at the fancy fitness tracker on his wrist. "According to my time, we've still got another fifteen minutes."

"That's okay. I'll review with her and show her the next series of moves." Kyle looked at Harper. "Harper, we need to get going."

"We do?" Harper swiped a hand across her brow.

"Uh, yeah. We have that other commitment this afternoon. Don't forget your camera bag."

A SLIGHTLY OUT-OF-BREATH Harper placed her equipment in the back of the SUV and got into the passenger seat. Kyle had the SUV running. She'd barely had time to wipe off her sweat and change clothes. She'd double-checked, there was nothing on her calendar until later this afternoon. What had she forgotten?

"Where's the fire?" she asked an impatient-looking Kyle, his expression reminding her of the grumpy guy she'd first hired.

"We promised Levi and Laney we'd go to their track meet this afternoon, remember?"

Harper did remember. That was the only thing she had on her schedule. She'd offered to take photos of the kids and the team. Frowning at the time on her phone, she calculated, "But that's not for another two-plus hours."

"Yeah, but I thought we should probably grab something to eat beforehand."

"Oh." Harper glanced over at him. Hands tight on the steering wheel, she wondered if he was trying to strangle the life out of it. Clearly, he was worked up about something. Harper stared out the window thinking this over. The last few days had been a little tense for her, trying to settle for a platonic closeness. Looking at the guy and *not* wanting to kiss him and touch him was a challenge, sure, but they'd both committed to friendship. And Kyle was shaping up to be a good friend, maybe the best she'd ever had. So what was up?

Today, they'd spent the morning on the beach, reviewed some safety lessons, then she'd done some editing until… Until her martial arts lesson. Hmm. Was it her imagination or had he seemed a little short with Terry?

"How do you think the session went today?"

"Fine."

"You can be honest, I'm hopeless, right? I've never been much of an athlete."

"No, Harper..." He let out a sigh as if the topic pained him. "It's not you. Terry was right. You're catching on quickly."

"Well, what, then?"

"I, um, I don't think... I don't think Terry is the right instructor for you. I'll take over your lessons." An almost pained expression crossed his face.

Huh. Harper stared at his profile, wondering. Waiting for him to explain. When no further rationale was offered, she turned over the possibilities in her mind; Terry was ineffective. Absolutely not true as she'd learned a ton. Maybe the track meet was being held at another school instead of home like she'd thought and they needed the extra travel time.

She asked, "Is the meet at home?"

"Yeah, at the high school," Kyle answered, still seeming distracted.

She studied his profile, noting his furrowed brow, the tightness around his jaw, the taut muscles of his neck. Tension emanated from him, and she couldn't help but wonder if it was possible that he was jealous? The thought sent a jolt of longing through her. Terry did seem to be interested in her beyond the teacher-student relationship. Before today's lesson, he'd suggested they meet for coffee and a chat. Had Kyle heard that?

Only one way to find out. "So, have you vetted him?"

"Who, Terry? Of course," he fired back quickly, tossing a fresh scowl her way. "Why?"

"Just wondering."

"Did he ask you out?"

There was a tone there, for sure. "Yes, sort of. I mean, he offered to buy me coffee and talk about martial arts stuff."

"Martial arts stuff?" Kyle repeated, with not a small dose of disbelieving sarcasm.

"Yeah, he said he would show me some websites and YouTube videos where I could read up on it and get extra practice."

"I bet." Then he muttered under his breath before asking, "Did you accept?"

"Is there a reason I shouldn't?"

"Yes," he snapped.

Harper's lungs constricted tightly as her pulse kicked up a few notches. "Okay…?"

Kyle huffed out an exasperated sigh. "I'm not saying he's a bad guy or anything. But he's a player, and I'd hate to see you get hurt."

Jealous. She barely smothered a satisfied, *Ha!* She let herself enjoy the moment. Just because they'd agreed that a romance wasn't a good idea, that didn't mean it wasn't what she wanted. Admittedly, she was struggling. So yes, maybe she wanted him to suffer a bit with wanting her, too.

After a pause, she said, "Thank you for the warning, then. Now I'm glad I turned him down."

"You're welcome," he muttered, the relief evident in the slight relaxing of his shoulders and the way he loosened his grip on the poor steering wheel.

CHAPTER THIRTEEN

"THAT'S THE BEST NEWS, Mia! No, of course,
it's not too soon. We'll see you in the morning." Harper clicked off the call, apparently
with his sister, and beamed at Kyle. "I did it!"

"What did you do?" Kyle put the last of the
dinner dishes in the dishwasher and checked
the time. Harper would likely be going to bed
soon. He needed to call Josh and give him an
update. Not that he had anything new to add,
but Josh had been urging him to deliver, and
he could at least report that Harper was beginning to soften toward him. Soften, Harper,
kiss... He let the memory swim before him.

"I can't believe it worked! The weather is
supposed to be clear. I hope the light cooper-
ates." Harper turned toward him and bounced
a little on her toes. "I wanted to surprise you."

"Surprise me?" he repeated, still not focusing on much beyond the shape of her smiling mouth.

"Kyle, everyone cleared their schedules so
we could do this before you leave. Josie had

to switch shifts at the hospital, and Levi was supposed to go to Portland with Ty's family. But when Ty heard about it, she rescheduled. Craig took a day off. And Mia pushed all her appointments back. She's got a vet colleague covering her emergency calls."

Schedule clearing? A vaguely itchy feeling crept over him as he absorbed her little speech. "Everyone did what? What's going on?"

She took a step closer. "Family pictures. At your sister's house. Tomorrow morning. Isn't this great?"

Irritation churned inside of him. He would never ask his family to disrupt their lives in this way, not for him. Frustration seeped into his tone as he said, "I wish you would have asked me first."

"Why? So you could shoot me down?"

He bit back the yes on the tip of his tongue.

"Kyle, this is going to be awesome. I promise."

Head shaking, he picked up his phone. "I need to call Mia." He needed to apologize for putting everyone out in this way.

"Put your phone down. You're not canceling. Everyone is excited about this." Pausing, she tilted her head. "Everyone except you, apparently."

"How did this even happen?" Throwing up his hands, he let them fall back down to his sides. "No, I am not excited."

Undaunted by his reaction, Harper calmly explained, "I got the idea when we were having lunch with your family. I was talking to your mom, and I asked what you were like when you were a little boy. She showed me your baby picture and then she mentioned that the three of you had never had a photo taken together—a professional one—which I still can't believe. Then Josie said that they'd never had a family picture taken either. I suggested a photo shoot. And since you're leaving, we thought it would be prudent to do it sooner rather than later. But it took a while to put it together. That's a lot of busy people to organize."

"Prudent?" Kyle repeated because he didn't know what to say. He didn't want to hurt her feelings, but this was not okay.

Harper frowned. "Yeah, it means wise, practical, sensi—"

"I know what it means, Harper," Kyle returned flatly. He could feel his composure slipping.

"Why are you upset about this?"

"I'm not upset!" he snapped. "Fine, I'm a little upset. I don't think... You didn't need to…" With a frustrated groan, he leaned back, resting his hips against the counter. "Everyone shouldn't have to rearrange their lives for me."

"They're not rearranging their lives, it's just one morning, for a family portrait." Harper narrowed her gaze thoughtfully and tapped a finger on the countertop. "You don't think your family thinks of you like family, do you?"

As unpleasant as this was, he could no longer keep this from Harper. Not when she kept assuming that things were better than they were. "I don't deserve for them to think of me that way. Certainly not Mia, and not my mom either, for that matter. Even though my mom is the most incredible human and forgives me for everything so easily. Too easily."

"Kyle, what are you talking about? Forgive what?"

"Since you're not going to leave this alone… I have been a terrible son and an even worse brother. I spent my childhood chasing after my dad and my entire adult life in the military. I basically blew them off—my own mom and sister. I never came home. I rarely contacted them at all."

"Your mom talks about you like you're her *everything*. You and Mia both. I'm not sure

I've ever seen a prouder mom. Deservedly so, you are both successful and accomplished and completely wonderful to her."

Slowly, Kyle shook his head. "You don't understand. I can promise you that Mia does not want to have her picture taken with me. She's doing this for you because you're difficult to say no to."

Harper exhaled a sound of disbelief. "What I don't understand is this thing you have about your sister. She clearly adores you!"

Kyle raked a frustrated hand through his hair. How could he make her comprehend this? "Harper, Mia does not adore me. She... the opposite of adores me."

"You're wrong."

Her expression and her tone were so confident, and yet so misguided that it pushed him over the edge. This was his Achilles' heel, *his*, and how dare she profess to understand an issue that had taken years of misdeeds and neglect, on both his own and Bill Frasier's part, to develop?

Kyle pushed off the counter to stand straight, the muscles of his neck and back screaming with tension. "Look, Harper, I know you're trying to help, but you cannot possibly understand my relationship with Mia. Growing up, I was...not nice to her.

She tried repeatedly to be a good sister to me, but I wasn't interested. For most of my life, my priorities were screwed up. I was obsessed with my work, with the military, with my dad. As kids, he treated Mia badly, ignored her basically. And I went along with it without realizing how hurtful I was being. I don't deserve for Mia to include me in her family photos."

Harper looked stricken and Kyle was, if not glad, then at least gratified. He deserved her contempt on this subject, just like he did Mia's. "But she loves you, Kyle. Anyone can see that. I think there's more to her feelings than you realize."

Kyle sighed and raked a frustrated hand across his jaw. "Harper, as the only child of a doting single father, I don't think you can grasp how complicated family dynamics can be. Of course, Mia and I love each other, but it takes more than that to make a relationship." A relatively simple concept that he was beginning to believe he'd learned too late.

"Maybe that's true." Harper shrugged, eyes flashing with frustration and what looked like sadness. "But empathy isn't exclusive to shared trauma, Kyle. You don't need to live through something yourself to understand it, to feel compassion, to want to help. If I see a train wreck, I cry for the victims because I imagine what they're going through. It hurts me to see you torturing yourself like this."

She went on before he could respond, "And I'll tell you another thing—I'd love to have this problem that you have. To have a family that's bigger than two people. Do you know how lucky you are to have so many people who love you just for being you? Do you have any idea what it's like to never have to doubt or wonder if they have some secret motivation for being kind to you? For wanting to spend time with you? Levi, Laney, Mia, Jay, Josie, Craig, even the little ones. Your mom! I can't even…

"I would trade everything I have in this world for five minutes with my mom. I don't remember her. I only remember a feeling, and it's so fleeting and frustrating because I can't hold on to it. It's like trying to grab smoke. Growing up, I used to ask my dad all the time what he missed the most about her. And you know what his answer was? Time. Just time." She added a helpless little shrug. "All the little moments that make up the time you get to spend with a person you love. That's something I'll never have with my mom. So maybe you didn't do that when you could. That's not cool. But it's not too late. You have that time now. And you could have it with Mia. If you guys would just quit avoiding the issue and talk."

Tears welled in her eyes and Kyle realized that she might be right. But still, he didn't appreciate her trying to fix this for him. It made him uncomfortable, how she'd nosed her way into his family business. Plus, she had no room to talk when it came to avoiding issues, prompting him to say the words, "You know all about that, don't you? Not talking about things that make you uncomfortable. You won't even tell me what happened with you and Owen."

Breaking eye contact, she turned around with a tired sigh that almost had him regretting his words. "I'm going to bed. I'm leaving for your sister's at 7 a.m. Whether you're with me or not is your choice. But I can say with absolute certainty that your family—particularly your sister—will be crushed if you're not there."

"OKAY, EVERYONE, SCOOCH together a bit more for this one. Levi, move a little to your left..." Harper called out bright and early the next morning while motioning with her hand. "Nora, if you could step to the right, you're hidden behind Dean. Yep, that way. Perfect!"

Harper clicked the shutter. First, she'd taken some shots with Mia and Jay's house in the background, then turned them all, so their backs were to the ocean. Then she'd herded everyone about fifty yards down the beach to a gigantic driftwood snag that had washed in against a stretch of pebbled shoreline.

"Jay," she called out in a teasing tone, "your dog holds still better than you do. Any chance you could look right here?" She waved a hand behind the camera. Everyone laughed. Excitement bubbled inside of her because she could see the group relaxing and that's when family photos turned out best.

In the soft light, mild temperature and barely discernible breeze, the session was going better than she'd hoped. Especially considering the strain between her and Kyle. They'd barely spoken that morning, but he'd come over freshly showered and dressed according to Mia's request of casual attire in neutral tones. He was gorgeous in jeans and a gray cotton sweater with the collar and tail of his white shirt showing.

She didn't regret what she'd said; he and Mia needed to talk. Between what she'd learned from Mia and Nora and what she'd heard from Kyle, their issue was fixable. If Kyle could learn to forgive himself. Although, his final words the night before kept running through her mind.

He was right; it was easy for her to say that he and Mia could resolve their issues when she wasn't the one who had to talk about matters that were painful for her. What he didn't understand was that the truth about Owen would be painful for him, too.

She repositioned everyone a few more times. Satisfied that she had plenty of good images, she moved on to divide the family into smaller groups in various combinations: Jay and Josie, Jay and Josie and their siblings, all of them with the addition of Mia and Craig, then Levi and Laney, Dean and Delilah, just the girls, just the boys, then Nora with Mia and Kyle, and finally Mia and Kyle.

When she finished, she encouraged everyone to mingle around and play on the beach so she could get some candid shots for a family collage. Dean and Delilah didn't need to be told twice. Levi ran up to the house and retrieved beach toys. Plans for a grand sandcastle were hatched, and construction was soon underway. Kyle might not be thrilled about this day, but the rest of the bunch were having a blast. That made Harper happy and strengthened her resolve. Now, if there was only some way to help Kyle accept that he deserved to be a part of it all.

"KYLE, CAN I talk to you for a minute?"

Kyle turned to find Mia standing behind him.

"Sure."

Mia glanced toward the group, some of whom were working on the sandcastle, others were sitting and chatting on a blanket. Laney and Delilah frolicked in the shallow waves with George. Levi played fetch with Coastie. Harper moved around the group photographing it all.

"Let's walk." Mia took off. Kyle followed.

They hadn't gone far when she asked, "You and Harper are more than friends, aren't you?"

"Yes," he said, "but it's not what you're thinking."

"What does that mean?"

Kyle felt an inexplicable urge to confide in his sister. Maybe Harper was right that he needed to take advantage of these moments when he could. "If I tell you, can you keep it to yourself?"

"Of course."

"I'm her employee."

Mia's head tipped back in surprise. "You're her employee? What kind of employee?"

"Security consultant."

"What, like a bodyguard?"

"Sort of, but it's more about teaching her how to keep herself safe."

"Why does a photographer need a security consultant?"

"Remember that news story a few weeks ago?"

"When you saved David Bellaire, you mean?"

"Yes. Harper is David Bellaire's daughter…" Kyle explained, doing his best to keep it brief and excluding the part about her being Owen's ex-fiancée.

"Wow. I had no idea."

"I know." Kyle smiled. "Harper likes it when people don't know who she is." He found himself repeating Harper's words, "It's surprising the problems that are unique to famous people."

After he'd cooled off last night, he'd thought about their conversation, trying to imagine how it would feel to always wonder if someone's friendship or love was genuine. Despite Harper's bravado and engaging spirit, he knew her life had been lonely. She alluded to it in ways that he wasn't even sure she was aware of. It made his heart hurt to think about what she'd gone through. And yet the loneliness, suspicion and uncertainty hadn't made her cynical. It hadn't hardened her heart toward people or dampened her enthusiasm for life as one might expect. The positive energy she exhibited was a lot like Nora's. You could even see it in the photos she took. It made him want to protect her even more, from the internal pain as much as the physical danger.

"She keeps expecting Levi to figure it out. But I think that's part of the reason she's fallen in love with you guys, because you like her for her."

"Yeah, that's it," Mia said with a sarcastic chuckle.

Kyle shook his head to intimate that he didn't get what was funny.

"Sure, we're awesome and all but the reason she's fallen in love with *us* is because she's in love with *you*."

A mix of longing and anxiety swamped him, nearly stopping him in his tracks. "Mia, I don't think that's true."

"Kyle, the way she looks at you, it's like… Well, it reminds me of the way I feel about Jay. Why else would she do this for you? You know how busy we all are. Organizing this took a lot of planning. Not to mention, she loses a perfect morning of work herself. I know what this nice weather means for her. Not to mention all the time and money that she'll put into editing and printing. Do you know how much a good photography session like this would cost? Plus, the prints? And she insists that this is a gift for us all. Mom is beside herself with joy. I can't believe I didn't think of this sooner."

Kyle did like how happy this seemed to make Nora. And everyone else for that matter, including Mia.

Mia added, "And you're clearly in love with her."

"What are you talking about?" Kyle asked the question, but not, he realized, because it wasn't true, but because he wondered how Mia had figured it out before him. He'd been fooling himself by thinking he could keep himself from falling for her. Not loving Harper would be like trying to stop the tide from rolling in. He so badly wanted to be the one to end her loneliness forever, to show her how much he didn't care about her money or who her dad was. To show her how much he loved her for her. To be the man who deserved her trust. But that was impossible. He'd already betrayed her; she just didn't know it.

"For someone as intelligent and stunningly capable as you are, you can be pretty dense, you know that?"

"Yes. I do know that. Especially when it comes to women." Kyle stared down at the smooth gray sand. "My own sister included, apparently."

"So, listen, about your girlfriend."

"Mia, I don't want you to get your hopes up there. Harper and I—"

"And I'm telling you, she should be your girlfriend if she's not. You would be a fool to let her go. Anyway, Harper and I have been talking. She's very perceptive about people and relationships, by the way. There are some things I realize I need to say to you." She inhaled a deep breath and then released it in a long sigh. "Things I should have said before now."

When she didn't continue, Kyle nodded.

"It's difficult to say something when you don't know how it's going to be received. You know what I mean?"

"Yes," he answered softly. "Very well. But I can handle whatever it is you want to tell me."

Mia stopped walking. So Kyle stopped,

too. She inhaled a breath, and he braced himself to hear exactly what he deserved. Which is not at all what happened.

She faced him. "Kyle, I love you."

"I love you, too, Mia," he fired back without hesitation.

Through a sheen of tears, she sniffled and nodded. Her face erupted with a huge smile as she threw her arms around him. He hugged her close, and Kyle thought his heart might explode.

Mia loosened her hold and stepped away but kept a loose grip on his arms just below his elbows. "I realized last night when I was talking this over with Jay that I don't think I've ever said that to you before. You said it to me, but I've never said it back to you, do you know that?"

He smiled sadly. It was after his dad's funeral. He'd felt so alone with his grief and had finally realized just how large the void was between himself and Mia and what—who—had put it there. He'd said the words to Mia that day. But he hadn't offered an apology to go with them. He hadn't explained that he'd since realized how the strain between them had come to be. "I do know that. But, Mia, that's okay. You had a lot of reasons not to say it. I should have—"

"No! No, Kyle, I didn't. That's just the thing. I wanted to say it. I felt it. The fact that Bill didn't love me had nothing to do with you. You were his son, and he loved you, and I'm glad he was good to you. It helped make you the amazing man that you are. But he deserves all my anger, not you. I should have talked about this with you a long time ago, but there's always been this…distance between us." Mia released him, and they started walking again.

Kyle said, "I think Dad wanted it that way. In his mind, you were Mom's and I was his."

"That's exactly how I see it now!"

"I was a terrible brother to you and son to Mom. My behavior was inexcusable. That was on me. I'm so sorry. All I ever cared about was my career, the next mission and my teammates in the military. I rarely came home. I justified my behavior with my sense of duty just like Dad did."

"I think you were exactly the brother and son Bill raised you to be. And don't get me wrong, I admire your loyalty and your unwavering honor. I'm so proud of you and your career. You can ask Mom. When I heard you were getting out of the navy, I was cautiously optimistic that you'd feel like you'd fulfilled that. Then, when you came here to Pacific

Cove, I let myself get excited. I thought there was hope for us to finally be a family."

"I want that, too. It's why I came here. I know it took me way too long to see it." Ironically, it was losing Owen and that brother-like connection they'd shared that made him realize how much he wanted his family.

"Too long would be never. I was so happy you came here. But I didn't know how to trust that feeling. I have to tell you that when you took the job with Dahlia, it felt like… It feels like you're going into the military all over again. That conversation you overheard between Mom and me the other night was about that. About how I've been 'unsupportive' of your new career choice. But it's only because I'm scared, Kyle. And not just because of the danger—I know you can handle yourself. And, no, I don't want you to leave. But what I *don't* want the most is for you to follow in Bill's footsteps. I don't want you to forgo the relationships in your life for the sake of your career. We want you here, and if that's selfish, I don't care. I felt like I had to say this because it's been weighing on my heart. The circumstances of our childhood, including the way both Mom and Bill handled things, are as much to blame as we are."

Kyle agreed. "I'm so glad you did. But, Mia, I'm not career military like Dad. I got out for that reason. I want different things. I want…" He couldn't bring himself to finish that thought.

He glanced back down the beach. Everyone was enjoying the morning. Now barefoot, Harper had a hold of Delilah's hands, swinging her around in the sand. Delilah giggled wildly, her unruly red curls loosening from her ponytail and fluttering in the breeze. Harper's smile was radiant.

Mia followed his gaze, and asked, "What *do* you want, Kyle?"

He didn't answer because what he wanted was complicated. He wanted to be like his dad in some respects but not others. He wanted a job where he felt useful, one where he could utilize his skills. But not one that would take him away from the family that he was just beginning to know.

He wanted the truth about Owen, but he also wanted Harper.

Getting out of the navy was supposed to simplify his life. Instead, it had created a whole host of new issues. One in particular felt truly insurmountable. How had it come to this, this impossible choice between his best friend and the woman he loved?

KYLE AND MIA headed back to the others. Mia immediately went to check on George. Digging in the sand, the dog had unearthed a suspicious-looking pile of feathers that Mia feared was a seagull carcass. Kyle joined the castle construction, which was shaping up to be quite a fortress. From his spot on one side of the project, he watched Delilah sidle up to Harper who was now sitting cross-legged in the sand scrolling through photos on her camera.

Harper wore a little smile as if she knew she was responsible for all the magic unfolding around them. It was possible he'd been a little hard on her about this photo shoot. He shouldn't have made that comment about avoiding issues, either. She had a good reason for not easily trusting. And the truth was that he didn't deserve her trust. Except that he could be that person she trusted. He wanted nothing more than to be exactly that.

Delilah peered over her shoulder. "Josie lets me take pictures with her phone sometimes."

Harper looked up at her and widened her smile. "Does she?"

Delilah nodded. "She's going to take pictures at my dance recital."

"When's your dance recital?"

"Tomorrow night. I'm really good. You can come and watch me if you want."

"Thank you. I would love to see you dance. I'll talk to your sister about it. Maybe I could take some pictures with my camera, too."

Delilah's grin was the approximate size and brightness of the sun. Kyle really couldn't blame her. Once Harper turned on her charm, she was impossible to resist. He was a grown man with an excellent reason to fend off her allure and he couldn't seem to manage it.

Harper asked, "Have you ever used a camera like this one?"

"Nope."

"Would you like to try?"

Delilah shrugged, but Kyle knew from experience that meant yes. Clearly, Harper got that, too, and patted the ground next to her. Delilah couldn't sit fast enough, folding her legs at the knees and plopping onto the sand beside her.

"See this part here?" Harper pointed at the viewfinder. Nodding, Delilah leaned in, hanging on every word. "You put one eye up to it like this and that's how you see what you're taking a photo of." She demonstrated. "Now I'm going to take a photo of you, okay?"

More nodding from Delilah, which was so

completely cute. Kyle loved the way she did that, chin tucked under, with quick little bobs of her head.

"Let me see that gorgeous smile. Got it!" Harper turned the camera over. "That turned out good. See?" She held it so Delilah could inspect the image. "You are very photogenic like your sister Laney. Now it's your turn. You can take one of me."

"Dee, are your hands clean?" Josie called from the blanket where she sat chatting with Nora. "Harper, you might want to inspect those little paws before you let them touch your expensive camera."

Harper laughed while Delilah stuck out her hands for inspection, an action Kyle could guess she performed on a regular basis.

"Ooh, I like your nail polish!" Harper said.

Delilah grinned. "Once, Uncle Kyle let me paint his toenails."

Beside him, Dean guffawed while Levi snorted out a laugh. Kyle didn't care because Harper looked up then, her gaze colliding with his, soft eyes full of approval and uncertainty. He hated that he was responsible for that hesitation. He owed her an apology.

Quickly, Harper turned her attention back to Delilah. Giving her hands a final squeeze, she released them and said, "These little grabbers look perfectly fine to me. Here you go." Harper shortened the strap and placed the camera around Delilah's neck. "This is so the camera is always right here when you need it. And in case it slips out of your hands it won't fall on the ground. Or into the ocean." Harper looked pointedly at Kyle. "As the case may be."

Kyle couldn't help but chuckle as Harper moved around behind Delilah and crouched low. "Go ahead and put your fingers here…" Harper placed Delilah's little hands accordingly and went on to explain how to make a box through the viewfinder take a photo. Kyle couldn't bring himself to look away.

"Enjoying the view?" Levi asked quietly.

"Absolutely," Kyle responded innocently. "The sunset is gorgeous."

"It's ten o'clock in the morning, dude."

"Whatever."

"You are so far gone," Levi joked. "I'm afraid you'll never find your way back."

Kyle didn't argue. But he felt the words as they uncovered a truth that he'd been keeping deep inside of him.

Levi emptied another bucket of sand on the castle's foundation as Dean instructed.

Dean patted it in place. "Grandma Nora

said she'd help shape the top into something supercool."

"Like a mermaid?" Kyle asked.

"Oooh! Gross!" Dean cried with the type of disgust that little boys excelled at. "No, like a battle station."

"Oh, of course, a battle station. What was I thinking?"

"I don't know," Dean said with a headshake as if Kyle's suggestion was indeed completely pathetic. "Do you think she can make a battle station?"

"I'm positive she can," Kyle said. A retired art teacher, Nora could create in just about any form or medium imaginable. Pencil, paint, charcoal, woodworking, it didn't matter. Since moving to Pacific Cove, she'd taken up sand sculpting and had already proven herself to be one of the finest around. Her team, the Sand Bandits, had placed in two categories at the Sandtastical Expo, a prestigious sandcastle competition, last year.

Dean's mouth formed a slow thoughtful frown. "Uncle Kyle, you should get some sand in your bucket. See, the way Levi does it?"

Kyle chuckled. "Levi thinks you might be an architect someday, but I'm guessing a construction boss like your brother Jay."

Dean nodded solemnly. "Yeah, I think I'd like to be the boss."

Levi laughed. "You will make an excellent boss, kiddo."

Kyle looked around and enjoyed the moment: the sound of the sea mixed with laughter, the feel of the warm sun on his skin and the cool, gritty sand between his fingers. The conversation with Mia was working through him, making him feel things. Realize things. Being here with his family suddenly felt different, right and…comfortable. The tension he'd been carting around eased a bit more.

His gaze found Harper again. He told himself it was his job to keep an eye on her. Not that the task was ever a hardship. He thought about Levi's earlier comment. Leave it to Levi. The kid had pretty much nailed how he felt about Harper with one simple observation. It was true; if Kyle was lost in Harper, he didn't want to find his way back. Not if it meant giving her up. For now, he could keep her close, but how in the world could he find a way to keep her like that forever?

CHAPTER FOURTEEN

"HARPER, ARE YOU absolutely certain you want to do this?" Josie asked Harper the next evening, handing her a program and staring earnestly into her eyes.

Mia had texted, asking that everyone meet outside the gym at the high school fifteen minutes early for Delilah's dance recital. Harper and Kyle were early for being early, and Josie had already arrived because Delilah had to be even earlier for group photos.

Harper studied the booklet. "*An Evening Dance Showcase,*" she read out loud. "What a lovely title. I adore the ballet."

"Hold up," Josie said, hands up, palms out. "Harper, this is not *the ballet*. Don't let that title in that fancy font fool you. This thing lasts like three hours and is essentially organized chaos. A veritable menagerie of tulle and satin." Josie added a helpless shrug. "Don't get me wrong—I love it. But one of those little tutu-wearing whirling dervishes is mine."

Laughing, Harper reached out and squeezed Josie's forearm. "Josie, please relax. I rarely do anything I don't want to do."

"I feel like Dee put you on the spot." She'd invited Harper at the photo shoot.

"She's six years old. Do you honestly think a six-year-old could talk me into doing something I don't want to do?"

"Wait, you've met Delilah, right?"

The two women shared another laugh.

Harper said, "Besides, I'm no stranger to dance recitals. Ballet is about the only thing I was ever good at that can be considered at all athletic."

Kyle gave her a curious sidelong glance. "You were a ballerina?" he asked, his brown eyes dancing with mischief. Harper was glad to see it. After yesterday's photo shoot, he'd been quiet for the rest of the afternoon, which had lasted all evening and into today. Not that he'd been visibly angry, just…broody. Harper considered apologizing, but she wasn't sorry. She felt bad that she'd upset him, but the family pictures had been the right thing to do. And everything she'd said to him was true.

"I was."

Josie waved at Nora, Mia and Laney, who were all walking across the parking lot. Lagging behind them were with Jay, Levi, Craig and Dean.

"How long?"

"Twelve years."

"Twelve years! You were a ballerina for *twelve years*? How did I not know this?"

"I have no idea, you've seen my bare toes." Years of dancing *en pointe* had taken a toll on her feet.

"Are there photos?"

"No," she lied.

"So if I ask your dad, he wouldn't be able to produce a single photo of you with your hair in a bun and wearing a fluffy skirt and dance gear?"

"I'm afraid not." Harper tried not to laugh. "And for your information, we don't wear *gear*. Those fluffy skirts are called tutus. Which are worn, along with leotards, tights, slippers and pointe shoes. Gear," she joked, "is for hooligan-type sports like football and hockey."

Kyle's grin was about a mile wide. "I don't believe you about the photo. And I'm so happy right now that I may have a line on my own pictorial gem. Possibly even a counter in case I'm ever blackmailed with unseemly photos."

"Go ahead and try," she bluffed. "Not a

single photo exists." That's because there was an entire wall of them. Including a few that were definitely worthy of a little blackmail.

"You made it!" A delighted Nora approached and wrapped Kyle and then Harper in huge hugs. Harper tried not to squeeze her too tight, but there was something singularly wonderful about a hug from Nora Frasier. Harper had never met anyone who conveyed as much joy and love as this woman did. Josie was next. Laney and Mia followed suit until greetings were exchanged all around.

Laney said, "Uncle Kyle, I want to show you something real quick." Laney produced her phone. "What do you think? Is this possible? Or is this like CGI?"

Kyle watched the martial arts video mashup, and said, "Bogus. Can't be done."

"I knew it! Thank you. I just won a bet."

"Hey," Nora said to Kyle, "that reminds me. It's a total bummer you're not going to be living here on a more permanent basis. Coby asked me if there was any chance you'd want to teach a class at the studio. Bring in more male clientele."

Harper was momentarily distracted by the vision of Kyle teaching yoga. She didn't know about more male clientele, but the place would be jam-packed with enthusiastic single women. An irrational spike of jealousy bloomed inside of her at the idea of perky Mandy making eyes at him from the front row.

The guys approached. Kyle whispered something to Levi that made him laugh, and Harper could see the admiration in the teen's expression.

A radiant Mia said, "Okay, now that we're all here, Jay and I have an announcement."

Harper pointed at the entrance. "Would you like me to wait inside?"

"No, Harper, stay. It's not a secret. Or at least it won't be in a minute. I realize yesterday would have been the perfect time to do this, but I wanted to wait until my doctor's appointment this afternoon to confirm. And since it'll probably be a week until our next gathering and Kyle will be gone by then, we decided tonight would work fine. I'll have to tell our tiny dancer after the show. But we're excited to share the news, so here goes… I'm pregnant. Jay and I are having a baby."

Laney squealed. Nora let out a happy scream. More hugging ensued. Nora and Laney both cried and hugged each other.

Nora said, "I'm finally going to be a grandma. I can't believe it."

"I like Nana Nora," Laney said. "Or Nano!

Or something. You're too cool to be just plain grandma."

"Oh, you sweet girl," Nora said, and hugged Laney again.

"How far along?" Josie asked. "Let me tell you right now that we are throwing you the baby shower I never had as an expectant big sister."

That produced more laughter.

"Due around the middle of November. Kyle, I hope you can make it home for Thanksgiving or the holidays so you can meet your new little niece or nephew."

"I'll make sure of it," Kyle said, and Harper wondered if everyone else could see how touched he was by Mia's words.

More questions were asked. Harper took it all in and felt honored to be a part of such a joyous occasion. Telling her "family" she was pregnant would constitute an audience of exactly one. Which was okay, of course. She wouldn't trade her dad for a thousand relatives, but she'd like more of them because this was unbelievably fun. She loved Kyle's family almost as much as she loved him.

"Hey, Kyle, any chance you could do me a favor?" Jay asked a little while later as they all made their way inside.

"Sure. What's up?"

"I've got a client who wants to install a top-of-the-line security system. I've worked with some companies that do standard systems, but nothing like this guy wants. Mia said you might know about them."

Kyle nodded. "Yeah, I do."

"Do you think you could meet him with me and talk it over?"

The two men proceeded to discuss security systems as they all trooped inside to find their seats. Harper felt gratified that Kyle finally seemed to be accepting the love and respect his family had for him. And he seemed comfortable giving it right back. As happy as she was for him, for all of them, it also made her long for more. She couldn't stop herself from wishing that Kyle loved her, too.

SEATED BETWEEN LEVI and Mia in a rigid, uncomfortable folding chair, Kyle contentedly watched the dance performance. It helped that from his vantage point he could also watch Harper. She'd spoken with one of the instructors, offered to take photos free of charge and proceeded to score two seats in the front row. Kyle insisted that Josie take the other spot next to Harper.

Harper was crouched in front of her tripod, completely focused on capturing this special moment for each and every parent. He was blown away by her generosity. Extreme wealth ensured that she could have or do anything she wanted. She could literally be in the south of France or lounging on a yacht somewhere. If she wanted, she'd never have to work again. And yet she chose to make her own way in the world. She was here, with him and his family at Delilah's dance recital in Pacific Cove. Volunteering at Lucky Cats, going to track meets, sharing family meals, taking photos... She'd chosen his family many times. She'd chosen to try and help him fix his relationship with Mia.

Imagining Harper as a ballerina wasn't difficult. He thought about what her recitals must have been like, with just her dad in the audience. She called her upbringing "nontraditional" and Kyle thought that must be an understatement. As the only child of a brilliant eccentric scientist, he'd told her she couldn't understand family dynamics. That had been unfair, too. She'd had her own share of difficulties. She'd talked about her childhood a little, the traveling, the lab equipment and microscopes that had been her toys. He remembered the discarded camera, a "friend" that had fueled her love of photography. He knew she'd been lonely. How had she endured it? Kyle had a million questions of his own and he was done denying himself the answers.

An hour into the performance, a pink-and-white-sequin-clad Delilah came prancing out onto the stage. Kyle was grateful for her bright red bun, making her easy to spot and keep track of in a sea of similarly dressed dancers. In a matter of seconds, she saw her big sister–mom Josie in the front row and lit up like a moonbeam. She proceeded to blow kisses to both her and Harper. Mia grabbed his hand and squeezed, and Kyle felt it right in the center of his heart.

Mia had wanted him there when she announced that she was having a baby. Kyle had nearly cried right along with his mom and Laney. His sister was having a *baby*. He was going to be an uncle to this little one, and he felt nothing but pure joy. And acceptance. More than acceptance. Mia wanted him home for the holidays. There was no way to explain that away or make excuses about not deserving her love. He had it, and now he needed to deliver.

And he had Harper to thank for forcing him to see it. An apology, a thank-you and a baring of his soul in one fell swoop. He was going to need to bring his A game.

That's when he realized that the answer to Mia's complicated question about what he wanted was, in fact, extraordinarily simple. He wanted Harper. His heart already belonged to her. He was sure she felt something for him, too. Mia was right; she wouldn't be doing all this if she didn't. Then there was that kiss… That kiss had told him everything he needed to know; he just hadn't been listening.

He'd find a way to make this work. He wished he could just be honest with her. But that was the one thing he couldn't be. Dahlia's instructions were clear, and he'd understood them at the time. But he knew Harper now, and there was no way she was involved in anything untoward with or without Owen. If he could just prove Owen's innocence, then Harper would be cleared, too. And then maybe…? Maybe he didn't have to choose.

What if Harper never found out about his involvement? Especially if there was nothing to find? He wasn't sure about those answers. But maybe the more important question was whether he could live with knowing he hadn't been completely honest with her. If that was the only way forward, then yes. With this assignment complete, he could spend the rest of their life together showing her how much he loved her.

He would spend the rest of his life deserving her trust.

SOMETHING WAS DIFFERENT, Harper could tell. All the way home, Kyle had been quiet. But not angry quiet like he'd been about the photo shoot. And not brooding quiet like he was all day today. He'd been giving her strange glances all evening and staring when he didn't think she was looking.

Like most evenings, Harper headed into the kitchen where she intended to put a pan of milk on the stove for hot cocoa.

Kyle followed her.

"Hot cocoa?" she asked him, removing a tin from the cupboard.

"Harper, we need to talk."

"Okay, what's up?" she said with way more bravado than she felt. Setting the tin aside, she faced him.

"Well, first off, I owe you an apology for the way I acted about the whole family photo thing. I'm sorry. You were right. It was great. And everyone loved it. Including me."

Harper was relieved to get this out in the open. "I appreciate that, but I understand, or at least I think I do, why you were upset. I don't regret arranging it, but maybe I shouldn't have sprung it on you like that. And maybe—"

"Nope," Kyle interrupted. "You were right to do it that way. If I'd known, I would have bailed, just like you said. More than that, Mia and I had a conversation that cleared a lot of things up, and I owe you a huge thank-you for that."

"Oh, Kyle, I'm so glad." A wave of relief flowed through her.

"Me, too. She told me you guys talked and that it was really helpful to her. And now I feel like a jerk for accusing you of getting in my business."

"You were right to accuse me. I did get in your business, but only because I want you to be happy." *Because I love you*, she added silently.

"I know, and I appreciate that. I'm... It's weird how well you seem to know me. We haven't known each other that long."

"Yeah," she agreed. Her stomach did another nervous dip because he was looking at her funny again. His eyes seemed to be asking a question that she couldn't decipher much less answer. What was going on here? She attempted to joke, but her voice was a little too wobbly to pull it off, "But add up all the hours we've been together. Most married couples don't spend as much time together as we have in the last few weeks."

With purposeful steps, he closed the distance between them. "True. But you're also extraordinarily observant and incredibly kind and…" His eyes traveled over her and lingered on her mouth. Her neck went hot. Now she was nervous for real. Accelerated-heartbeat, rapid-breath, fluttery-butterflies nervous. "Well, um, being observant is who I am. I'd say it's part of my job, but I think it's the other way around for me. I turned what I'm already good at *into* my job." She stopped babbling when she realized he hadn't finished his thought. If he was going to pay her another compliment, she kind of wanted to hear it. "And, what? I'm sorry—I think I interrupted you."

One more step and she could smell his enticing, comforting scent and feel his heat. As if that wasn't enough, he bent his head so that his lips were practically brushing her ear, sending her pulse racing all over again. "*And* I was going to say beautiful, but then I changed my mind. *Stunning* is the word I'm using because *beautiful* doesn't quite cut it. You are stunning." Then he kissed her neck.

She inhaled a little gasp and tipped her

neck to make it easier for him to reach. "Kyle, um…" But she couldn't finish the thought because his mouth was moving, lips brushing softly up the column of her neck and along her jaw and cheek until his mouth met hers. He kissed her and… And then she had no thoughts at all.

"Harper," he finally said after a good long while that wasn't nearly long enough.

"What?" she muttered in a smoky movie star voice that would have embarrassed her if her emotions weren't already in such upheaval.

He smiled against her lips. "Are you okay?"

"I don't know yet. Are you going to tell me this was a mistake?"

"No."

"Okay, then I'm fine."

He chuckled. "I do need to tell you something though."

"Oh, no," she said. "Are you quitting? Is this my goodbye?"

"No. Harper…"

She squeezed her eyes shut.

"Open your eyes, please."

She did.

"It's not bad news, or at least, *I* don't think it is. I've been trying to deny my feelings, but I've done a lot of thinking the last couple of days. My conversation with you and then my discussion with Mia and something Levi said made me realize a few important things, and I don't want to push them away anymore. Even though I know this isn't ideal, logistically speaking, I just… I love you."

The rush of joy Harper felt at those words was unlike anything she'd ever experienced. It quickly combined with a dose of shock to leave her…stunned. And thrilled. And overjoyed. And shocked. And…

"You, we, I…" She held up one finger in a "just a sec" gesture.

"It is indeed a rare occasion that renders Harper Jansen speechless."

"No." She shook her head. "Nope. That's not what this is. I have all the words. They just keep colliding with my feelings, making it difficult to arrange them in speakable form."

His eyes danced with humor and his expression was so full of affection that it set her back again. Harper didn't think it was possible for her heart to feel any fuller than it did at that moment.

She was wrong.

"Okay. Maybe, just start with three little ones, then? If you feel inclined, that is."

"Kyle." She gripped his shoulders because

that made her a little weak in the knees. "That has got to be the sweetest thing anyone has ever said in a moment like this. And I mean anyone ever. Greeks, Romans, love-struck medieval knights, Renaissance poets, I'm counting them all. If I wasn't already smitten, I would have fallen. Just now. With that one sentence."

Eyebrows nudging up, he said, "I'm waiting."

"I love you, too. So. Incredibly. Much."

He gave her a playful frown. "You couldn't just stick with the traditional three, could you?"

"What can I say? I'm an overachiever."

"That you are, and I like that about you, along with about a million other things." Tucking a lock of hair behind her ear, he turned serious. "Listen, I know we're facing some complications here, with me leaving soon, but I think we can work through them."

Harper desperately wanted that last part to be true. Nodding, she said, "Before this goes any further, I need you to know something."

She felt his muscles tense beneath her fingertips, but his voice was calm as he said, "Okay?"

"I was never in love with Owen. I had feelings for him that I recognized later were infatuation. He was charming and smooth-talking and good at putting his best foot forward. Later on, I learned things about him that I didn't like and ultimately, I realized that I never actually knew him. He only let me see what he wanted me to see. I would never have married him. We broke up, and no matter what he led you to believe, we would have stayed that way. Forever.

"This might be difficult to believe considering my romantic track record, parts of which I clumsily and embarrassingly divulged to you at Rhys's, but I've never felt like this before. I've never loved anyone like I do you. I *wanted* to be in love, which I realize sounds a bit silly, but I don't think is all that unusual. But more than that, I trust you. And that is so huge for me. I didn't think I'd ever be able to say that to another man again."

"I trust you, too."

Harper felt something unfurl inside of her, comforting her right at her core. She hadn't considered that aspect before, how it would feel to have Kyle trust her, too. But it was what prompted her to tell him everything.

CHAPTER FIFTEEN

THE RELIEF KYLE felt at Harper's assertion caught him off guard. He'd assumed that her grief had faded, but to know that her feelings for Owen were never as strong as he'd believed them to be was even better. Truthfully, he was elated.

"I'm sorry that things didn't end well between you two, but I'll admit that makes it easier for me, knowing that I'm not competing with the memory of my best friend. He would be a tough act to follow."

Silently, Harper took his hand and led him to the sofa. She sat, urging him down next to her. Shifting her body, she tucked one leg under the other, so she was facing him. "I hope you mean that because I'm going to tell you what happened between me and Owen and why I ultimately came to despise your best friend."

Despise? A tingle of dread slid up his spine and traveled across the back of his neck. How could anyone despise Owen?

"Owen had a side business in Africa. He was a broker, dealing in the wildlife trade."

"What do you mean, like ivory and rhino horn?"

"Yes. At least, he told me he'd dealt in some ivory when he first started, but it was becoming much more troublesome. The laws are strict regarding the sale and trade of ivory, but there are loopholes. Loopholes everywhere. But he said there were plenty of other highly profitable items from all over the world that are perfectly legal to buy and sell, if you know how. He certainly seemed to know the laws inside and out.

"Those details didn't matter to me though because it was all unethical, what he was doing. And I didn't want any part of it."

Kyle knew he should say something, but his brain couldn't seem to make sense of what Harper was describing. There had to be an explanation that didn't include Owen buying and selling endangered animal products.

"I hope you believe me."

"I do. I believe what you're saying, it's just… so hard to believe of Owen. It goes against everything we stood for. Or, I stand for."

"I'm glad. There's more…" By the time Harper was done describing what she knew,

Kyle's skin was crawling. He asked the questions he knew Dahlia would want him to ask.

Harper answered, revealing her suspicions and the reasons behind them. Confusion and disgust warred with doubt inside of him. "But I don't understand why he would do this? Take this kind of risk…?"

"It's a multibillion-dollar industry. The profits are outrageous. If you knew him like I think you did, then you know money was very important to Owen. It was his number one priority. From what I could see, there wasn't much he wouldn't do to get it. This was another area where we disagreed. He wanted to use my father's jet to transport some of this stuff. Again, he told me it was all perfectly legal, but it felt like smuggling to me. Why would he keep it a secret? Why wouldn't he arrange transport himself? It felt wrong and his reaction to my hesitation only heightened my concerns. He wouldn't answer my questions about what he was shipping. I…" Harper trailed off and looked thoughtfully out the window toward the ocean.

Facing Kyle again, she inhaled a deep breath, and went on, "We fought. I wouldn't budge. He was very, very angry. He threatened me and said if I didn't help, he'd leak it to the media that I was already involved. As it turned out, I had inadvertently introduced him to one of his best suppliers, a man named Dale Freeman. He was a businessman I met, along with his wife, in Singapore on a trip with Dad on BEST business. Owen flew in for a day and the five of us spent an evening together. I never saw Dale again but that's how Owen met him. And once before that, I had allowed Owen to ship some cargo on my dad's jet."

"Like what?" Kyle asked.

"Wood products and furniture—responsible, sustainable items. I think now that he'd probably accepted them as payment and re-sold the stuff in the States. Because I trusted him, I hadn't documented it like I should have. I was terrified of how he could make it look, but I called his bluff. He told me I was a selfish, rich b—" She cut the word off. "That part doesn't matter. I was already done. That was the end for me."

Kyle didn't like that, the words or the way she said them. The idea of anyone, Owen included, attempting to manipulate her, calling her names, mistreating her made him want to lose his own temper.

"I left Africa the next day. But first, I went to Owen's supervisor, Drew Louis, and told him what I suspected."

Kyle nodded, trying to absorb this information. Harper added, "It's an extremely dangerous business. I've wondered if it's what got him killed."

Now Kyle wondered, too. Undoubtedly, so did Dahlia. "What did Drew say?"

"Not much, to be honest. He pretty much ignored me. I also emailed Travis Shupe, the CEO, but I never heard back."

"What did you tell Drew?"

"That I had concerns about Owen's business dealings. That I suspected involvement in the wildlife trade. I suggested it might not look great for them if one of their employees was found to be connected to something like this. He didn't ask me any questions or if I had proof or anything else for that matter. I was frustrated by his reaction. But I'll admit that I was also relieved that it seemed to blow over after Owen's death. I was really worried about all of it harming my dad's reputation in some way."

Kyle suspected the opposite was true. Instead of blowing over, it had blown up. No doubt, Drew wished he would have asked more questions. The only reasons he could think of that he hadn't followed up was that he didn't want to let on to Harper that he already knew about Owen's venture. Or he could have even suspected that Harper was involved. Either way, he wouldn't have wanted to put the investigation in jeopardy. Dahlia had extensive resources. Kyle wondered what they'd uncovered. Obviously not enough or they wouldn't have asked him to help. Or possibly their leads hadn't panned out. He studied Harper carefully. He could see how difficult this was for her. But he had to keep pushing if he wanted answers.

"Why didn't you tell me this sooner?"

"At first, I didn't tell you because I didn't know what you'd think about it, like if you'd agree that what he was doing was wrong. I was hopeful when I heard your sister was a vet. Then I met your animal-loving family and saw you all at Lucky Cats. That was further evidence, but I wasn't positive. You and Owen were so close.

"There was also the issue of who was I to tell you this about your friend? If Owen had wanted you to know, he would have told you. And if you did believe it was wrong, was it my place to tarnish your memory of your friend? From our first conversation, I could see how much you loved him and how highly you thought of him. I didn't—I don't—want to take that away.

"Later, after I found myself falling for you,

I also had the thought that you might not believe me. I don't have any real proof. It's been awful keeping this to myself."

"There's no doubt about that," Kyle said.

"Honestly, the part about you thinking that I was so in love with him was the worst." Harper buried her face in her hands. "But I didn't know how to tell you that part without telling you the rest."

Kyle gathered her in his arms. "I love you even more for trying to save my feelings." She melted into him, and he held her for a long moment.

Harper sat up. "I make my living photographing nature and wildlife. I donate a lot of what I earn to various wildlife conservation causes. To have my name associated with something like that would be devastating. But that doesn't even touch what it could do to my dad. Can you imagine if the daughter of environmental scientist David Bellaire was found to be involved, even peripherally, in the sketchy world of the wildlife trade? If his aircraft was even suspected of having transported souvenir animal parts from threatened species?"

After the news coverage that the salmon egg episode garnered, Kyle could only imagine.

But the bottom line here was that despite what Harper suspected, for Kyle, it didn't answer exactly what Owen had been doing. Not by a long shot. His gut told him his friend had had another motive. The fact that Dahlia was still investigating backed that up. Harper had said herself that Owen's actions were "technically legal." This could suggest that Owen had been acting in the name of a larger operation. The logical explanation was that he'd been on the trail of illegal wildlife traffickers himself. No way was his best friend a criminal. That had to be it. It wouldn't surprise him if Owen had been single-handedly trying to bring down a crime ring. Surely, this is what Dahlia was working to prove. Regardless, Harper didn't know anything concrete and she didn't possess any hard evidence. Relief swept through him like a cool breeze loosening the anxiety that had been tying his insides into knots.

He would report this news to Josh and be done with this deception where Harper was concerned. He and Harper could move on without her ever knowing the part he'd played for Dahlia. For the first time, Kyle could see a clear path to a future together.

"FAVORITE KIND OF CHEESE?" Kyle asked.

"That's a tough one," Harper answered. "I like all the cheeses, but I'll go with Gruyère."

"Would you rather be too hot or too cold?"

"Hot. I hate being cold. I especially hate cold water. Please don't ever ask me to do one of those polar plunges. I was cold just watching you fall overboard."

"Duly noted."

"Since we're on the topic of water, I'm also terrified of sharks."

"Harper, they're more afraid of you than you are of them."

Harper frowned. "I don't believe that."

"Good, because it is not true. Shark fear is healthy and confirms your high level of intelligence."

She laughed and gave him an approving nod. "That was a good one."

"Thank you. Favorite color?"

"Orange, like the sun."

That made him grin. They were seated in matching chairs outside on the deck. They'd spent the morning on the beach and returned to enjoy a cup of coffee before Harper went to work in her office until lunchtime.

Leaning over, he took a break to kiss her, before continuing, "Who was your favorite teacher in school?"

"Sister Mary-Margaret."

"Why?"

Harper looked thoughtful for a few seconds. "She was brilliant and funny, treated us all the same and taught us girls not to be afraid of math."

"Then I like her, too. Favorite steak?" He loved that she was a carnivore.

"Filet mignon."

"Mine, too." Kyle nodded. "That's an excellent pick."

"I'm glad you approve."

"I can't wait to make it for you. We'll have Levi over. He loves it, too. Favorite fabric?"

She snuffled out a laugh. "Um, cotton? Organic, obviously."

"Do you prefer cats or dogs?"

"Hmm. Do I have to pick?"

"You absolutely do have to pick. That's the way this game is played."

"I didn't know it was a game. It feels like an inquisition."

Kyle frowned. "Does it? I'm sorry. I just want to ask you all the questions that I've been dying to ask since I met you but was too afraid of letting on how attracted I was to you."

A blush spread across her cheeks as her expression softened. Reaching over, she entangled her fingers with his. "No. Not at all. I was teasing. I'm enjoying it, even though I have a hard time believing that you've spent the last month being curious about my favorite cheese."

"Hey, cheese consumption says a lot about a person," he joked. "Your preference for Gruyère tells me you're classy yet earthy at the same time."

"Okay. Sure." Then Harper laughed and shook her head. "I'll go with cats. I've really come to love them."

"Me, too."

"Really?" Eyebrows drifting up, her expression matched the surprise in her tone.

"Why does that surprise you?"

"I don't know. I guess because dogs are so dependable. You know, kinda like you, they're all about loyalty, devotion, obedience."

"You think I'm obedient?"

She shrugged a shoulder. "Don't you kind of have to be to succeed in the elite realm of Special Forces?"

"Maybe. To a degree. But I think that's why I like cats. Because they're not. They don't *have* to be anything—they don't *try* to be anything. They just are who they are, and they don't apologize for it."

"That's so true," Harper said.

"You're a cat." He kissed her again.

Harper pulled back a little to smile at him.

"You are seriously the best with compliments, do you know that? I mean my heart just did this flippy thing inside my chest because you called me a cat."

Kyle grinned. He wasn't trying to be good at compliments; he'd never been a flatterer. That was for guys like Owen and Terry who were all about the game. "I'm just being honest."

A slow smile spread across her face. "I told you if you were honest with me then we'd be fine. Do you remember that?"

"Of course," Kyle said, hating the uncomfortably familiar twinge of guilt-ridden apprehension that flowed through him. He kept telling himself it would fade with time.

The app on Harper's phone chimed, indicating someone was on the property. Kyle tensed. His job here might be winding down, but his focus on Harper's safety was not. That concern, he realized, would be a part of his life forever. It was one that he welcomed because he was completely confident that he was the best man for the job.

Harper picked up her phone and studied the screen. "Delivery," she said, and then touched the screen, enlarging the focus. "This app is so cool. I didn't even know it did this until you showed me. I can see the brand of shoes this guy is wearing and that he's got a tattoo on his left forearm. It's a whale. That's cute. Whales will forever remind me of you now, you know that?" Kyle loved that she was taking in every detail, using the skills he'd taught her. "I can even zoom in on the shipping label… And, I see that it's for… Kyle Frasier. From…" Slowly, she lifted her head and furrowed her brow in question. "Who is Sheila Broderick?"

Kyle had almost forgotten about the package that Sheila was sending. Followed closely was the startling realization that Harper didn't know the name of Owen's mom. He wondered if she knew about Mattie.

"OWEN HAD A CHILD? A little girl? How old is she?"

Kyle had peeled an envelope from the top of the package. Tearing it open, he removed the contents and riffled through the small stack of papers. Setting the box aside, he handed Harper a recent photo of Mattie that Shelia had included.

"Yes, her name is Mattie. She's eight years old. You're so good with Delilah, I wondered if you'd spent time with Mattie. I almost asked you…" He gave his head a little shake. "She lives with Owen's mom, Sheila.

And Owen when he was home. Sheila called me a while back and told me she was sending me a package. I gave her this address and then sort of forgot about it."

This didn't make sense. "Why is the return address from New Jersey?"

"That's where they live."

"But Owen was from California."

"California? No… Owen bought Sheila a house in Camden after he got custody of Mattie."

"Camden, New Jersey?" Harper repeated.

"Yes. That's where Owen grew up."

"He told me he grew up in Newport Beach, California. We flew home from Africa for a week and spent two days there… He showed me the neighborhood. He said his house had been torn down, but he planned to buy a place there one day."

"No. He *wanted* to live in Newport Beach, California, someday. That was his dream. 'To earn a spot in Newport Beach.'"

"What? I don't understand why he would lie about this…? It's like everything about him was a lie."

Kyle looked uncomfortable by that assertion. She didn't care. She was angry all over again.

He said, "I think… Did he tell you this stuff when you first met?"

Harper thought back. "Yes, he did. We met in the lobby of my dad's office building. I dropped a box of doughnuts, and Owen helped me clean up the mess. We chatted. He asked me out. He said he was leaving for Africa in a few days, so it had to be soon. He was sweet and very persistent. We had dinner that night. He…he talked about himself a lot, and before he knew anything about me, like who my dad was, he'd already told me all of this."

"Yeah." Nodding, Kyle explained, "He, uh, he used to do that. He had this story he would use…"

"To impress women?"

"Yes. My guess is that he rattled all that off before he realized that you weren't one of his…"

"Conquests," she finished for him.

Kyle gave her a little grimace. "And then he didn't know how to get out of it."

She didn't bother to mask the bitterness she felt. "And then he found out who I was, or more importantly, who my dad is, and decided I was worth a little more of his time."

"Harper, I don't doubt that he loved you," Kyle countered gently. "The way he talked

about you, I'd never heard him talk about another woman like that. But he was a proud
guy. And more insecure than I realized. He
hid it well."

Harper scoffed. "Yeah, he was a very good
liar. He told me his parents were dead. He
said his dad had been a wealthy investment
manager and his mom an attorney. He said
he inherited a 'nice chunk of change.'"

"He was embarrassed about his childhood
as it was, and then to realize who you were…
That you had money. That would make him
even more determined to be worthy of you.
I'm not trying to make excuses for him, but
Owen grew up very, very poor. His dad left
when he was ten. Sheila worked as a clerk
in a convenience store. Owen was the oldest
of three, and after his dad left, he helped his
mom raise his two little sisters."

All these details that Harper hadn't known,
and that Owen had lied about, flooded her
thoughts. Why would he lie about having a
child? "Was he married to Mattie's mom?"

"No. Mattie was the result of a brief relationship. Mattie's mom was young and not
interested in being a mother long-term. She
gave custody to Owen when Mattie was only
a few weeks old. Sheila has cared for her
granddaughter ever since, with Owen's finan-

cial support. Owen adored Mattie. He talked about her all the time. I'm surprised he was able to keep her existence a secret."

"That poor girl." Harper felt a mix of sympathy for Mattie and anger toward Owen. His lies were just further proof that he'd been using her. And despite how she felt about him now, it hurt that he hadn't cared enough about her to be honest. Even more than that, in Camden, New Jersey, there was a little girl who'd lost her dad. Harper couldn't help but empathize.

"She's a sweetheart, too. Owen made a huge mistake by not introducing you to her. She would have been better off knowing you."

"Why do people feel like they need to lie to me about who they really are?"

"I wish I could make this all go away for you," Kyle said as he wrapped her in a tight hug.

"You are," Harper whispered. Gratitude flooded in to replace her anger. It felt so good to be secure in the knowledge that those days were behind her. So good that she didn't even notice that Kyle never answered her question.

CHAPTER SIXTEEN

THAT EVENING, MIA, Nora, Josie and Laney were coming over to view the family photos. Kyle could tell Harper was nervous, which only made him love her more if that were possible. Before their arrival, Kyle vacuumed the floor and arranged chairs before three huge monitor screens in Harper's office. Harper made snacks, including peanut butter cookies. Kyle "taste-tested" four of them while he inspected the rest of the edible assortment she'd arranged on the table.

He pointed at a dish containing light brown goop. "What is this? Baby food?"

"Don't tell me you've never seen hummus."

"I'm sure I've seen it, but I obviously repressed the memory."

Harper laughed. "I know your mom doesn't like sugar and eats only healthy food."

"This is true. She's very disciplined these days."

"These days? You mean, you didn't grow up eating this way?"

"Uh, no." Kyle chuckled and grabbed another cookie. "We grew up eating burgers, bacon, biscuits and fried chicken. Mom's health fixation came along after my dad died. It was a heart attack. My mom felt guilty about it, like if she would have cooked differently, then he wouldn't have died."

"Are you kidding me? That is so incredibly sad."

"It was. She was distraught. Grief can make people question themselves in all sorts of ways."

Harper got that look like she wanted to say more but wasn't sure if she should. She finally went with, "I imagined Nora as this hip and cool mom doing yoga and making healthy treats for all of you and Mia's friends."

"Nope. Well, yes, she was pretty cool. She was this creative, free-spirited art teacher and all my friends loved her. But the snacks weren't healthy. The yoga came along later, too. In conjunction with the healthy eating. She was devoted to my dad, and when he died, she was a little overweight, too, and not very healthy. Like she mentioned, I got into yoga in high school. Sometimes we'd do it together. Not long after Dad died, I came home on leave. She was just…despondent. I talked her into going to yoga class with me. She met an instructor who inspired her. They became friends and the blend of healthy eating and yoga snowballed into the Nora you know today. If Nora does something, it's with her whole heart. Like you."

Harper smiled. "But you said you never came home when you were in the service."

"I didn't mean literally never. I meant rarely. I didn't come home often enough."

"But weren't you stationed overseas?"

"Yes, but that's not a valid excuse. I went home with Owen to visit Sheila and Mattie more than I did my own family."

Harper stepped into his arms and kissed him. "Well, you're here now. And you're doing everything right."

"That's what Mia says, too." Kyle felt a catch in his chest. Soon, he promised himself, he really would be doing everything right.

The doorbell rang. Harper immediately headed toward the sound.

"Where are you going?" Kyle asked, knowing his tone would be enough for her to rethink her steps.

Muttering under her breath, she marched back into the kitchen. "Oh, you know, taking the long way around to get this." Picking up her phone, she swiped the screen, and then exclaimed sarcastically, "Oh, my gosh, it's your family, can you believe it? I would never have guessed."

Kyle barely resisted the urge to chuckle and shook his head. "You have to use the app *every* time someone is at the door, even when—"

"I'm expecting someone," she finished for him.

"Especially when you're expecting someone. A skilled criminal would know to strike when your guard is down and—"

She finished his statement with a resigned, "And they're the most dangerous ones. I'm sorry. I know you're right, it's just… Ugh."

"I don't want you to be sorry. I want you to be alive."

Harper studied him for a beat before giving him a firm nod. "Okay." She gave him a quick kiss and added, "With so few words, you do such a good job of scaring me straight." Then she headed to the door to welcome his family.

After the women took a tour of the house, they gathered in the dining room to sample the food.

"Harper, this hummus is delicious," Nora gushed. "Is it homemade?"

"Thank you, Nora. It is. I think everyone should add a little hummus to their diet."

Harper smiled smoothly at Kyle as she scooped some onto a plate. When she reached for his favorite chips and dumped a few next to the dip, he could see what she intended.

"Laney," Kyle said, in an effort at distraction, "you should slip a few of those cookies into your backpack and take them home for Levi and Jay."

"That's a great idea," Harper agreed. "I'll get something to put them in." She hustled into the kitchen, passing Kyle the hummus-laden plate on her way by. With a wink, she said, "Here you go. Help yourself."

"Sneaky," he whispered.

When they'd eaten their fill and caught up on small talk, they all headed into Harper's office. Kyle couldn't believe that the woman he loved had so effortlessly gained his family's favor. He couldn't make out what they were saying, but he savored the sound of their animated conversation and laughter. He decided he could listen to them for hours. But he needed to utilize this moment of privacy. With the package from Sheila in hand, he quietly exited the house, locking the door and setting the alarm behind him. He wouldn't be gone long, and with any luck, he'd be back before he was ever missed.

Once inside his cottage, he took a deep

breath and stared at the box. After Harper's reaction to Owen's lies about his family, he hadn't thought it wise to open the package in front of her. He had no idea what to expect and suspected he might prefer to be alone with his reaction. He couldn't help but feel like Owen was reaching out to him from the grave.

Tearing off the brown paper and opening the box, he found an envelope on top with his name printed in bold black letters. Inside, he found a letter dated only two weeks before Owen died. Emotion clogged his chest as he read the words from his friend.

Dear Kyle,
If you're reading this, then things probably aren't great. I'm either dead or dying in a hospital. (I hope it's the first one because you know how I feel about hospitals and dying slow.) Either way, I hope Mom came across this package and sent it to you before much time passed. Knowing her, I'm afraid you're reading this, and I've already been gone for months—or years. Ha-ha! In the grand scheme of things, it shouldn't matter, it would just be nice for you to be able to pick up where I left off as soon as possible.

But first, I need to tell you a few

things. We're different, me and you. I wish I was more like you even as I wish you were more like me. Mostly I wish I was like you because you're the best man, the best friend and the best SEAL I've ever known. But if the second were the case, you would be with me right now and this letter wouldn't be necessary. We'd already be partners in this. But that's okay, we both have always done what we felt was right. Even if it didn't always match up completely.

Now I'm going to say the hard stuff because it's easier to write it down— I love you. You are the brother of my heart. You know that, right? That's why I'm turning this operation over to you. You're the only person I can trust. But I gotta be honest with you here, I may be in over my head a little and taken chances that I shouldn't have taken. Not that that matters now. What's done is done. Nothing ventured, nothing gained, and all that.

But it's also the reason I'm writing this letter. You know, in case. Always have a plan B, right?

I know you'll be able to straighten things out if I've gone too far. I can't say much more in this letter in case someone else finds it before it finds you.

Take this key and figure out the code. Go there! You'll find everything you need.

Please remember that I'm trying to give Mattie all the things I never had. You know how much I want that. You know how much I love her. So, I'm also asking you, if something happens to me, to help Mattie remember me through your eyes. That's how she'll see me the best because no one really knows me like you do. I'm counting on the fact that you'll do this. You've never let me down. Your friend,

Owen

PS: I hope you never read this! Someday when we're old men, I'll show you this letter and tell you about this time of my life while we're sitting on my porch and talking about the good old days.

Kyle wiped the tears from his eyes and read the letter again. He knew his friend wasn't perfect, but he loved him.

And Owen loved him, too. He knew it with all of his being. Owen had risked his own life to save Kyle. Kyle made a vow to spend time with Mattie doing exactly what Owen had asked. It wouldn't be difficult for him to do it, to help her remember all the best parts of her dad. Harper was right that she hadn't known the man Kyle had. *This* was the Owen he knew.

This letter was cryptic, yes. But Kyle was confident that this was Owen's way of telling him that he was on to something big. If something happened to him, he wanted Kyle to see it through. Kyle felt his stomach churn at the thought of Owen trying to uncover a dangerous smuggling operation all on his own. Had this, as Harper feared, been what got him killed?

Inside the box, Kyle found a bag of mementos stretching back through the years of his and Owen's friendship: a bottle cap from their favorite bar in Coronado, a business card from a paintball place they'd frequented in San Diego, a pouch of shells they'd collected on the beach for Mattie, on it went. Kyle was touched that he'd saved the items. He found the key inside a baggie that was wrapped up in two US Navy T-shirts. A slip of paper was tucked in with it.

Kyle unfolded the note, chuckling when he saw the "coded" message. He and Owen had invented their own code when they'd first met. Before SEAL training, after basic, they'd both been stationed in San Diego. They'd had a nosy, jealous roommate who was constantly trying to get them in trouble. They'd devised the code both to communicate confidentially and to irk their annoying roommate. They'd eventually unloaded the roommate, but the code had lived on.

Whatever Owen had left for him was in a safe-deposit box in Newport Beach, California. And there was no doubt in Kyle's mind that it was there that he'd find the proof he needed to clear Owen's name.

THEY WERE OUTSIDE in the yard when Kyle noticed the strange car creeping close to the end of Harper's driveway. He and Harper had gone grocery shopping that morning and stopped at a nursery on the way home. Harper was preparing to plant some flowers. She was happy, and he loved that. He wished with all his soul that he could relish the domestic simplicity of the outing, but he was too busy trying to decide whether he should tell her about the safe-deposit box.

Should he explain what he believed Owen was really up to? Or wait until he had the proof in hand? Probably the latter, he decided. She hadn't known Owen like he had and might not see things the same way.

His contract with David was up in two days. He'd detour to California before going to Seattle. He'd hand over the proof and tell Travis that he wasn't taking the job with Dahlia at the same time. Then he would surprise Harper and his family with the news that he wasn't leaving Pacific Cove. But first, he wanted to solidify his new plan for employment. He looked forward to a time when Owen would no longer be this looming presence in his relationship with Harper.

The ominous car turned into the driveway and distracted him from his thoughts.

"Are you expecting someone? Do you recognize the vehicle?" Kyle asked Harper, positioning his body so that he stood in front of her.

"No, on both counts," she said.

The car stopped behind Kyle's pickup.

"What do we do?"

By that time, Kyle already recognized the man behind the wheel. But what in the world was he doing here?

"It's okay," Kyle said. "I know him. That's my friend Josh." He kept his tone casual, but his mind was busy spinning through possibilities. Did Josh have news about Owen? The double threat weighed on him instantly. He didn't want Josh to know that he and Harper were romantically involved. Not until he had a chance to explain about her and Owen. And he didn't want to tell Josh what he suspected about Owen until he had the proof in hand.

Of course, the bigger danger was that Josh would let it slip that Kyle had been working for Dahlia. He needed to get rid of him. And he needed to do it fast. Maybe he'd invite him out for coffee. That would be good; he and Harper had been talking about simulating situations that might arise when he was gone. That would be his excuse.

"Oh, how nice. A navy friend?"

"Yes, but he works for Dahlia now. I don't know what he's doing here."

"Kyle! Hey! Looks like I have the right place?"

"Yes, you do. Hi, buddy!" Kyle said enthusiastically when he approached. "This is a cool surprise," he lied and shook his hand.

Motioning between his companions, Kyle said, "Josh Avery, Harper Jansen. Harper, Josh."

"Nice to meet you, Josh."

"You, too," Josh said with a sheepish smile. "But I kinda feel like I know you already."

"Oh?"

"Yeah, I was a friend of Owen's, too. Like Kyle here. And then, of course, Kyle has told me about you."

Kyle could see the curiosity flickering in Harper's eyes. He braced himself because he knew that expression. It was the one that preceded the question blitz. But it didn't happen. What she did instead was way, way worse: she invited him in.

CHAPTER SEVENTEEN

HARPER BEGAN HER inquiry in the kitchen while she made a pot of coffee. The CIA or the FBI should hire her, Kyle thought, to perform all their interrogations. He could see Josh warming to her, falling under her spell. Within minutes, he was providing details about his family and childhood in Green Bay, Wisconsin.

Kyle hadn't known that Josh had had a dog named Stan who'd once gotten stuck in a frozen pond. According to Josh, he and the dog had both nearly drowned, and the harrowing experience had resulted in his desire to become a navy SEAL. Kyle would have laughed if there wasn't so much at stake here.

The thing about Harper was that she was genuinely interested in people. She had such an engaging way about her that it made you want to answer. But still, Josh should know better than to willingly divulge so much about himself to an unknown entity. And that's when he realized that maybe she wasn't an unknown at this point.

Kyle fought off the panic and tried to think. He wanted to stop this conversation and push Josh out the door. If she found him out, his only hope was that she would trust in his love enough to forgive him. Since she knew how much Owen had meant to him and that he'd been doing a job for his new employer… What was he thinking? None of that would fly if he were in her situation. What he needed was for her not to find out at all.

Harper poured coffee and arranged cookies on a plate. They settled in the living room, Josh in one of the easy chairs by the fireplace, he and Harper on the sofa. An easy hour passed, with Harper encouraging them to share stories about their time together as SEALs. They acquiesced, and by silent mutual consent they stuck to the funny and more lighthearted stories and avoided much mention of Owen. Kyle started to relax. He should have trusted that his friend would know better than to give him away.

As the second hour came to a close, Josh announced that he needed to hit the road. His next stop was an aunt and uncle in Newport where he was expected for dinner.

Harper said to Josh, "I'm so glad you were

able to stop by for a visit, but I just realized you never mentioned what you were doing here on our little stretch of coastline? Did you come all the way here just to see Kyle?"

"Basically. My sister's baby is being baptized this weekend in Salem, and I'm the little guy's godfather. When I realized how close to Pacific Cove that was, I decided to zip on over here in my rental car and see the Oregon coast. Visit Kyle and meet you. My new hero."

Hero? Kyle tensed. Where was he going with this?

"You're just saying that because I showed you the photo of Kyle when he fell overboard," she joked.

And that's when things began to fall apart.

Josh laughed. "Well, yeah, there's that. But I also want to thank you on behalf of Dahlia for the tip you gave Drew Louis before Owen died."

"Oh," Harper said, belying her clear surprise with a little shake of her head. "I didn't think anyone was listening."

"Like I told Kyle the other day, Dahlia took that information very seriously. Drew had to play it cool at the time because of your close association with Owen. You know, in case you were somehow involved." Josh added an apologetic smile. "I'm sure you understand."

"Of course," she returned smoothly, but Kyle could see the wheels spinning in her mind, no doubt homing in on that phrase "Like I told Kyle…" She'd be wondering why he'd been talking to Josh about anything Harper had reported to Drew. It was more than enough for someone as intelligent and perceptive as Harper to put together.

"There will be a formal thank-you coming your way." Josh tossed a smile at Kyle but didn't focus long enough to notice that Kyle didn't return it. Kyle stared at Josh and willed him to stop talking. If he stopped right now, then maybe Kyle could salvage this somehow.

Instead, Josh said to Harper, "That part of the investigation is finished. There won't even be a hint about you or BEST between the pages of the report, no matter the final outcome regarding Owen.

"I have news about that, too. Good news, sort of. The investigation into the cause of death is complete. It's been confirmed that Owen's car wreck was an accident." Directing his next statement to Kyle, he said, "We should have the answers on the rest of it soon. Hoping for more good news."

Harper nodded and looked at Kyle. For a

split second, Kyle was afraid to meet her gaze as if avoiding it could stave off this nightmare. But he did. He had to. Anyone else would see a beautiful woman relaxed and enjoying Josh's speech. Kyle saw a fake smile frozen in place on features unusually pale. The usual sparkle had dimmed in her blue-gray eyes. She knew. Kyle's chest hurt like his heart was being crushed from within. He recognized the pain for what it was, all the while hoping she'd give him a chance to explain. To apologize. To promise…

Josh stood. Harper followed suit. Kyle forced himself to move. Such a strange sensation, he thought, to have your dreams, your deepest hope for the future, crumble down around you and not be able to do anything about it. His life was all about action, moving, doing, preparing, fixing. But if time in the military had taught him anything, it was that some things you just couldn't fix. Because when he thought about this from Harper's point of view, he didn't see forgiveness and understanding in the cards. And honestly, he didn't deserve either.

"Let me get you some of those cookies for the road," Harper said and headed into the kitchen where she packed a bag for Josh. Kyle noticed the slight tremble in her hands.

"Thank you so much," Josh was saying. "I can't remember the last time I had homemade peanut butter cookies…"

Kyle felt like he was watching himself from above, giving his body commands: walk to the kitchen, take a sip of coffee, laugh at Josh's joke… Somehow, he managed to escort his friend to the door. They said their good-byes and expressed how they both looked forward to Kyle's first "official" assignment with Dahlia. Kyle shut the door, locked it and found Harper standing in the dining room.

BEFORE THIS MOMENT, Harper would have considered herself an expert on betrayal. But one who would never allow herself to be subjected to it again. Positive that she'd finally met an honorable man who truly loved her, she'd been growing smug in the knowledge, and the security Kyle provided. And not the physical kind, but the bone-deep confidence that she could trust this man with her life, her fears, her deepest secrets. It was darkly, horrifically comical when she thought about it. How she'd believed that Owen had broken her heart when in reality, he'd only damaged her pride and wounded her soul. That experience was nothing compared to what Kyle had done. Owen's betrayal felt like a stroll on the beach compared to this.

Trembling with a combination of shock and rage and disappointment, she stared at Kyle unsure where to begin. Maybe he didn't deserve any words. In his eyes, she certainly hadn't.

Finally, she asked, "Have you been working for Dahlia in some type of information-gathering role while you were working here for me?"

"Yes."

"I am such an idiot."

"Harper, no, you're not. Let me explain."

"Okay." The word came out involuntarily. It was just there without any thought on her part. Evidently, her heart was doing the talking, because she realized then that she desperately and irrationally wished for the possibility of an explanation. "Let's hear it. I would love for there to be an explanation that doesn't include you spying on me for Dahlia while you were purportedly working as my security expert. Getting close to me, being nice to me, letting me fall for you, all the while allowing me to believe we might have a future together. No wonder you haven't seemed concerned about a long-distance relationship. You were so confident that would work out because all along you knew it didn't matter. You got what you wanted, and you were leaving, right? Now that I think about that, I need to ask you a question—when did they ask you to do this?"

Kyle's head began a slow, resigned shake. "Does it matter?"

"Yes! To me it does. The least you can do is be honest for two minutes here. Apparently, it's mission accomplished. No need for secrecy now. When did they ask you?"

"Josh called the first night we went to yoga class."

"I knew it. That's when you started being nice to me. I should have known your Jekyll and Hyde transition was too smooth. Do you have any idea how stupid I feel? Telling me you liked me, comforting me and holding my hand on the boat, setting up that photo shoot at Rhys McGrath's?" She paused to let out a disgusted groan. "Ugh. I was so smitten by the whole show. How humiliating. I kissed you in that bunker. And you let me! I confided in you. I told you things I've never told another human being. I fell in love with you. Meanwhile, you were just doing your job and reporting it all to Dahlia."

"I was doing a job, yes. But I also—"

Harper waved a hand to stop him. "And

you don't believe me, do you? About Owen? Josh said that you guys are still hoping for an explanation—for 'good news.'"

"I have reason to believe that he may have been working undercover. Possibly trying to infiltrate a smuggling operation."

"He wasn't, Kyle. If he had been, why wouldn't he have told me? I would have been way more inclined to help him if I'd known that."

"He wouldn't jeopardize an investigation. As soldiers, it's drilled into us to disclose as little information as possible. He was trying to protect you."

Harper scoffed. "How is using my father's jet protecting me? How is threatening to ruin my professional reputation protecting me?"

Kyle looked uncertain. "I'm not…sure yet. I'll have the answer soon. There has got to be a good explanation for all of this."

"A good explanation. You're right," she said bitterly. "You were about to explain. I'm ready for that explanation now."

Kyle stared at her as if frozen. His dark brown eyes were calm and stony just like the guy she'd first hired. She'd actually believed she'd broken through that shell and gotten to know the man inside when the truth was, he'd been playing her all along. Her initial impression had been spot-on; this emotionless robot was the real Kyle Frasier.

With biting sarcasm, she asked, "Is this the fight, flight, freeze scenario where the teacher freezes in front of his star pupil? I'm guessing this is the one scenario you never planned for, isn't it? That I'd find out you were using me, too, just like your best friend did. Too bad Owen wasn't still alive so you boys could have a nice laugh about this."

He squeezed his eyes shut for a few seconds, opened them and said, "Harper, you have to believe me. I never meant to hurt you. That was the last thing I wanted. It was not all lies. I didn't—"

"You didn't think I'd find out, so that would make it all okay? That's what you were thinking, right?"

"I'm so sorry."

She noticed he didn't deny this assertion. He'd never meant to tell her, because none of this was real. Not for him. She pressed two fingers above her eyebrow in an attempt to ward off the stabbing pressure there.

"I don't want your apologies. I want to hear this explanation of yours that is going to make this better. The one that will make this all go away. Because I cannot handle the idea that the man I love—I thought I loved—the man I literally *trusted* with my life, not to mention my heart, would do this to me." She felt her control slipping as her heart splintered and shattered inside her chest. Her entire body was shaking now. Reaching out, she grabbed the back of the chair in front of her. Jaw clenched so tightly it throbbed. She forced herself to meet his eyes. "Does that explanation exist?"

The silence stretched between them for so long it felt loud in her ears like the entire ocean had moved inside her head and was now pounding against the inside of her skull.

"No," he finally answered. "It doesn't. In a couple of days, when my contract here is up, I'm going to go get the answers about Owen. And then we should talk about all of this."

"What does that mean, go get the answers? Where?"

"I can't… I don't want to say. In case Owen…"

"Oh, of course. Owen. I get it. By all means, let's keep protecting the criminal. What are you waiting for? Go. Go get your answers, whatever that means."

"Harper, I made a commitment here and I would never break that. Not even for Owen."

"Well, lucky for you, then, you don't have to break anything. Except my heart. But even that's worth it for your precious Owen, right?"

At that, he winced a little. Harper knew it was harsh, but she couldn't seem to stop herself. She'd done nothing to deserve this pain and everything to earn his love.

"Harper, please don't do this."

"I'm doing you a favor, Kyle. You're fired. Go. Find the truth. Because it's exactly what you need. Although, there's no doubt in my mind that you're going to discover that the man you worshipped is not the man he truly was. And then you can live with that. All alone."

Then, without another word, he walked out the door and out of her life.

KYLE WENT TO the cottage, stuffed his few belongings into his backpack, grabbed his keys and hit the road. He briefly considered going to his mom's or Mia's but didn't want to have to lie about why he was there. There was no way he could hide his misery. He felt like he was moving through quicksand as it was; every movement took effort as he continued to give his body commands. In a way, it reminded him of navy SEAL training. Putting his body on autopilot, pushing through the pain, focusing on the next task.

He drove east until he hit Interstate 5, then north to Portland where he checked in to a hotel. Once there, he searched for the closest airport to Newport Beach and booked a flight to California. Then he lay down on the bed with a pillow over his head and tried to make peace with what he'd done. It was a battle he knew he'd wage for the rest of his life. At least he could finally make things right where Owen was concerned.

THE CHIMING OF her phone woke Harper. Again. It wasn't the first time she'd heard it from its spot on top of the dresser across the room. Staring at the clock, she calculated that she'd slept for a paltry four hours. Vaguely, she recalled getting up for long enough to use the restroom, down some pills for her headache and drink a glass of water. Then she'd crawled back under the comforter and into welcome oblivion. Understandable, considering that after Kyle left, she'd sat frozen on the sofa for hours until darkness had fallen around her. And still she'd sat there, cold and hurt and lonely. At some point in the night, she'd managed to move into her bedroom where exhaustion had finally, blessedly given her a brief respite.

She knew she could only put off the inevitable for so long. The inevitable, in this case, being life. Feeling sorry for herself wasn't going to help. Well, maybe it would help a little in the short-term. Putting one foot in front of the other was paramount at this point. A loud growl from her stomach suggested a muffin would also be beneficial. She'd barely eaten yesterday. She wasn't counting the crackers and water she'd ingested to choke down the headache medication. At least an appetite meant she was still alive.

Dragging herself out of bed, she brushed her teeth and headed into the kitchen to make coffee. She snagged her phone off the dresser on the way. A tap of the message inbox showed her that the latest text was from Laney: Hey! Any chance you could help in the cat room this morning? Two of our regular volunteers are out with a stomach bug.

Harper had offered to fill in whenever they might need her. There was no way she could say no. Harper responded with an immediate affirmation. Laney texted the four-digit access code to the cat room's outside entrance.

A quick glance at the clock told her she had just enough time to take a shower and grab a box of pastries on her way.

A last glance at the clock told her she had just enough time to make a shower and grab a box of pastries on her way.

CHAPTER EIGHTEEN

HARPER ARRIVED AT Lucky Cats and punched in the code to unlock the cat room door. She stepped inside and unloaded her backpack and the box of pastries she'd purchased. A familiar black-and-white cat ran to her with a toy in her mouth, which she dropped at Harper's feet. Threading in and out of Harper's ankles, she let out a loud meow.

"Annie?" Scooping the cat up, she glanced around but didn't see anyone else in the cat room. The cat's purr was like a balm to the ache inside of her.

Laney walked through the door of the clinic. "Hey! Good morning, Harper. Are those doughnuts? Please tell me there's a maple bar in there."

"Hi, Laney. Yep, extra maple bars because I know they are your favorite and Levi's. I've seen you fight over them. Why is Annie back? I thought she'd been adopted."

Laney nodded sadly. "She was. They returned her."

"Returned her? What do you mean?"

"It happens sometimes. This couple adopted her, but then they split up. The woman moved out. The guy travels for work and was leaving Annie alone for days at a time and having the neighbor check in on her."

"Days! All alone? Why didn't the woman take her?"

Laney shrugged. "We don't know. If a person isn't willing to expend the effort to take care of a cat, then we don't want them to have one anyway. I'm glad he brought her back instead of continuing to leave her alone like that. He felt bad about it. Can you imagine how lonely that would be? We'll try again."

Harper sank down onto one of the benches that lined the room. The tears were on her cheeks before she realized they'd formed. The sob was out before she could stop it.

Laney rushed to her side. "Harper? Are you okay?"

"I'm… I…" Annie rested her head on Harper's shoulder. "That isn't right, Laney. To leave a cat all alone like that. Being lonely is torture, and I mean that literally. It's been a very effective form of torture in many societies throughout history. That's why they put prisoners in solitary confinement."

Laney went a little wide-eyed. Harper

couldn't blame her. She was crying and talking nonsense.

"Let me get Mia." Laney was up and gone before Harper could stop her.

Mia showed up less than a minute later. "Harper?"

Harper looked up at her. "Mia, can I have an adoption application, please? I'm taking this cat. I mean, I want to adopt her, if I'm acceptable. I don't know a lot about cats, but I'm learning. And you guys are here if I need you, right?"

"Yes, of course, you can. You and Annie would be a great fit. We're here for anything you need. You have lots of people here who care about you. And Annie. Let's go into my office and talk about it. You can bring her."

Harper followed Mia into the clinic and down a hallway.

"Have a seat," Mia said once they were inside her office.

"Thank you." Harper settled on the sofa where Annie seemed content to stay in her arms. "You guys are so...amazing. You and your entire family. Do you know that? I've never... I don't have much family. It's just my dad and me. I don't have that many people in my life actually... I mean, I have friends, of course. Not super close ones though, and none that live nearby. You know what? Honestly, I've never really needed other people that much. Until…" Until Kyle.

That's when she realized that, thanks to him, she now had a new nemesis. Loneliness. Since childhood, being alone had been a routine part of her life. So much so that she hadn't recognized it for what it was.

She'd gotten so good at being alone, at figuring out ways to pass the time, that it became a part of who she was. It was what had attracted her to photography in the first place.

Not only had photography given her a solo activity to engage in, but the end product— the photo itself—had helped her to capture a moment, an emotion, a memory that she could visit anytime she wanted. It was a means to ease the loneliness without giving in to it. She could see now that she'd counted on that lifeline. But now it was gone, too. Or at least she knew it would never again be enough.

Because Kyle had shown her how it felt to truly share her life with another person. Even the idea of work, of taking photos, felt different because of him, because of the memories they'd made. Reminding herself that it hadn't been real only helped a little. It had felt real. For the first time in her life, she'd been genuinely *not* lonely. Bottom line: she was both weirdly thankful for and mad at Kyle for coming along and showing her what the opposite of loneliness felt like. Looking at Mia, she realized his family had helped with that, too.

This revelation caused a fresh bout of tears because was it weird to have a relationship with Kyle's family and not with him? Did that make her even more pathetic?

Mia sat next to her and slipped an arm over her shoulders. "This has to do with my dumb brother, doesn't it?" She pulled a tissue from her paw-printed doctor smock and handed it to Harper. "I told him he was a fool if he let you go. Do you want to talk about it?"

"Sort of. But I'm not sure it's right to talk to you about your brother. I'm not even sure if I should be here, hanging out with you guys. I don't want to make things awkward for you. Or for him."

Mia gave her a gentle smile. "I can promise you that nothing you can say about Kyle will make me love him any less if that's what you're worried about. And we love you, too, Harper. With or without Kyle. You and I are friends. Now tell me what happened, if you want to?"

"I do. It's kind of a long story. We… He

didn't start out as my houseguest or whatever he told you."

"He was your bodyguard."

"Wait, you knew? How much do you know?"

"Yes, but I didn't know all along. He told me the day of the photo shoot and asked me not to say anything. No one else knows. He didn't tell me much. You know how secretive he is."

"Ha! Yeah, I certainly do."

Mia gave her an encouraging smile even though Harper knew she probably sounded like she was coming unhinged.

Gathering herself, she wiped at her nose, and asked, "So, you know who I am?"

"Yes, Harper, I do know who you are. But I already knew *you* by then. As a person. As my friend. But if you mean, do I know who your dad is, then yes. But that doesn't make any difference to me, and it won't matter to the rest of this family either."

Harper smiled at the Kyle-like compliment.

"Although, I'm warning you that when Laney finds out, she will undoubtedly have questions."

"Laney's questions I can handle. Her curiosity reminds me of me. It's not malicious. She'll make a great detective someday."

Mia smiled. "Yes, she will. She's taking shooting lessons right now from a friend of Craig's to prepare. And while it makes me cringe inside, I can see she's serious about this career choice. She idolizes Kyle, and he's such a great role model for her. I'm working on getting my fears under control. Go on when you're ready."

Harper said, "The fact that you know a little background makes this easier to tell. In addition to helping me with personal security, Kyle was already working for Dahlia, and I didn't know it."

Mia frowned. "What do you mean already working for Dahlia?"

"He was being paid by Dahlia to spy on me while he was teaching me the security stuff."

"Spy on you?"

Harper tried to keep it short while explaining the best she could, including her suspicions about Owen. Mia asked questions. Harper answered them.

Mia said, "So, did he finally confess all of this to you?"

"I found out by accident." Harper went on to tell her about Josh's visit.

"Wow."

"Yeah. I have trust issues that go way back. I've had bad experiences with people trying to take advantage of me for my dad's wealth or connections. Including Owen. I thought Kyle was different. He knew who I was, and he acted like none of that mattered. He told me he loved me, and I believed him." Harper's cheeks went hot with embarrassment, and she felt the need to explain. "He was so different than any man I've ever known. He didn't treat me like I was special. I mean, special because of my dad's money or fame. He was like you guys—I was just Harper, and he had no problem teasing me and pointing out my mistakes. I loved that he liked *me*. And then I found out it was all a lie."

"Hmm. Harper, listen to me, this is all fantastically terrible. But I know my brother. He would never use another person in that way. I'm not saying that he wasn't trying to find out what happened with Owen. Undoubtedly, that was, is, a priority. But if he told you he loves you, he means it. And that person, that amazing guy you got to know is real."

Harper didn't respond. She didn't believe it. She couldn't. He'd admitted that he'd been using her to get the information he wanted to clear Owen, that he'd gotten too close to her for that reason.

"Have you considered this from Kyle's perspective? Falling in love with the woman he was being paid to protect, who also happened to be his best friend's fiancée? While he was being paid to spy on her? I can promise you any one of those issues would go against my brother's unfailing sense of honor. I'd be willing to bet he struggled and fought to *not* fall in love with you. Now that I think about it, I could see him doing that very thing the day we talked on the beach when I accused him of being in love with you."

"You accused him of being in love with me?"

Mia smiled. "Yeah, and just so you know, he didn't deny it. I thought it was odd how miserable he seemed to be about something that should be making him happy, but now I get it. His loyalty toward Owen versus his love for you must have been eating away at him. Not to mention his obligation to Dahlia. Please don't think I'm defending what he did, but I know how my brother thinks.

"Kyle values duty, honor and loyalty above all things in this world. His dad made sure of that. Bill was a perfect role model of putting duty and honor before *anything* else, even his family. Even his wife, our mother, who doted on him. He attempted to mold Kyle into his image. For a long time, it worked. But then Bill died, and Kyle realized his dad wasn't quite the pillar of perfection he'd grown up believing he was. It's been very difficult for him to reconcile all of this. It took me a while to realize how much. Even with all of that, he still has that sense of duty and responsibility. You can't shake that. It's ingrained in him. Even Jay has it from his time in the Coast Guard. They do the 'right thing'—" she paused to add air quotes "—'no matter the personal cost.' Through all of that, Owen was there for him. I don't know if you're aware of this, but Owen saved my brother's life."

Harper nodded. "Yes, but I never heard the details."

"Owen didn't just save him. He risked his own life to go back for Kyle under impossibly dangerous circumstances. It was truly heroic. They both should have died. Owen might have been involved in this shady business, but he loved Kyle. He was loyal to Kyle. There was bravery and honor in there, too. There had to be in order for him to do what he did. If there's even the slightest chance that Owen is innocent of this, Kyle will hang on to that thread. He'll do everything in his power to prove that before he accepts his guilt."

Harper could see how some of this might be true. Most of it, probably. And it only strengthened Kyle's goodness. His ability to see right into the heart of a person was one of the reasons she'd fallen in love with him. That's what he'd done with her, wasn't it? Seen her for who she really was and loved her anyway. He'd done the same thing with his dad. Harper felt her cheeks burn with a combination of regret and shame. If only she'd been able to see this sooner. If only he hadn't left without explaining some of this to her. But she hadn't let him, had she? Nope. She'd fired him and kicked him out.

And when Kyle discovered the truth about Owen—and Harper had no doubt he would— he would be devastated all over again. To once again discover that a man he idolized was not the person he believed him to be. She knew what that was like; to find out someone wasn't who you thought they were. It took time to work through those feelings, to acknowledge them, to accept that they were about that person's actions and not a reflection on you. She'd lived it more times than a person should have to. And yet she hadn't allowed herself to see that Kyle was going through that very thing. Or would be as soon as he discovered the truth.

A sense of urgency rushed through her so quickly it left her a little shaky. Turning so that she faced Mia, she said, "Mia, I need to see him but he's gone. He left yesterday. Do you know where he is? Has he left for his job with Dahlia?" She needed to apologize, to explain, to tell him she loved him. She needed to be there for him when his world came crashing down.

"Harper, he didn't take the job."

"What?"

"He didn't take the job with Dahlia. He hasn't signed the contract. Technically, he has until the end of the month to decide, and he decided to take the extra time."

"Then where is he?"

"Newport Beach, California. I have no idea where exactly or why he's there."

But Harper did. At least, she knew the why part.

HARPER BROUGHT UP a map on her tablet and tried to think calmly and rationally. Kyle had said that after his contract with her was complete, he would "go get answers" about Owen. The inference being that the information he sought resided elsewhere. That had to be why Kyle had gone to Newport Beach.

Harper had to get there as quickly as possible. She tried to calculate Kyle's timeline. It was roughly a two-and-a-half-hour flight. The closest airport to Newport Beach was

LAX, approximately an hour's drive. He'd likely rent a car when he arrived, which would also add time. With efficient planning and a little luck, she could be there at the same time if not get there ahead of him. She cringed thinking about the angry words she'd spoken to him just before he'd walked out her door. How could she get him to talk to her?

Pulling up her contacts, she tapped on her dad's number.

He answered on the second ring. "Hi, honey. How are you? What's up?"

"Hey, Dad. I'm fine. I'm calling because I need your help."

"Okay."

"Aren't you going to ask what this entails before you commit?"

"Harper, you rarely ask me for help. So if you're asking for something, then I know it's important."

Harper felt her anxiety ease a little. No matter what happened in her life, at least she had her father on her side. "Thanks, Dad. It is kind of important. Are you home right now?"

"I am. Just reading the paper."

"Oh, great. That means you're in the family room, right?" Lounging in his recliner and reading the paper was one of his favorite things.

"Yep."

"Here's what I need you to do. Stand up and go over to where all my photos are hanging."

"Uh, okay." Harper could hear him shuffling around as he set the paper aside, adjusted the recliner and stood. A moment later, he said, "I'm there."

"I need you to take down one of the photos hanging there, scan it and send it to me."

"I'm on it. But which one?"

Harper told him.

A few seconds of silence ensued while Harper tried to imagine what her dad was thinking. "Um, honey, are you sure this is the one you want? It's not exactly the best photo you've ever—"

"Believe me, Dad, I know. I'm positive."

"Are you going to tell me what this is about?"

"It's about Kyle. But I don't have time to explain right now. Trust me, I know what I'm doing." Maybe. Hopefully. If this plan worked.

"All right," he said. "I'll trust you. I like Kyle."

That made her smile. She suddenly realized that in all the time she'd dated Owen her

dad had never said that. "I'm glad," she said.
"I like him, too. One more thing?"

"Anything."

"Can I get a lift in one of your airplanes?"

CHAPTER NINETEEN

KYLE APPROACHED THE National Hometown Bank of California and silently reviewed his strategy. Internet searching the night before told him that he'd need a picture ID and a signature to access the box. Because he hadn't initially opened the box with Owen, he had no idea how he was going to get access. The idea of forging Owen's signature didn't sit well with him. He doubted that speaking with the bank manager would do much more than arouse curiosity.

He couldn't help but think that Owen would have been aware of these issues. In the end, he decided he'd attempt to follow Owen's request exactly as he'd laid it out. Kyle put his casual "I belong here" face on, reminded himself to dole out information only as necessary, and casually strolled through the bank's sliding doors. He took his place in line and waited to see a teller.

A cheerful woman with long, glossy black hair called him forward. Her name tag read

"Stacy," and on the wall of her station, she had photos of two little boys who may have been twins. "Hello, sir, how can I help you?"

"Hey, Stacy," he said, returning her friendly smile. "I'd like to access a safe-deposit box."

"Oh, okay, um, let me send you over to customer service. They do our safe-deposit boxes."

Stacy clicked her mouse, pressed buttons, spoke into her headset and then pointed the way. A plump, middle-aged woman with curly red hair met him outside a small office.

"Hi, I'm Renata. I understand that you need access to your safe-deposit box today?"

"Hi, Renata. I'm Kyle. And, yes, I do."

"Okay, follow me. I'll get you set up."

Kyle did as she instructed.

"What's your last name? And do you have your picture ID and box number?" she asked once they were on opposite sides of a counter. Kyle could see the vault behind her.

This is where things got tricky. Was the box in Owen's name or both his and Owen's names? He went back to the basics of keeping it simple. "Kyle Frasier. Box number 1499." He set his ID on the counter between them.

Renata glanced at his driver's license, then did some clicking with her mouse, *mmm-*

hmmed a few times, then unlocked and opened a drawer beside her. She pulled out a card and slid it across the counter. "Here you are."

Staring blankly, Kyle grappled with disbelief. His name was the only one on it, the signature so remarkably like his that he would have sworn under oath that it was his handwriting. Apparently, he'd accessed his box three times in the last two years. Huh. Kyle memorized the dates. One of them clicked into place. The first date fit. He'd had training in San Diego that week. Owen had been between jobs. He'd flown in for the weekend, and they'd stayed with Josh at his place. Kyle remembered it well because he'd "lost" his driver's license. He now surmised that Owen had commandeered it, driven north and opened this box in Kyle's name.

Analytically, he could see how Owen could pull this off. According to their IDs, their stats were very similar. Both had brown hair, and although Kyle's was darker, when it was cut military-short, you couldn't tell. They both had brown eyes; again, Kyle's were darker, but the photo was small. A mere ten pounds separated them and while Owen was a couple of inches taller, who would stop to measure?

Likely, only someone with security or intelligence training would note the differences strongly enough to be alarmed. He wondered now if ID comparison was something he should have covered with Harper. Pain sliced through his chest at the thought of her and how much he'd hurt her. He knew that raw look of devastation on her face would haunt him forever.

Renata laid a pen on top of the card. "Sign right there in that box, please. Just under your last sign-in."

Kyle picked up the pen, marveling one last time at Owen's forging ability. Vaguely, he wondered what else his friend had perpetrated in his name. Renata seemed to study it for a split second, and Kyle almost laughed at the irony of being accused of forging his own name.

"Perfect," she chirped. "If you want to grab your key and follow me, we'll head left through that door like last time."

HARPER SPENT PART of the plane ride tracking down Kyle's hotel reservation. The thought occurred to her that he could be intending to stay with a friend or relative, but she couldn't recall either him or Owen mentioning anyone they knew nearby. A hotel seemed more likely.

Kyle knew about Owen's preoccupation with Newport Beach better than she did and so might naturally gravitate toward the upscale area Owen preferred. She started with the swanky beachfront resort where she and Owen had stayed when he'd ushered her around the city, pointing out sights like he'd been born there. Even though she suspected Kyle wouldn't stay at a hotel as expensive as that one, especially when he was likely in town for an entirely different purpose, she called anyway. No luck.

She worked her way inland from there. On the fifth call, she hit pay dirt at a smallish boutique-style hotel three blocks from the beach. Rooms were available so she secured a reservation for herself. Then spent the remainder of the flight trying to decide how to approach him and what she'd say. She'd considered calling but felt better about seeing him in person. Her greatest fear was that he'd refuse to talk to her.

Since her plane had taken off from a private airfield near Pacific Cove and would land right in Newport Beach, Harper estimated that she'd arrive just before Kyle. After taxiing to the hangar, she thanked the pilot, texted her dad to let him know she'd made it and then hired a car to take her straight to the hotel.

The ride was short and once in the lobby, Harper greeted the clerk, gave her name and handed over her credit card. "I'm meeting a friend here. His name is Kyle Frasier." Harper briefly considered making up a story about being his sister or girlfriend and asking for his room number, but she knew hotels weren't supposed to reveal information about their guests. Instead, she asked, "Can I have a room near his?"

"Sure. Just a sec. Uh, let's see… Mr. Frasier hasn't checked in yet, but I'll make sure you're in the same wing."

Harper smiled in relief. Just that simple amount of information gave her what she needed to proceed. "That would be perfect. Thank you."

"No problem." The clerk finished checking her in, gave her a quick overview of the hotel's amenities and handed over a key. "You're all set, Ms. Jansen. Enjoy your stay here with us at the Beach Whistle."

Harper thanked the young woman and headed to her room where she changed her clothes and twisted her hair up into a bun. Her hope was that a few simple changes would ensure that the employees behind the front desk wouldn't recognize her and, thinking they were being helpful, point out Kyle to her when he arrived.

Tucking the envelope with the print of the photo from her dad into her handbag, she set off for the hotel bar, conveniently located just off the lobby. She took a seat in a corner where she could watch the door. And wait.

But not for long. Less than an hour later, Kyle walked into the lobby, worn backpack hanging heavy over one shoulder. In his hand he held a small duffel bag. His expression was set to his default of somber intensity, making it difficult to get a read on his emotions. But Harper thought the tension emanating from him indicated stress. He definitely looked tired.

She wished she could go to him and wrap her arms around him and pretend that none of this had ever happened. Of course, that was impossible. But she was determined to find a way to make things right between them.

Check-in complete, Harper watched Kyle head toward the same wing where her room was located. Harper forced herself to stay another ten minutes before she removed the manila envelope from her bag and went over to the concierge's desk.

Kyle stared at the stack of items he'd removed from Owen's safe-deposit box: some envelopes, three ledgers and a couple of small boxes he hadn't opened yet. In the bank, he'd thumbed through the first ledger, scanning the countless rows and columns of numbers, desperate for the explanation he sought. He didn't know what the numbers meant, but he couldn't ignore the bad feeling as it rapidly pushed his hope aside and spread through him like a cold dark cloud.

The next ledger had only heightened the sensation. It contained pages and pages of coded names to decipher. Names that didn't mean anything to Kyle.

The final ledger had left him reeling. The entries were written in his and Owen's invented code. Kyle quickly translated enough to validate, and likely prove, Harper's assertion. Kyle knew he'd need more time to analyze everything to be certain but the final thread he'd been grasping for disintegrated into the truth.

There was a part of him that wanted to shove all the material back inside the box, leave the bank and pretend like he'd never received the key. He could send it to Dahlia or the FBI and let them figure it all out. But he knew he couldn't do that. The authorities would need his help to interpret all the information. They'd need his help to prove his best friend was a wildlife trafficker. A criminal, just as Harper had asserted.

Standing in that little room at the bank he'd begun to feel claustrophobic. Chest tight, he'd focused on simply breathing as he transferred everything to the small duffel bag he'd brought along and went to his hotel.

Now here he was, in his room staring at the items and feeling like a fool. Should he call Dahlia first? Or the FBI? He should probably confirm his suspicions before he called anyone. He was trying to decide where to start when a knock sounded on his door.

A look through the peephole revealed a young guy wearing a hotel uniform and a wide smile. He was holding a manila envelope.

Kyle opened the door. "Can I help you?"

"Hello, Mr. Frasier?" At Kyle's nod, he went on, "I'm Sean, one of the concierges here at the Beach Whistle. I have a package for you."

"From who?"

"Uh…" Furrowing his brow, Sean studied the envelope. A white sticker on the front bearing Kyle's name was the only marking on it.

"Do me a favor and open it, will you, Sean?"

"Who, me? Are you sure?" Sean's happy-go-lucky smile morphed into one of abject concern. "Do you think you're being served with divorce papers? Or a subpoena? What if it's poison? Or a bomb? It could be anything… If you're worried about the contents, we should probably call the cops."

"No." Kyle couldn't help but chuckle. "Sean, buddy, relax. None of those things have crossed my mind. I bet it's a mistake. No one in my life knows I'm here. Nobody I know would be sending me anything. I'm just saving you a trip of having to hike back here and fetch a package that was delivered to the wrong room. And, in case it's valuable, I'd like a witness to the contents."

"Oh, cool. I get it," Sean said, nodding, smiling again. He opened the envelope. His face scrunched with confusion as he removed the contents, which from what Kyle could see was a photograph. Then his head began a slow shake. "Dude, it's definitely for you. At least, your name is on this sticky note here. But I've got bad news for you. It's worse than a subpoena. Looks like maybe you've got yourself a stalker. And not even a hot one. This chick is kinda homely…"

Kyle could see it was a photo of a young

woman in a pink tutu. Harper? He reached out and took it from Sean. An interesting mix of confusion, amusement and affection swirled through him as he recognized a teen-aged Harper posing in her ballet gear. Reaching for his wallet, he pulled out some bills and passed them to Sean.

"This is for me after all. Thanks, man."

Sean grinned and handed him the envelope. Kyle shut the door and crossed the room to sit in the only chair.

With a grin that reached all the way inside his heart, he stared at the extremely unattractive photo of the most beautiful woman he'd ever met. He'd learned enough from Harper to know that the lighting in the photo was bad. But that was far from the only issue. The very pale shade of pink washed out her complexion, effectively accentuating several angry red zits on her face. Her hair was pulled back into a sleek bun, but with the background nearly the same color as her hair she appeared to be bald. Her skirt was too big and hung crookedly from her hips. It was the cutest, sweetest, most precious photo he'd ever seen. Of the woman he loved.

With shaky hands he read the accompanying note.

Dear Kyle,
Please accept this photo for your personal blackmail file. Clearly, it evens the score.
With love from,
your awkward ballerina
#photographerinbadlighting
PS: If you'll give me a chance to apologize, maybe we can call a truce?

His awkward ballerina? Love from? Could she possibly mean this? Each beat of his heart seemed to carry a fresh surge of hope through his body. Why was she doing this? What did this mean? How had she found him? Another knock on the door sounded before he could even begin to sort through all his questions and thoughts.

He hurried to the door. "Yes," he whispered, when he looked out and saw Harper standing in the hall.

He opened the door. "Hey."

"Hi," she said, and Kyle's heart softened even further because he could see she was nervous. He barely resisted the urge to gather her close and kiss her anxiety away. But he no longer had that right. He hadn't ever really deserved to have it in the first place. And that's when reality hit him. No matter what she was doing here, he couldn't hold her ever again.

"Kyle, thank you for opening the door. Can I?" She gestured at the room beyond.

"Of course." A part of him wished she wasn't here while a much bigger part of him wanted her to stay. "Come in."

Harper walked across the room to the table where he'd set down the photo. "I see you got it."

He followed her. "I did. Thank you. I love it."

"Really?" She sank into the chair. "Because in my fantasy you looked a lot happier to see me in this moment."

Kyle sat on the edge of the bed so that they were only a few feet apart. He knew these next words were going to be the most painful of his life. "Harper, I am happy to see you. I can't imagine a world where I would ever not be happy to see you. That's not it."

"What does that mean? That you still love me or that you never did?"

Kyle struggled to find the right words. How could she doubt that he loved her? He'd done this. Made her doubt that he ever loved her at all. Even if she forgave him, he couldn't be with her and have her doubt him.

And she would. No matter the reason for it,

that's what his deception had wrought. "Love doesn't have anything to do with this. I need to know why you're here?"

"I came to apologize."

"For what?"

"For the things I said to you. And because I didn't see how badly you needed to find the truth about Owen—for yourself as much as for Dahlia. All I could think about was myself and how much you'd hurt me. I didn't consider what it was doing to you. I'm so sorry for that."

"Harper, I lied to you. I deceived you. What you did—this note and the photo? It's a perfect example of what I love about you. Your kindness, thoughtfulness, sense of humor and complete lack of pretension. But this—you— are way, way more than I deserve. And the fact that you're here right now is tearing me up inside. It is killing me to sit two feet from you and not touch you and kiss you and tell you the million other things I love about you. But the fact is, I don't deserve it. Any of it. Not your apology or your kindness. And I definitely don't deserve your love.

"And no matter how I spin this, what you said keeps coming back to me. No explanation will take it away or make it right. I did exactly what you think I did. You trusted me, and I destroyed that trust. It's unforgivable, and I want you to know that I don't expect you to forgive me. I'm not asking for that. There is no forgiveness in this equation."

"That's not true. You didn't have a choice. I see that now."

"No, I did have a choice. And then I said and did certain things based on that decision, just like you accused me of. You were right when you said that I started being nicer to you after Dahlia requested information."

"So, that's the only reason you were nice to me?"

"No, you know that's not the only reason. I wasn't lying that night after yoga when you called me on my behavior. When I said that I liked you, that was the truth. I already liked you too much at that point. The reason I wasn't being nicer to you before then was because my feelings already went way beyond like. But I wouldn't let myself act on it. It felt wrong. In my mind, you belonged to Owen—you belonged to each other. When I said it was easier to keep you at arm's length, I meant that. It was. Except, that it wasn't…

"Honestly, the assignment from Dahlia just gave me the excuse I needed to get closer to you. I told myself I could handle it, that I could keep distance between us and get to know you at the same time. What a joke. Basically, I deluded myself. You were…impossible to resist. And when you kissed me, I just… I caught this glimpse of how things could be between us and I wanted that. I wanted it so much that I talked myself into believing it was possible. I told myself that if you never found out I was spying for Dahlia, then maybe I could pretend like it didn't happen. I fantasized about making it up to you in a million different ways. But I realize how stupid it was to think that we could have a relationship based on a lie. What I did was unforgivable, and I want you to know that I accept that."

Harper had tears shining in her eyes and Kyle hated that he'd put them there. A woman as full of joy and life as she was should never cry. Especially not through any fault of his.

Her gaze locked on to his and a fierceness that Kyle had never seen before flared in her blue-gray gaze. Like a storm rolling in from the Pacific she seemed to be gathering strength and courage.

"So," she finally said, "if all of that is true, then why can't I forgive you?"

"What do you mean?"

"You keep saying that what you did is unforgivable, but shouldn't that be my choice?

I'm the one who was wronged here. Don't I have a say in all of this? Shouldn't I get to be the one to grant the forgiveness?"

Hope flared to life inside of him, but he quickly tempered it. There was no way she could forgive him so easily. He couldn't allow it.

"You should know that I talked to Mia about all of this. About you. And she helped me see the situation more clearly. It's not that I agree with what you did, but I understand why you did it. And it's not like you told Dahlia anything that harmed me. If anything, it helped me."

Kyle shook his head. She needed to understand that the content, the outcome, didn't matter. "But I would have, Harper. If you had done something wrong or suspicious, I would have reported it. That's like saying that it's okay to break into someone's house intending to steal something, but then you don't take anything because there's nothing there to steal."

She answered with a gentle smile. "I understand what you're trying to say. But at the same time, you wouldn't be the man you are if you didn't do the right thing. It's who you are. You do the right thing, Kyle. No matter what it costs you. And that's part of what I love about you."

It would be so easy to go to her and kneel in front of her and kiss her and embrace what she was saying. But he knew it wouldn't be fair to her. She deserved a relationship based on trust.

"I'm going to ask you a question and you have to answer it honestly."

"Fine," he said quickly.

"If I say I forgive you, can you forgive yourself?"

"I don't…know. What does that mean?"

"It means that you're too hard on yourself. Anything less than perfection and you think you've failed. And then it affects the people around you, too. Everyone thinks forgiveness is a two-step process. Forgiveness and acceptance. And sometimes it is that simple. But sometimes, like with you, it's not. It's a three-step process. If you wrong someone, it isn't up to you to decide if they should forgive you. You apologize, and then they get to decide what to do with it. But it doesn't work unless you then accept their forgiveness. Whether you think you deserve it is irrelevant.

"You did the same thing to your mom and Mia. You decided that you were such a bad son and brother that you didn't deserve their forgiveness and for a long time you dictated the relationship based on that. Kept them both at a distance because you felt like you didn't deserve their love."

Harper was right; he'd done that. It was only because of her facilitating a dialogue between him and Mia that his relationship with his sister was changing. And he'd finally accepted that. He'd also begun to accept his mom's doting pride and…mom-ness toward him.

"You managed to forgive your dad for being a jerk to your sister and not a perfect husband to your mom. You even forgave him for manipulating your behavior. You've forgiven Owen for being a jerk to me. You owe yourself the same consideration."

This was also true. "But, Harper, I love you so much. I'm an honest and trustworthy person. I pride myself on those traits. But I blew it with you. Trust is the thing that you need most in your life, in your relationships, and it's something I could give you. Something I wanted to give you. I wanted our relationship to be built on that. Every relationship should be built on that. But for us, it's gone. I destroyed it, and I don't know how to get it back."

"So, what I'm hearing is that you love me,

but because our relationship is no longer perfect, you don't want to try?"

Kyle felt himself fighting a smile. She had
such a way of summing things up, of getting
to the heart of an issue. "Maybe." He sighed
and scrubbed his hands over his stubbled jaw.
"I can't stand it that I've hurt you. I don't
want to do it again."

"Well, you better get over that because
chances are you will hurt me again. And
I will hurt you. But not on purpose. And
maybe not get paid for it." She smiled at her
own joke.

"Harper, I don't understand how you can
kid about this."

She shifted forward and Kyle knew that if
she reached out to him, that if she touched
him, he wouldn't be able to resist her. "I don't
understand how you can say you don't want
to be with me if you love me."

"I do want to be with you, but I don't think
you…"

"You think I shouldn't want to be with
you?" she finished for him.

"Yes."

"See, you're doing it again, deciding for
me."

"Okay. You decide."

"Good. Here's my decision." She got up

and moved to sit next to him on the bed. She took his hand and held it between both of hers. "And remember, you have to accept it."

Kyle laughed. "Fine." There was no way he was going to disagree with her now. He couldn't have ever pictured Harper Jansen Bellaire would be here with him after everything that had happened.

"I love you, and I'm willing to give you a third chance."

Kyle didn't think it was possible to feel such happiness after the crushing disappointment of Owen. "A third chance?"

"Yes, I already gave you a second chance. After yoga, when you apologized and told me you liked me."

"Oh, yeah. That means you better screw up soon. I don't like how uneven things are between us."

Harper climbed onto his lap. "I'll see what I can do. I adopted a cat, does that help? The couple who took Annie brought her back and I've got her now."

Kyle hugged her tight and nuzzled her neck. "No. That does not help. But it makes me very, very happy. I love that cat."

Harper grinned. "I know. I'm hoping she can be our cat."

"I would like that," he said. And then, because he couldn't wait one second longer, he kissed her.

They were both breathless when he finally pulled away. "Harper, I love you and I wish we could do this all day, but... I'm sorry, I'm afraid I'm under a bit of a time constraint here."

Her response was a rush of words, "You don't need to hurry. You can call the airline and cancel your flight. We can fly back whenever we want on my dad's plane."

"It's not that. I, uh, I need to call the FBI."

"Oh, no. Kyle, you got proof about Owen?"

"Yes," he said, "I don't know what it all means yet, but I'm certain you were right all along."

"I am so sorry," she whispered. "I was honestly hoping I was wrong." Kyle watched her expression darken, sadden, and he knew she meant it. He loved her even more for it.

"Me, too. And now I need to call...somebody."

She nodded. "I'm staying with you. No matter what this entails. I will be here for you."

"Thank you," he said simply, because he wanted that, he realized. He didn't want to face this alone. The reality of who Owen really was began to crowd his thoughts again.

As if reading his mind, Harper said, "I

figured out something else throughout this whole ordeal. I spent a lot of time being angry with Owen about what he did. Granted, some of it was deserved. But I also wasted time feeling resentful of him for coming between us. When really, I should be grateful because ultimately, he's what brought us together. If it wasn't for him, we would never have met. I would never have known what it was like to love someone like I love you."

Kyle stared at her with a mix of wonder and affection. Gratitude bubbled up inside of him. Gratitude toward Harper. Kyle knew it would take time to learn to separate the criminal Owen from the friend he once knew. And it was going to be hard. But, for now, the idea that he had this reason to remember Owen fondly nearly overwhelmed him.

Pressing his forehead to hers, he whispered, "Thank you for that. You're amazing."

"Yeah, well, you're pretty great yourself. And just for the record, I will never let you go again."

"In that case, I suppose the FBI can wait another minute..." Kyle kissed her sweetly. "Or two."

EPILOGUE

A few months later

HARPER GLANCED AT the clock for approximately the seven hundredth time. Five more minutes. Kyle had said he'd pick her up at three and she knew very well that he was never late. Just one of the many things she loved about him. Dating the man she loved was a lot more fun than she'd ever imagined. Kyle had insisted they needed a restart. He wanted time to prove that she could trust him, that he was willing to put her first. Harper had assured him it wasn't necessary, but he'd been adamant. Ultimately, she'd agreed. The last thing she wanted to do was make him feel rushed.

Three months into their courtship, and she was having the time of her life. Kyle was romantic and creative in the activities he planned for them. But it didn't matter to her whether they were climbing mountains or strolling hand in hand on the beach. As long as they were together, every minute felt like a perfect adventure. Although, admittedly, she'd liked some outings better than others. The camping trip she'd adored, the deep-sea diving, aka posing as shark bait, not so much. But she'd promised him she'd try anything once and Kyle seemed determined to take that literally. Their flexible schedules helped.

Kyle hadn't signed the contract with Dahlia. After coming forward and helping the FBI sort through Owen's ledgers and notes, he'd announced that he had different plans. Unbeknownst to her, Jay had given him the idea to start his own security consulting business.

Frasier Security offered everything from basic alarm system installation and top-of-the-line video surveillance to personal safety consultations. No surprise, he enjoyed being able to help people while sharing his knowledge and skills. Thanks in part to Jay's contacts in the construction business, he was already booked out for months. The job entailed some traveling. Harper often went with him, incorporating photography stops along the way. But yesterday, he'd left early and was gone all day. He hadn't returned until she was already in bed and then he'd worked on a job all day today. Secretly she hoped there wouldn't be a lot of days like that in their future.

He'd texted this morning and told her to dress comfortable and casual and be prepared for adventure. Harper was tying her sneakers when the doorbell rang. Habit had her picking up her phone to check the security app where she discovered Santa Claus standing on her porch. He was holding a bouquet of flowers.

Laughter bubbled up inside of her. She tapped the button to activate the intercom. "Go away, Bad Santa. I'm on to you. No one wants your lousy gifts around here."

Of course, "Santa" knew the exact location of the camera lens. Grinning, he put his face right in front of it, real close so his nose looked distorted. "Hey, you used the app when you were expecting someone. This is a very proud moment for me."

"Well, I've been living under the enthusiastically watchful eye of this security expert guy, and he gets a little testy if I'm not hypervigilant."

"Hmm. He sounds awesome. You're lucky. He must care about you a lot."

"I am pretty lucky."

"Can I come in now?"

"What's the password?"

"I love you, Harper."

"That's close enough." Harper unlocked and opened the door. Kyle came in and locked it again behind him. He handed her the flowers, then peeled off his suit to reveal jeans and a T-shirt. Annie trotted over and stepped on his shoe. He picked up the cat and cuddled her close while Harper admired the colorful mix of flowers.

"Thank you. These are gorgeous."

"I realized today that I've never asked your favorite flower."

She thought for a second. "I don't think I have one. When it comes to flowers, I'm all-inclusive."

Kyle leaned over and kissed her. "That's going to make my job easier going forward."

He followed her into the kitchen where she retrieved a vase for the bouquet. "Where are we going?" she asked.

"Out for sushi," he joked.

"So should I call in a burger order to Tabbie's right now?"

Chuckling, he put Annie down. She pounced on her ball and wrestled it to the ground. "I was thinking we'd go bungee jumping and zip-lining."

"Really? 'Cuz I've heard that's more of a first-date type of thing."

"Funny," he said drily, but she could tell he wanted to laugh.

"Here. You should open this." From his pocket he produced a small square box, which he handed to her.

Despite her now-racing heart, she joked, "Um, Santa, this box is too small to be a wide-angle lens."

Kyle grinned. "Maybe it's a really tiny lens."

Harper laughed.

"Open it."

Nodding, she opened the box. She let out a gasp, recognizing the contents instantly. A simple platinum diamond-studded band lay sparkling inside.

"This was my mom's."

"It was. Your dad gave it to me. The reason I left yesterday was so I could meet him in Seattle. I had no idea how to ask a billionaire genius for permission to marry his daughter. When I got there, I realized I've never really cared about money until that moment. I've never thought of you as the daughter of a billionaire, as an heiress. To me, you are the kindest, smartest, most talented, beautiful and amazing person on the planet. But I went ahead with it anyway… I told him that I have nothing but my love to offer you. But that I will cherish you and do my best to take care of you and keep you safe."

"Kyle, that's perfect."

"I thought so, too," he joked. "The problem was that it didn't sound that great to me when I delivered it. I wanted to get up and leave and tell him I'd come back when I had more to offer." Kyle took her hand. "But you know what he said?"

Harper shook her head, but she didn't speak. Tears filled her eyes, and she blinked them away. She didn't want to cry in the happiest moment of her life.

"Time. He said all I needed to receive his blessing was to give you my time. To promise that I'd always be there for you, to choose *you* over everything and everyone else." Harper could see the tears gathering in Kyle's brown eyes along with the love she knew he felt for her. "Do you know how easy that was for me, Harper? To promise that, when you already own my heart, when all I want to do is be with you, and keep you close to me forever?"

Swallowing the emotion clogging her throat, she managed to say, "I think I have an idea."

"And I will, Harper. If you agree to marry me, I will do that, and I'll cherish every second that we have together. So, will you marry me?"

"Yes, Kyle. Of course, I'll marry you. I can't wait." One step and she was in his arms for a kiss made all the sweeter knowing she would soon be his wife. With her mouth still close to his, she whispered, "Nothing will make me happier than to help you keep that promise."

* * * * *

For more great romances from Harlequin Heartwarming and author Carol Ross, visit www.Harlequin.com today!

Get 4 FREE REWARDS!

We'll send you 2 FREE Books plus 2 FREE Mystery Gifts.

Love Inspired® books feature contemporary inspirational romances with Christian characters facing the challenges of life and love.

FREE Value Over **$20**

YES! Please send me 2 FREE Love Inspired® Romance novels and my 2 FREE mystery gifts (gifts are worth about $10 retail). After receiving them, if I don't wish to receive any more books, I can return the shipping statement marked "cancel." If I don't cancel, I will receive 6 brand-new novels every month and be billed just $5.24 for the regular-print edition or $5.99 each for the larger-print edition in the U.S., or $5.74 each for the regular-print edition or $6.24 each for the larger-print edition in Canada. That's a savings of at least 13% off the cover price. It's quite a bargain! Shipping and handling is just 50¢ per book in the U.S. and $1.25 per book in Canada.* I understand that accepting the 2 free books and gifts places me under no obligation to buy anything. I can always return a shipment and cancel at any time. The free books and gifts are mine to keep no matter what I decide.

Choose one: ☐ **Love Inspired® Romance**
Regular-Print
(105/305 IDN GNWC)

☐ **Love Inspired® Romance**
Larger-Print
(122/322 IDN GNWC)

Name (please print)

Address   Apt. #

City   State/Province   Zip/Postal Code

Mail to the **Reader Service:**
IN U.S.A.: P.O. Box 1341, Buffalo, NY 14240-8531
IN CANADA: P.O. Box 603, Fort Erie, Ontario L2A 5X3

Want to try 2 free books from another series! Call 1-800-873-8635 or visit www.ReaderService.com.

---

*Terms and prices subject to change without notice. Prices do not include sales taxes, which will be charged (if applicable) based on your state or country of residence. Canadian residents will be charged applicable taxes. Offer not valid in Quebec. This offer is limited to one order per household. Books received may not be as shown. Not valid for current subscribers to Love Inspired Romance books. All orders subject to approval. Credit or debit balances in a customer's account(s) may be offset by any other outstanding balance owed by or to the customer. Please allow 4 to 6 weeks for delivery. Offer available while quantities last.

Your Privacy—The Reader Service is committed to protecting your privacy. Our Privacy Policy is available online at www.ReaderService.com or upon request from the Reader Service. We make a portion of our mailing list available to reputable third parties that offer products we believe may interest you. If you prefer that we not exchange your name with third parties, or if you wish to clarify or modify your communication preferences, please visit us at www.ReaderService.com/consumerchoice or write to us at Reader Service Preference Service, P.O. Box 9062, Buffalo, NY 14240-9062. Include your complete name and address.

LI20

Get 4 FREE REWARDS!

We'll send you 2 FREE Books plus 2 FREE Mystery Gifts.

Love Inspired® Suspense books feature Christian characters facing challenges to their faith... and lives.

FREE
Value Over
$20

YES! Please send me 2 FREE Love Inspired® Suspense novels and my 2 FREE mystery gifts (gifts are worth about $10 retail). After receiving them, if I don't wish to receive any more books, I can return the shipping statement marked "cancel." If I don't cancel, I will receive 6 brand-new novels every month and be billed just $5.24 each for the regular-print edition or $5.99 each for the larger-print edition in the U.S., or $5.74 each for the regular-print edition or $6.24 each for the larger-print edition in Canada. That's a savings of at least 13% off the cover price. It's quite a bargain! Shipping and handling is just 50¢ per book in the U.S. and $1.25 per book in Canada.* I understand that accepting the 2 free books and gifts places me under no obligation to buy anything. I can always return a shipment and cancel at any time. The free books and gifts are mine to keep no matter what I decide.

Choose one: ☐ **Love Inspired® Suspense Regular-Print** (153/353 IDN GNWN)   ☐ **Love Inspired® Suspense Larger-Print** (107/307 IDN GNWN)

Name (please print)

Address   Apt. #

City   State/Province   Zip/Postal Code

Mail to the Reader Service:
IN U.S.A.: P.O. Box 1341, Buffalo, NY 14240-8531
IN CANADA: P.O. Box 603, Fort Erie, Ontario L2A 5X3

Want to try 2 free books from another series? Call 1-800-873-8635 or visit www.ReaderService.com.

---

*Terms and prices subject to change without notice. Prices do not include sales taxes, which will be charged (if applicable) based on your state or country of residence. Canadian residents will be charged applicable taxes. Offer not valid in Quebec. This offer is limited to one order per household. Books received may not be as shown. Not valid for current subscribers to Love Inspired Suspense books. All orders subject to approval. Credit or debit balances in a customer's account(s) may be offset by any other outstanding balance owed by or to the customer. Please allow 4 to 6 weeks for delivery. Offer available while quantities last.

Your Privacy—The Reader Service is committed to protecting your privacy. Our Privacy Policy is available online at www.ReaderService.com or upon request from the Reader Service. We make a portion of our mailing list available to reputable third parties that offer products we believe may interest you. If you prefer that we not exchange your name with third parties, or if you wish to clarify or modify your communication preferences, please visit us at www.ReaderService.com/consumerschoice or write to us at Reader Service Preference Service, P.O. Box 9062, Buffalo, NY 14240-9062. Include your complete name and address.

LIS20

THE FORTUNES OF TEXAS COLLECTION!

18 FREE BOOKS in all!

Treat yourself to the rich legacy of the Fortune and Mendoza clans in this remarkable 50-book collection. This collection is packed with cowboys, tycoons and Texas-sized romances!

YES! Please send me **The Fortunes of Texas Collection** in Larger Print. This collection begins with 3 FREE books and 2 FREE gifts in the first shipment. Along with my 3 free books, I'll also get the next 4 books from The Fortunes of Texas Collection, in LARGER PRINT, which I may either return and owe nothing, or keep for the low price of $5.24 U.S./$5.89 CDN each plus $2.99 for shipping and handling per shipment*. If I decide to continue, about once a month for 8 months I will get 6 or 7 more books but will only need to pay for 4. That means 2 or 3 books in every shipment will be FREE! If I decide to keep the entire collection, I'll have paid for only 32 books because 18 books are FREE! I understand that accepting the 3 free books and gifts places me under no obligation to buy anything. I can always return a shipment and cancel at any time. My free books and gifts are mine to keep no matter what I decide.

☐ 269 HCN 4622   ☐ 469 HCN 4622

Name (please print)

Address   Apt. #

City   State/Province   Zip/Postal Code

Mail to the **Reader Service:**
IN U.S.A.: P.O Box 1341, Buffalo, N.Y. 14240-8531
IN CANADA: P.O. Box 603, Fort Erie, Ontario L2A 5X3

THE CHRISTMAS ROMANCE COLLECTION!

10 FREE BOOKS IN ALL!

'Tis the season for romance!
You're sure to fall in love with these tenderhearted love stories from some of your favorite bestselling authors!

YES! Please send me the first shipment of three books from the **Christmas Romance Collection** which includes a FREE Christmas potholder and one FREE Christmas spatula (approx. retail value of $5.99 each). If I do not cancel, I will continue to receive three books a month for four additional months, and I will be billed at the same discount price of $16.99 U.S./$22.99 CAN., plus $1.99 U.S./$3.99 CAN. for shipping and handling*. And, I'll complete my set of 4 FREE Christmas Spatulas!

☐ 279 HCN 4981   ☐ 479 HCN 4985

Name (please print)

Address   Apt. #

City   State/Province   Zip/Postal Code

Mail to the Reader Service:
IN U.S.A.: P.O. Box 1341, Buffalo, NY 14240-8531
IN CANADA: P.O. Box 603, Fort Erie, Ontario L2A 5X3

---

*Terms and prices subject to change without notice. Prices do not include sales taxes, which will be charged (if applicable) based on your state or country of residence. Offer not valid in Quebec. All orders subject to approval. Credit or debit balances in a customer's account(s) may be offset by any other outstanding balance owed by or to the customer. Please allow 3 to 4 weeks for delivery. Offer available while quantities last. © 2019 Harlequin Enterprises Limited. ® and TM are trademarks owned by Harlequin Enterprises Limited.

Your Privacy—The Reader Service is committed to protecting your privacy. Our Privacy Policy is available online at www.ReaderService.com or upon request from the Reader Service. We make a portion of our mailing list available to reputable third parties that offer products we believe may interest you. If you prefer that we not exchange your name with third parties, or if you wish to clarify or modify your communication preferences, please visit us at www.ReaderService.com/consumerschoice or write to us at Reader Service Mail Preference Service, P.O. Box 9049, Buffalo, NY 14269-9049. Include your name and address.

XMASR19